African Ming

Two Continents, Two Centuries
Dramatically Converging

Mark J Cotterell

2015

ISBN: 978-1517457198

Readers of this novel might be interested in the companion
story, "African Duel" – ISBN: 978-1484915400.

Further details of books by this author may be found on the
website: http://colliercreations.weebly.com.

These publications are all available as either e-books or
paperbacks from Amazon.

1 2 0590207 1

Chapter List

Chapter 1

Auspicious Date

Little did he realise that his world would collapse so catastrophically within twenty-four hours. It was beyond his wildest imagining that he could tumble from the secure, familiar life he enjoyed, to become a wandering outcast, constantly looking over his shoulder. After all, the following day promised to be one of the happiest days of his life, though perhaps touched with a degree of nostalgia.

His beloved sister had been his constant companion throughout childhood, and they had forged a strong bond. By this time on the morrow she would belong to someone else. Not that he objected – he knew she was marrying a delightful young man from a village a few valleys to the north.

On this particular day he had stayed late in his workshop, partly because he had many stone artefacts for which his customers were clamouring, and because he needed to put the finishing touches to a jade figurine of the goddess Guanyin. He modestly conceded to himself that, even at twenty-five years, he was probably the best stone mason in the area, and consequently he was fairly well-known. As well as major stonework projects, his expertise in producing small, highly intricate carvings of gods, goddesses and animals was becoming known even beyond the boundaries of his native Shandong Province.

Another reason for his delayed return was that there would be chaos at home that day. With a wry grin, he visualised the fact that the house would have been cleaned several times, the excessive quantities of food prepared, and the special wines purchased. He was better out of the way while the preparations for the wedding were in progress. His father and mother would be in a constant sweat, and the two servants would have been bombarded with instructions from dawn to nightfall.

As Jinwei threaded his path along the muddy street of Split Mountain village towards the family home on the hillside, he was repeatedly greeted by acquaintances.

"Congratulations to you, Kong Jinwei! Best wishes for your sister's ceremony tomorrow – and for her future happiness."

He smiled and acknowledged their acclamation politely. It gave him a warm feeling to be surrounded by so many friends, all of whose roots went back into the prestigious past of that district.

Suddenly the air was full of loud, rough shouts. Round the corner between two hovels came a pair of burly, brightly-dressed men bearing pikes. He recognised them as the guards of the one who kept the whole village in terror and subservience.

"Make way for his Honour! Make way!" they bellowed, as they strode through the throng of pedestrians. The crowd quickly scattered, leaving a clear passage down the middle of the street. One ragged old woman, either through deafness or distraction, failed to heed the command. She continued to stumble along the thoroughfare clutching three eggs in her hand. With an abrupt shove, one of the guards pushed her into gutter, where she fell with a scream, the eggs smashing against the wall of a house and running in a yellow rivulet into the mud.

Jinwei moved to the side of the road, as a richly-decorated palanquin came into view, borne by four coolies. Rapidly the bearers trotted through the village, and as they passed Jinwei, he realised that the side curtains had been drawn back, no doubt because of the excessive heat. Glancing into the vehicle, he was met with such a venomous expression that he quickly looked away. Lounging on the cushions was a man who looked like an overfed pig, and his face bore the signs of the alcohol and debauchery which doubtless accompanied his high office. The Landlord had obviously recognised Jinwei, and the hatred portrayed in his visage chilled the young man's blood for a moment. Even when the little procession had passed out of sight and sound, he still found himself trembling slightly, and leant against a wall to recover. Of course he knew what lay behind the animosity. Several years previously, the Landlord had moved the boundary of Jinwei's family land, in violation of the long-standing lease that they held. Jinwei's father, himself a well-known craftsman in wood-carving, had taken the case to the magistrate in the nearby town. Despite the Landlord's handsome bribe to the legal officer, the judgment had been handed down in favour of Jinwei's family. In fury, the loser had publicly vowed vengeance against those who had disgraced him. Subsequently the family had tried to minimise their contact with the Landlord, but lived in some trepidation about possible reprisals by that odious official.

That one glimpse of personified hate had rather unnerved Jinwei, and at the same time he began to feel rather hungry. He recalled that, in the haste of finishing his work during the day, he had not eaten since dawn. Thus he felt he could spare ten minutes for a little refreshment, and made his way to one of the more substantial buildings in the village, which served as a cheap restaurant. Under the awning which projected out over the street, he settled himself on the stool beside an empty table. Immediately the proprietor bustled up with a warm welcome.

"Good to see you, Kong Jinwei. This is a happy day for you indeed!"

"Well, tomorrow actually."

"What can I bring you?"

"A bowl of something. Do you have chillied chicken noodles?"

"Surely. Just a moment!"

A waiter plonked down onto the table a pair of chopsticks, a porcelain spoon, a teacup and a kettle of hot tea. As was customary, Jinwei poured some of the tea into the cup, and then used his fingers to wash the chopsticks and spoon in the teacup. Throwing the liquid away, he refilled the cup and began to drink, and shortly his noodles arrived.

"Kong Jinwei! Fancy seeing you here!" came a shout, as a young man approached.

"Can I join you?"

"Of course. Sit down! Wonderful to see you. It's been a long time."

"I hear your sister is marrying tomorrow. Who's the lucky guy?"

"He's called Wang Maqiang. Lives just over the hills. Bright fellow. Specialises in calligraphy, and well educated. I like him very much – and I reckon my sister will be happy with him!"

"Sounds like a good match. Why did you choose tomorrow?"

"We asked the shaman, and he studied the dates carefully. This one is the most auspicious around this period."

"I suppose that the date does not have a 'four' in it!"

They both laughed, for it was well-known that the Chinese sound of "four" was similar to that of "death", and it was bad luck to choose such a date.

"He also made sure that tomorrow is the eighth day of the month – so that it rhymes with our word for 'prosperity'. Such a lot of myths to follow! It's difficult to get it all right, especially as each district has its own local traditions," added Jinwei.

"Have you fulfilled all those Six Etiquettes? Letter, presents, visits, matchmaker – and so on?"

"My father has been scrupulously careful about the details, and the other family has done its part well. We now have a house full of the gifts that they've kept sending us during the last year."

"Talking of dates," his friend interrupted, "I learned something rather odd on my recent trip to Beijing."

"Why did you go all that way?"

"We are in the textile business now. I took a bundle of cloth to a customer in the capital. While I was there I had my first sight of a devil."

Jinwei started. "D'you mean a 'foreign devil'? I've heard about them – but never seen one. What are they like?"

"Just near the gate of Cheng Tian Men, I saw a couple of them. Despite what people say, I think they are human. They are taller than most Chinese, and have long noses and very white skin. They speak in a rather strange way, and then sometimes make weird sounds to each other. It's said that they have a language of their own."

"What's that to do with dates?"

"Oh, I forgot! Someone told me that these devils don't count the years in the proper way. We all know that we are now in the fourteenth year of Emperor Yongle's reign. But the foreigners say it is year 1417."

"That's impossible. No emperor can live for a thousand years!"

"They don't measure the time by their emperors. Their years are counted from an event when some god came down to earth. That's why it is so long."

"Very interesting," Jinwei said. He glanced at the setting sun. "By the way, I must be getting back. Nice to see you again."

As he tramped homeward, his thoughts turned to his sister, Meili. He imagined the sense of excitement, trepidation and hope that would be overwhelming her at this time. Not that he had any qualms about the life that lay ahead of her. Although the marriage had been arranged by the two families without the bride having any awareness of the negotiations, it happened fortuitously that Jinwei knew the bridegroom through several business operations that they had jointly undertaken. His sister's future spouse was a handsome specimen of manhood in his mid-thirties, tall for a Chinese, and respected as a teacher in the area. In fact he and Jinwei had worked together on some construction projects in a neighbouring city involving carved lettering, where their complementary expertise had produced impressive decoration in stone on the city walls.

His arrival home was greeted with the news that the pressure and anxiety had caused his mother to take to her bed. But it was confidently expected that she would be up early the next morning to oversee the finishing touches to decorations, food and drink.

For a while after the evening meal, the brother and sister sat together and reminisced about their lives. They had grown up in this corner of north China under the beneficent rule of the Ming emperor. Although Meili was not supposed to know anything about her husband of the following day, Jinwei tried to paint a word picture of the man, and give her an insight into the kind, sensitive person that he appeared to be.

They talked late into the night, Jinwei prolonging this last opportunity of seeing her, before she was whisked over the hills to her new life.

Chapter 2

Woeful Wedding

The next morning dawned bright and clear, taken as a sign that heaven was smiling on the wedding day. Long before the sun, the household was up and about – and the air of expectancy was tangible. Meili was meticulously enrobed in several layers of ceremonial red clothing. Her hair was intricately plaited with coloured threads, and her face heavily made-up with red and pink cosmetics. Then she was plunged into semi-darkness as a large red headdress enshrouded her down to the shoulders, giving her only a dim appreciation of the outside world through the thick veil. She was to be condemned to this discomfort until the evening, when her husband would gain his first view of his bride.

Soon after the appearance of the sun, the village people of Split Mountain began to stream towards the Kong's home, full of laughter and banter. The earliest arrivals settled themselves in the main reception room of the house, the centre-piece of which was Meili in all her carmine glory. As was customary, she was convulsed with sobs, with tears dripping through the veil in places. This was a proper acknowledgement that she loved her family, and was making a sacrifice in leaving for another home.

Soon the crowd, laughing and joking, had overflowed into the grounds of the house. Their hosts served wine and sweetmeats to the growing horde. Periodically, eyes would turn towards the eponymous gap in the opposite mountain, through which the expected procession would come.

As midday came without any sign of the wedding party, lunch was served to satisfy the voracious appetites of the hundreds of supporters, motivated to be there either by heart or stomach.

Late in the afternoon as the sun was beginning to dip towards the horizon, a group of little boys came running along the track, shouting "They're coming! They're coming!" Some of their elders had to quieten their boisterous enthusiasm, since by that time everyone had got the message. Conversations ceased, as everyone strained their ears for the anticipated sounds.

Then the wind brought the echo of a drum, followed by a trumpet and cymbals. Up in the defile between the mountains a small group of brightly-dressed dancers could be seen, heading for the village. As they neared the waiting throng, it became clear that there were several cavorting young men surrounding a tall lithe figure, who walked with easy grace. Behind them, four burly young fellows were carrying an empty sedan chair.

At the entrance to the Kong's courtyard, the little procession stopped, and all the young men bowed to the waiting company. After returning the gesture, Meili's father stepped forward and addressed the groom and his attendants.

"Welcome, Wang Maqiang, to my humble house. May you and your companions be pleased to enter my home."

Smiling broadly, the husband-elect passed through the courtyard into the doorway of the house. Immediately, he fell flat on his face with a cry. The people roared with laughter, as he carefully removed the slimy banana skins that had been laid across the entrance. It was customary for various impediments to be put in the way of a bridegroom seeking his betrothed. Ultimately, he obtained his first sight of his future spouse – albeit only a red-clothed, plaintively-weeping form.

The bridegroom's party was then entertained for a short while, until sufficiently fortified with food and drink to begin their return journey over the hills.

At this point it was the role of Jinwei, as the elder brother, to gently guide his sister out of the house to the inviting sedan chair. There was much cheering as she took her seat, and the stolid porters prepared for their arduous walk to take Meili to her new home.

But then the atmosphere changed. Gradually the hilarity subsided, and was replaced by an awesome silence. One by one people nudged each other, and pointed towards the road leading up from the village. A few began to cry out in fear, and the family seemed to have turned to stone as they stared at the unwelcome scene.

Marching up the roadway were four uniformed, armed men. Jinwei recognised them at once – they were the guards of the Landlord. The image of that hostile face in the palanquin came back to Jinwei, and his stomach began to churn.

The four soldiers did not stand on ceremony, but marched straight into the courtyard of the house. Each held his halberd upright, allowing the sun to reflect off the polished surface of the blade, and reveal its finely-honed edge.

Nobody moved.

The sergeant took a small scroll from his pocket, and began to read in a taunting voice.

"Listen, all you who hear! By order of the Landlord of this district, we are to convey one Kong Meili to the house of the aforementioned Landlord."

"What nonsense is this?" shouted Jinwei's father. "Get off my land at once!"

The soldier continued to read, "Since the bride dwells within the jurisdiction of the Landlord, he is claiming the 'first-night privilege of carnal knowledge' on her wedding night."

With a smirk, the man rolled up the scroll, and handed it to the head of the family.

"This is preposterous!" screamed the bridegroom. "Nobody is going to take my wife from me! That custom is simply an old myth that was never carried out."

"We have our orders, and will obey them," barked the sergeant. "Seize the chair!"

With a rapid jump, the young man leapt in front of the sedan, shielding his intended from the attackers. Like lightning, one of the soldiers reversed his halberd, and brought the thick shaft down on the head of the bridegroom. Without a sound he collapsed on the ground and a great wailing rose from the onlookers, while a stream of blood oozed from the injured man's skull.

Jinwei readied himself to leap forward to his sister's defence, but his father's hand gripped his wrist.

"No more bloodshed, my son! These men mean business. We must find another way."

"Ready, lady?" the sergeant cried mockingly, as the soldiers lifted the four carrying-poles of the sedan chair. "Our master can't wait to get to know you!"

The response was a terrified scream from within the red veil. Dumbly, the assembly watched the armed men carry the chair and its frantic occupant down the road.

"You can have her back in the morning!" was the final taunt. "She'll be better educated then."

The family quickly turned its attention to the injured bridegroom, who soon regained consciousness. Despite a considerable amount of bleeding, a doctor among the guests declared that the skull was not actually fractured, and that the young man would soon recover.

The crowd of well-wishers soon melted away, leaving the depleted family in a state of absolute dejection. Meili's mother had fainted at the sight of her stricken future son-in-law, and was being careful attended by the servants in her bedroom. Her husband had reacted with great anger, and seemed to have lost his rationality.

"We must do something!" he stormed. "Send a messenger to the city. See the mayor! Tell him to stop this thing!"

The others tried to reason with him. "But the city is a long way off – and those officials won't move fast. Anyway, the present mayor is a crony of our Landlord. We can't rely on him."

Someone put in, "I hear that he also has strong connections in Beijing."

"Do it anyway! Send someone quickly!"

Reluctantly, with no hope of success, arrangements were made to seek aid from the main municipality. But it was obvious that help could not arrive in time to save Meili from the intentions of her captor. The youngest son of the family was given the fastest horse, with instructions to do all he could to rouse a response from the city officials.

Nobody noticed that Jinwei had quietly slipped away. Unobtrusively, he followed the group of soldiers as they carried the sedan chair like a piece of booty through the village. On the far side stood the mansion of the Landlord. It was surrounded by a high stone wall, surmounted with sharp iron spikes. Jinwei watched helplessly as the sedan was carried with triumphant shouts through the entrance archway. Then the great wooden gates slammed shut.

Jinwei sat despondently on a rock, while the sun slowly departed from that sad day. It was all too easy to visualise that horrible monster putting his hands on his beloved Meili. But she was incarcerated behind the thick walls of her captor's home – and Jinwei felt totally helpless.

Slowly a vague memory stirred in his mind. Several years before, he had done some repairing of stonework on the Landlord's estate, although he had never been paid. But while working there, he had noticed a large oak tree standing just outside the property. Its sturdy limbs had projected over the wall, and Jinwei had surmised that it could provide a possible route into the garden from the outside world. Now he wondered if it was still there, and whether he could find it in the gathering darkness.

Stepping gingerly across to the wall, he began to follow it

towards the point where the tree might be. Just before dusk fell, he reached the ancient trunk, and quickly began to climb. He was pleased to find that one thick branch extended over the wall in a downward direction. Quickly he clambered along it, and dropped into the gloom of the Landlord's garden. Raking the poorly-lit area with his eyes, he remembered the layout. It was a typical landscape garden of the period, with ponds, rocks, trees, shrubs and flowers. Among these ran a maze of paved paths and stone steps. Around the area were several single-storey pavilions. One, in particular, was swathed in muted light emanating from the lattice windows. He headed towards it, guessing this might be the Landlord's bedroom, although moving cautiously because of the convolutions of the pathways.

On reaching the building, Jinwei stepped up to the main window. Curtains were drawn across it, but several gaps enabled him to see inside. One glance sufficed to reassure him that his guess had been correct. He was staring into a lavish chamber. As his eyes became accustomed to the light, he could pick out ornate chairs, lacquered tables and intricately-carved artefacts. Suddenly, to his horror, he saw a large bed against the far wall. Lying on it, partially covered with a sheet, was his sister.

At once a great rage swept through him, overpowering him with emotion. He wrenched open the flimsy casement, and climbed through the opening into the bedroom. The figure on the bed gave a startled scream, as he darted across the room to the bedside. Immediately, he heard the sound of approaching footsteps. Next moment Jinwei was confronted by the bear-like body of the Landlord, clad only in a thin robe. With a bellow of rage and recognition, the monster leapt towards Jinwei, but not before drawing a short dagger from behind a pile of books. Jinwei looked in vain for a weapon, or at least a means of defence. The best he could do was to grab an alabaster statue of a young warrior. Even in that instant, his brain registered that it was one of his own creations. He threw the sculpture with all his might at the approaching menace, hitting him on the chest. This did not stop the headlong rush of the infuriated

Landlord, and the projectile crashed to the floor at his feet. Judging by the colour of his face, the assailant had been drinking heavily, and this worked for Jinwei's salvation. Not perceiving the broken statue on the floor, the Landlord tripped over it, fell forward, caught the corner of a table with his forehead, collapsed on the carpet, and lay still.

"Meili, be quick! We must escape before he comes round," Jinwei gasped, breathing heavily.

"But I have no clothes," came the whimpered reply.

"Where are they?"

"Over by the window, I think."

Immediately, Jinwei grasped a bundle, and threw it onto the bed. Turning his back on his sister, he urged her to enrobe as quickly as possible. Meanwhile he watched the recumbent form on the floor for any signs of returning consciousness.

"Ready now," breathed Meili through tears.

With a fair amount of help, she managed to negotiate the splintered window. Guiding her with his hand, Jinwei led her along the narrow paths between the shrubs. After a while, he realised he was lost, and they found themselves on a tiny peninsular in a small lake. Retracing his steps, he tried to reorient himself with respect to the buildings surrounding the garden. After several false trails, they reached the garden wall, where the oak tree bowed to them invitingly.

Silently they edged their way along the branches, and descended to the ground outside the wall. At once, Jinwei picked up his shattered sister, and carried her through the night back to their home.

As they approached the house, they could hear their father raving. On seeing them, he quietened down and listened to the tale of Jinwei's exploit.

"Of course, the Landlord will be after us in no time." Jinwei panted. "What can we do?"

"Just wait for the city to send someone out to put things right. Your brother must have arrived hours ago, and is probably on his way back with a contingent right now. Let's hope they get here before the Landlord," he said, full of unfounded hope.

Meanwhile, the servants took Meili to her room, and with the aid of a draught of opium, sent her off to sleep. Jinwei himself was hit by a wave of nausea and exhaustion. Taking to his bed, he promptly dropped off - trusting that the morrow would be a better day.

Chapter 3

Frightened Felon

Jinwei was awakened by the jingle of harnesses and the pawing of horses. At first he did not realise where he was, but then the memory of the previous night hit him. He hoped that he was hearing the sounds of help from the city, so that their confrontation with the Landlord could be concluded. Rising with alacrity, he peered out into the courtyard. A squad of the city-militia was standing truculently before Jinwei's father, and an oxcart stood in the gateway.

"I am ordered to arrest Kong Jinwei," announced the senior officer. "He is charged with the murder of the Landlord of this district."

Jinwei's blood turned to ice. He had not imagined that the fall in the bedroom could have been fatal, but someone had obviously been sent to the city with a report to that effect.

"But - we can explain..." began his father.

"No explanations. Leave that for the judge!" shouted the man. "Search the house and grounds at once!"

Realising the hopelessness of the situation, Jinwei stepped out into the courtyard, and said in a low voice "I am Kong Jinwei."

Without allowing a moment for discussion, the soldiers seized Jinwei, clamped iron manacles onto his hands and feet, and threw him bodily into the back of the oxcart. Despite his father's desperate entreaties, the group whipped up the two oxen, and lumbered away in the direction of the town.

It seemed like the longest three hours of Jinwei's life, bouncing on the rough boards of the cart, as it corkscrewed along the rutted road. Soon he was covered in bruises, and his bonds prevented him from moving to a more comfortable position.

Eventually the nightmare ceased, and the small troop entered the forbidding gates of the city jail.

But the ending of one trauma was the beginning of another. He was dragged along a corridor of cells, and then thrust into a small cubicle. After the removal of his manacles, a warder brought a wooden board about fifty centimetres square with a central hole. Jinwei recognised this as the dreaded "canque". The device was in two parts which hinged open, allowing it to be put round his neck and then closed. After it was locked, Jinwei found that his hands were unable to reach his face, making it impossible to feed himself or blow his nose.

He was then led out into a public square in front of the jail, where he saw several other prisoners wearing canques. They were kept under the watchful eye of a guard, while a number of philanthropic citizens put food into their mouths. It was patently clear that this was the only way that these convicts received any sustenance. At the same time, an unruly group of small boys ridiculed the prisoners, and threw mud and rotten eggs at them. Jinwei endured all this with a sinking heart, and eventually was taken back to a cell in the main penitentiary.

As he tried to sit on the stone floor with bruised limbs and the heavy canque round his neck, he gave up all hope of life - or even any desire to live longer. He knew that the next day he would face a court where he would get no justice, and he trembled at the thought of the hideous forms of execution specified for murderers. He pondered the fact that he had fallen so far. Two days ago, he had been a proud member of a family that had the same surname as China's greatest thinker. Then a maxim, purportedly from that august precursor, came into his mind, "Our greatest glory is not in never falling, but in rising every time we fall." It all seemed so simplistic, but how could he ever escape from this situation? However, he resolved that if the chance ever came, he would rise again from his fallen state.

****

It was impossible to sleep in the filthy dungeon, with his many bruises aching every time he tried to find a comfortable posture, and the canque chaffing his neck whenever he moved. Several times he heard the warder making his rounds, and trying the doors of the cells.

After the night had dragged on for many weary hours, the sound of footsteps indicated the guard was still on patrol. But this time, the steps stopped at his door, and he discerned the muted sounds of the lock being turned. A figure was silhouetted against the dim light from the corridor.

"Jinwei are you there?" came a whisper.

"Yes, yes, who is it?"

"I'm Wang Maqiang. We must move quickly."

It took several seconds for the incongruity of the situation to register with Jinwei - and he concluded that he must be dreaming. There was no way that his prospective brother-in-law could be here in the same cell. Then his uncertainty vanished, as his rescuer crept up beside him, and started to unlock the canque from his neck. After being gently helped to his feet, Jinwei found himself being guided out of the cell, and towards the entrance of the prison. On reaching the main gate, they stepped past the recumbent form of the jailor lying in a chair by the open door. Leaving the prison, they slunk furtively along the darkened streets. Eventually, they came out of the suburbs of the town onto a narrow muddy path. Only then did Jinwei believe that this was reality and not fantasy, and immediately his voice came back.

"Maqiang, is this really you?"

"It certainly is – and I'm heartily glad to have got you out of that place."

Until this moment, Jinwei had only casually noticed the white turban that his companion was wearing, but then he realised it was a large bandage covering much of his head. Recollection of the events of the previous day flooded back.

"But how did you achieve this? That was the city's main jail."

"Well, it happened that I knew the warder on duty tonight. Not personally - but my brother did a service for him once. You know our tradition of 'guanxi', honourable indebtedness. Well in this case we were able to ask for repayment by helping you to escape. Don't worry about him – he agreed to accept drugged wine, and will only get a reprimand and a demotion for it. But he is now considerably richer for his cooperation!

On their brief walk, they had met no one. But Jinwei jumped nervously when he heard the whinny of a horse just ahead.

"Don't be afraid. That is your horse - tied to a tree over there by the main road. If you ride west, you'll be in Jining in a couple of hours. The Grand Canal runs through there, and you can probably get a passage on a boat going down to Suzhou. After that, you'll have to start a new life – and we hope the authorities will not catch up with you. With your skills you should find a job easily. Stone masons are in great demand. Of course…," he said wistfully, "our family will miss you, but it's your only chance."

"How can I thank you enough, Maqiang – for taking this great risk to save me from such a ghastly death?"

"I'm the one who is grateful. You saved my wife from something worse than death…"

"What do you mean - your wife?" Jinwei interrupted testily.

Maqiang laughed. "Last night I had a long talk with your father. Your sister has been dishonoured, but fortunately you rescued her before that monster could violate her. I am quite prepared to go through with the marriage. In fact, your father considered that really the ceremonial process was virtually complete. Meili and I only had to bow to the household gods to be joined as one. In view of these strange circumstances, your father agreed that we complete the ritual last night. And now Meili and I are husband and wife."

"That's amazing... I'm so glad for you... I mean, congratulations!" Jinwei stammered. "But can you still live in this area after all that has happened?"

"Not with all this gossip and innuendo around us. We think it best if we too go away to start a new life. Our plan is to travel across the mountains into Shanxi, and there I will seek a teaching position. Shouldn't be difficult."

By this time the clouds had moved across the sky, allowing a full moon to illuminate their surroundings. Jinwei saw a fine horse tied to a tree.

"But this must have cost you a great deal."

"Don't worry about it. Count it as my gift to my new brother-in-law," Maqiang joked. "Now, listen carefully. In the saddlebags you will find some food and money – enough to keep you going for a while. Also, there is a suit of clothes, which I hope will make you blend in with other people. You can make out that you are a travelling salesman for an agricultural company – or something like that,"

"But, where should I go?"

"Follow this road for about thirty miles. As soon as it is getting light, turn the horse loose, put on your disguise, and walk into Jining town. Try to find a barge going south that will take you. May heaven go with you!"

"And you too. I will never forget your bravery and kindness - and will tell my children of it. But go carefully yourself, and look after my sister."

"Rest assured of that. Now - away with you! The hunt for you will be on very soon."

The two men clasped hands, then embraced. Jinwei mounted quickly, and cantered away along the road. Sensing that pursuit would come before long, he was tempted to travel at full gallop, but realised that a degree of circumspection was needed. Although he was on a main road, the surface was still rough enough to cripple a horse if not ridden carefully. Also, he felt that a galloping horse would attract more attention in the villages than one going at a moderate pace.

****

Happily the bright moonlight assisted him on his way. Several times he passed through small villages, where dogs barked furiously - but no one appeared or challenged him. Mostly the roadway ran along dykes between paddy fields, and only towards the last part of the route did he begin to climb through low mountains. Eventually he saw a cluster of lights on a hillside ahead of him, and guessed that he was approaching Jining. At the same time, the greyness of the night was replaced by the peculiar light of the false dawn, and he acknowledged that it was time to abandon his steed. Finding a small copse, he dismounted and removed the pannier bags from the saddle. Then giving the horse a smack, he sent it trotting away into the fields.

Inside one of the bags, he found a fine blue "zhishen" whose name literally meant "straight body", and denoted a full-length robe with side slits below the waist. It was the traditional casual attire for men of breeding, but not sufficiently ostentatious to arouse comment. Many a traveller would be wearing such clothing, and once he added the black hat that he found in the bag, Jinwei would look like thousands of other Chinese males. Rummaging further, he found several packages of sticky rice wrapped in lotus leaves, as well as a sack containing a supply of steamed-bread buns. It appeared that Maqiang had thoughtfully selected the bags, since they looked like the usual receptacles carried by travellers, and did not betray their equine connections.

After dressing carefully and adjusting his baggage, Jinwei stepped out onto the road, and strode purposefully towards the town. Unfortunately, a peasant from one of the little shacks by the road spotted him, and stared in puzzlement at such a well-dressed man coming out of the woodland. Jinwei feared that this man might alert his pursuers, but there was no time for concerns on that score.

A further matter of significance suddenly struck him. It was obviously vital that he should avoid using his true name. Doubtless the story of his escape would ripple through the countryside in no time, and there would be official posses sent in all directions. After musing for a while, he decided that he would be renamed as Wu Fashang, and he carefully repeated the name until he felt confident that he would automatically use it in preference to his previous moniker.

By this time, he was entering the streets of the town, where people were beginning the day's activities. Not wishing to get into conversation with anyone, he walked confidently along the main street, and out into the country beyond. He continued onward until rewarded with a rather strange sight. On the far side of a paddy field he saw an earth embankment, along the top of which a set of coloured sails was gliding. Thankfully, he turned towards the spectacle, climbed the bank, and found himself on the edge of the Grand Canal.

Despite having heard many people discussing this remarkable engineering achievement, he was quite overawed by the scene before him. What looked like a river, two hundred metres wide, was studded with a plethora of boats of many designs. Small sampans were being rowed between the shores, middle-sized junks were making their way along the waterway, and huge grain barges with high sterns were moored along the towpath. It was evident that some of these vessels were preparing to get under way. Since the wind was blowing down the canal from the north, a couple of barges were preparing to be towed upwind by means of long ropes extending to teams of men on the banks. Wu Fashang, as he was now called, noted with appreciation that his journey to the south would have a following wind, which he trusted would be advantageous to his escape.

On one of the barges, the sails were being bent on, indicating that it would be sailing very soon. Fashang walked along the bank, and hailed a man on the vessel.

"My man, are you going south today?"

The man looked up. "We are, sir."

"Can you give me a passage to Hangzhou?"

"You'll have to ask the captain," he said, as he ducked into a hatchway.

Fashang, his new name gradually becoming more familiar, had assessed the dangers of giving away his intended destination. So he had deliberately mentioned the remotest point on the canal. Actually, he was planning to leave the boat earlier than that, and immerse himself in a large city.

"Good morning to you, sir!" came a strong voice, and an agile, middle-aged man, having the bearing of a captain, emerged onto the deck. "How can I help you?"

"I am looking for a passage southward. Are you able to take a passenger?"

"Come aboard, so I can see you better."

Gingerly, Fashang made his way along a single swaying plank leading from shore to boat. Arriving on deck, he was confronted by the master of the vessel. "I'm going as far as Suzhou – if that's any help to you. I can take you there in about ten days, if the wind keeps up."

"That would suit me very well. And what would be the cost?"

"Depends what you want. I have a spare bunk in a small cabin next to mine in the poop. If you want food, you can mess with the crew – just like I do."

Then he named a price which, although high, was within Fashang's financial means.

"I'm not made of money," he said wryly, and named a much lower sum.

The captain chuckled. "Why not split the difference?"

"That sounds reasonable. I'll be happy to join you. My name is... is Wu Fashang."

"Pleased to have you aboard, Mr Wu. We're returning from carrying wheat to Beijing, and so are travelling empty at the moment. With a fair wind, we should make good time, but we have to moor up every night. This barge is too big to go rushing on into the darkness."

The captain ordered one of his men to show Fashang to his simple quarters. "We will sail in about an hour. You can get some noodles at that place on the wharf if you're hungry," he added.

Chapter 4

Grand Canal

With much shouting, and some singing, the sails on the four masts of the barge were hoisted. Since each sail had five long bamboo battens sewn into the heavy canvas, the task was onerous. Amid repetitions of "Yi, er, san... Yi, er, san...," each sail crept slowly up its mast, while the ten men on the halyard sweated and strained. Then the lines running from the ends of the battens were carefully sorted and cleated.

On the captain's command, mooring lines were cast off, and the bow of the craft pushed out into the canal, using long poles. With a favourable wind on the quarter, the skipper was able to set a steady course down the waterway. The crew scurried about with the ropes from the sail-battens, adjusting the sail shapes for the fullness or flatness required by the master. The broad reach was the fastest point of sailing for this type of vessel, and soon a bow-wave was frothing past the sides.

Fashang realised that his presence would be an encumbrance to the delicate task of getting under way, and so secreted himself in a corner of the poop deck. He observed the strained features and the intense concentration of the captain as his vessel flew down the crowded waterway. A sailor had been stationed on the bow next to a large gong, and with a hefty club sounded a warning to other users of the channel. Most of the small sampans and junks took flight towards the shores at the approach of this voluminous grain barge.

After about an hour, the canal widened considerably, and Fashang noticed that they appeared to have joined a wide river. Thus the complexity of the navigation diminished, and the captain called out.

"Mr Wu, would you care to join me up here?"

Fashang climbed the ladder to the control platform, where the master was standing beside the huge tiller that was being manned by two men. He instructed the helmsmen to keep a tower on the shore in line with a mountain peak, and then turned to Fashang.

"This is your first voyage on the Canal, Mr Wu?"

"It is. And I'm finding it very interesting. How long is the whole waterway?"

"In total it is about a thousand miles. But it was only last year that the whole length became continuously navigable. When the Emperor moved from Nanjing in the south up to Beijing some twelve years ago, there was a problem getting grain up there. The old system used a lot of trans-shipment of cargoes from one river to another, but now the route links all the lakes and tributaries of the various deltas – including the Yellow River and the Yangtze.

"That's an impressive piece of engineering."

"And when you think there are ten thousand grain barges like this plying up and down, you appreciate there must be a lot of hungry people up north," he laughed.

The further south that the wind carried him, the more Fashang's sense of unease began to dissipate. The memory of recent days diffused slightly, and he began to plan ahead for a new life, confident that he had left his pursuers in the hills of Shandong.

He decided to explore the barge, which took the standard pattern of ships in the Ming Dynasty. The bow was relatively low, while the horseshoe-shaped stern carried a large aftercastle containing the captain's cabin, chart-room and passenger accommodation. Above this, lay the poop deck from which most of the navigation was undertaken, and which could provide a measure of defence in case of boarding by attackers. The middle section of the vessel was divided into covered cubicles, which acted as grain-bins. The crew of thirty brawny, coarse sailors slept in the forepeak of the barge, well away from the captain's quarters. Meals were taken communally under a canopy on the central deck.

Before long, the craft turned into a much narrower man-made waterway, and then Fashang noticed what appeared to be a gate right across the canal. He stared with perplexity at this obstruction, while noting that the sails were being lowered.

"Never seen a lock before, Mr Wu?" the captain enquired.

"It's quite new to me. What happens now?"

"Wait and see!"

The barge pulled into the bank, and the majority of the crew climbed on shore. A thick rope was passed to them, and they stood waiting. After a furious ringing of the gong from the boat, the large gate started to move, and gradually opened to reveal a long rectangular pool. At once the crew began to tow the vessel through the opening, and to a mooring along the internal wall. At the same time, several other smaller boats, that had been waiting, crowded in as well.

"The principle of the lock is this," explained the captain as the huge wooden gate shut behind them. "We are now trapped between these two gates across the canal. As you can see, the man over there is turning a windlass. That opens a tunnel to let the water out."

"Already we are beginning to drop down," observed Fashang.

"And once we reach the level of the water downstream, they can open the lower gate – and we'll be on our way again."

"Incredibly ingenious!"

"One more feather in the cap of Chinese engineers. The first lock was built on this canal four hundred years ago. The reason we need this system is that the canal rises quite high halfway along its length. In fact, where you joined us, Mr Wu, at Jining is the highest spot. They built massive reservoirs there to provide water for the canal."

"I'm learning every day," replied Fashang.

During that day they negotiated two more locks and then moored for the night. Fashang joined the crew for the simple evening meal of rice and fish, but found it was quite adequate. He struggled with the conversation of the sailors which was hard to understand, since most of them had a strong southern dialect. He guessed that the majority came from Suzhou.

"And where d'you come from, friend?" one of them asked suddenly. "Your accent is very strange to us."

Fashang caught his breath, knowing that his speech could betray his origin. Having anticipated this situation, he had an answer ready, assuming that these men were not very conversant with the geography of north China.

"My home is Kaifeng in Hebei province," he replied calmly.

"I had a friend from Hebei," pondered one of the sailors, "but he didn't sound at all like you."

"Almost every town has a different dialect in our area," Fashang responded hastily.

"Oh, that's it then."

Fashang realised that his distinctive Shandong accent could be the cause of his undoing in the future. There were certain sounds, such as "sh" that were never used in his home area, and he was quite incapable of articulating them. His only hope was to bury himself in a cosmopolitan city where his speech would be less noticeable.

****

For several days they continued their southward journey along the Grand Canal. Having left the mountains behind, the waterway ran for long distances between raised dykes through fields of corn or rice, which extended in monotonous flatness to the horizon. Periodically their route took them through large, shallow lakes before joining up with man-made channels again.

After a few days of fair wind, they awoke one morning to a flat calm, and the sails were not hoisted. The captain ordered his crew onto the embankment to start towing the vessel with a long rope, which had a series of loops for the men to put round their waists. After several hours of this strenuous labour, the sailors were beginning to flag, and the speed was too slow for the captain's liking. He decided to release the two steersmen to join the dispirited gang on the towpath in order to keep the craft moving.

"Mr Wu. I wonder if you would care to try your hand at steering. We are moving quite slowly, and it won't require great effort. I will go forward and shout directions from the bow."

"Certainly, Captain, I'll be glad to assist," replied Fashang.

And thus it was that he learned how to steer a large boat, and to take orders for changes of direction to avoid obstructions and sandbanks. It was a new experience for him, and little did he anticipate that this skill might in the future prove of crucial value.

The following day proved even more difficult, as the wind sprung up from the south, directly opposing their course. After towing for several hours, they reached one of the shallow lagoons where it was impossible to haul by rope. The sailors spent most of the day punting the vessel across with the aid of long poles.

Happily, the wind backed to a more agreeable direction after that, and their passage continued quite speedily along the canal. A memorable distraction occurred one afternoon, when the sounds of trumpets and drums could be heard behind them. The captain reacted immediately by ordering the sails to be struck, then steering towards the bank, and quickly mooring alongside. Fashang noticed that all the other boats on the river were taking similar action.

"Everyone on the centre deck!" ordered the skipper. "Everyone kneel – now, heads on the floor!"

Fashang delayed his obedience long enough to glance up the canal at the cause of this commotion. Bearing down on them along the centre of the channel was a luxurious barge, glistening with gold and carrying a suit of emblazoned sails. The middle section of the vessel took the form of a raised pavilion, within which richly-ornamented furniture could be seen.

"What is it?" he murmured, as he lowered his face to the floor.

"It's the Imperial Barge," replied the captain. "No one is allowed to look at it, on pain of punishment. Keep your head down, Mr Wu. You can look when it's gone past."

When the reverberations of the drums began to diminish, everyone cautiously raised their heads. Observing the stern of this elaborate pleasure vessel, the captain commented, "It seems the Emperor was not on board. Perhaps it's going to bring one of the princes back from Hangzhou."

After several days of this pleasant outdoor existence with the panorama of countryside and town sliding slowly past them, Fashang felt his sense of fear slip away completely. He analysed his own feelings - anger towards the Landlord, apprehension for his sister, and trepidation about his own future. But, remembering the slogan of the esteemed philosopher, he promised himself that even though he had fallen, he would rise again. Thus he began to feel a measure of excitement about the challenges and opportunities of his new life. That night he slept very peacefully – but it would be the last time for many days.

Next morning, as the boat's company was breakfasting under the central awning, they heard noises on the far side of the canal. Several boats were moored there, and the sight of horsemen riding, shouting and stopping on the bank could be vaguely discerned through the morning mist.

"Fetch me my sighting-tube!" ordered the captain, and soon he was peering through the long wooden tunnel of this apparatus. Although the image was not magnified, the exclusion of all extraneous side light did make it easier to see an object at a distance.

"Very strange! Looks like soldiers. But it's not an attack. Something is going on," he pondered. "You there, take the sampan and scull across to find out what's up!"

Soon one of the sailors departed on his mission, and was seen talking with the crew of a junk on the opposite shore. Then he rowed back to report. When he climbed on deck, he was shaking and stammering.

"Well, what is it?" demanded the captain.

"Well, sir, they say…"

"Get on with it. What did they say?"

"I don't believe it – but they said…"

"Come on, man! What did you learn?"

"Jinyiwei…"

"Say that again – you don't mean Jinyiwei, do you?"

"That's what they said. They were checking all the boats."

The colour faded from all the faces of the crew.

"By heaven, we're lost. Get rid of all that illicit spirit we're carrying," expostulated the captain. "At once!"

"But what's the matter, captain," asked Fashang.

"Don't you know who the Jinyiwei are?"

"Yes, we've all heard of them. But surely they only stay in Beijing. They're the Emperor's secret police. Why would they come this far from the capital?"

The captain interrogated the sailor again, "Are you really sure they said it was the Jinyiwei?"

"One of the men on that large junk over there said they were wearing the special embroidered uniform, and he saw the gold tablet on the torso of one. That shows they were genuine." He added, "And someone saw one of the blade weapons that only they may carry."

"Anything else?"

"It seems they were searching for a criminal, but nothing more. A murderer who killed a landlord in Shandong."

With concern in his voice, the captain said, "Mr Wu, are you all right? You seem in a state of collapse."

"Oh, yes, Captain. I think something in the breakfast upset my stomach. Maybe I'll lie down."

As Fashang departed to his bunk, the captain continued to try and solve the puzzle. "Why would the Jinyiwei bother with a provincial murder case? That's for the local authorities."

"Apparently this landlord was related to a senior eunuch in the court," volunteered the sailor, "and they are taking it seriously. They're working their way down the canal, and will come up this side before long."

Fashang had heard many rumours of the vast intelligence network of the Jinyiwei, and of their cruelty and violence in upholding the security of the state. He trembled at the very thought of falling into their hands. And yet he knew he was trapped. He lay on his bunk, emotionally and psychologically exhausted, knowing that the end was near. His desperate ploy to start a new life was about to be extinguished.

The captain entered the small cabin, and sat on the bed.

"It's you, isn't it?"

"What d'you mean?"

"You are the one – the one they're looking for. I guessed something like this."

"Well, what will you do? Turn me in to them? That's your duty," Fashang said weakly.

"I'm not sure. You don't look the type to do a thing like that. Anyway, some of those landlords deserve it. Let me think for a moment."

After what seemed like an eternity, the captain looked Fashang in the face.

"I don't believe you're a criminal – and I will help you. What d'you plan to do?

"I hope to reach Suzhou. It's so big, and so mixed up, that I could probably disappear into the crowd there."

"That's what I guessed you would try. Look here, I have an idea…"

Sails were hoisted, and the barge began to surge onward down the canal. At one point in mid-morning they passed a moored junk on which they could clearly see the activity of uniformed men. The sun reflected off their brightly-coloured garments, and there was little doubt that this was a Jinyiwei search party.

In late afternoon, the captain ordered the men to moor up near to a large village. He made sure that he was on the opposite bank from where the searchers had been seen. Just as mooring lines were being tightened, the crew was surprised to see Fashang appear on deck wearing his travelling clothes and carrying his bags.

"Well, Captain, I must thank you for your hospitality. I trust that we are settled up financially."

"Indeed, Mr Wu. And it's been a pleasure to have you as a travelling companion. May heaven go with you, and bless you."

Looking around at the crew members who had become his

friends, Fashang bade them all goodbye, and then stepped ashore. Without looking back, he strode out towards the village, and was soon lost to sight in the jumble of houses.

****

That evening, the captain was feeling in a particularly generous mood, and doubled the usual allowance of grog for all his sailors. Consequently, the rowdiness in the forepeak did not last so long as on most nights. Sitting on the deck in the darkness, the captain eventually concluded that the men were all sound asleep. Taking a lantern, he shone it towards the silent shore, and after a while was rewarded with the slight swaying of the boat as someone came up the gangplank. Without words, he hustled Fashang into his quarters in the poop, and then locked the entry door securely.

"So far, so good. Where did you go?"

"I passed through the village, and saw another on a hilltop. So I headed in a determined way for that. When I reached a copse of trees, I hid there till nightfall - and then crept back here."

"There's some food on the table. Help yourself. I've told the cook that I want to eat in my cabin from now on – so there will be plenty for us to share."

"I do appreciate what you are doing – and the risk you are taking."

"No matter. Now get to your bunk. You will be up early tomorrow."

Fashang retired at once, but failed to find sleep throughout the long hours of the night. Just as light was filtering into the cabin, he was roused by his host.

"Time to move your dwelling," the captain said sardonically.

He led Fashang to a spot in the lower deck near to the sternpost of the vessel. Carefully removing a panel of the flooring, he revealed a small cavity below. It was just sufficiently large for a man to sit, despite being partially filled by a thick wooden beam running vertically through the space.

"This is the rudder stock, which is held in place by those two large bolts. If we ever run aground, then we come down here to unship the rudder, so that we can get off. But that is very rare, and you will be quite safe here."

Cautiously Fashang climbed into the tiny space. Handing down a bottle of water and a small bag of food, the captain replaced the wooden panel, leaving Fashang in semi-darkness. As his eyes adjusted to the light, he found that he could monitor the outside world through a few small holes in the planking. The compartment had never been intended for human occupation, and soon Fashang was feeling very cramped as he sat on the rough woodwork.

Before long, he could feel the motion of the boat changing, as it got under way again. The thick timber passing vertically through his limited space began to rotate back and forth as the helmsman moved the tiller on the deck above. He also began to feel rather sick in the enclosed unventilated environment. However, he was thankful to be alive, and still clinging to the remote possibility of escaping his awful predicament.

And so began a painful, wearying existence. By night Fashang could sleep comfortably in his bunk in the lower poop deck. But, paradoxically, the days were the nightmares. Hour after hour, he sat curled up in the rudder chamber, listening to the water cascading past the transom of the boat. His health began to deteriorate, and he felt nauseous and weak much of the time.

However, the stratagem proved effective. Late one afternoon, as the barge was passing through a lock, he heard strident shouts. Peering through a suitable aperture in the woodwork, he saw a collection of horses and richly embroidered cloaks. Within minutes, he heard heavy footsteps and angry voices above him. There was much banging of the deck, and sounds of lockers being opened. Fashang froze, and prayed for invisibility. After an apparently interminable period, the voices ceased, and the footsteps died away. From his spy hole, he could see the Jinyiwei officers conversing together on the shore, followed by mounting and riding away.

Chapter 5

Suzhou Fugitive

The days became a confused blur, and he lost count of time as the plunging vessel ate up the miles of the Grand Canal. One evening, after emerging from his rabbit-hole into the captain's quarters, he was surprised to hear where they were.

"Mr Wu, tomorrow we will enter Suzhou. That's where you leave us, I understand. Do you know the area?"

"Not at all. Can you advise me?"

"In fact, our destination is some way from the city centre - and you must get away from the barge as soon as we moor up."

"What's the best way to travel?"

"Plenty of oxcarts will give you a ride if you agree a price. That's probably safer than walking in your case. But beware of your speech – you sound too much like a northerner."

The next day, Fashang listened from his tiny enclosure as the sounds of a big port grew nearer. Peering through the cracks in the stern he saw a vast expanse of water, and deduced that this was the famous Tai Lake, which the captain had described to him. The barge had obviously sailed into a large basin on one shore, and was threading its way through a tangle of piers and docks to find its mooring. Shortly after making landfall, Fashang heard sounds suggesting that another group of officials was inspecting the barge, but Fashang did not know whether it was related to him. He remained hidden till night had fallen.

All through the hours of darkness, he waited for the captain to release him from his tiny prison. It was not until the small hours of the morning that he sensed the rush of fresh air that indicated the panel was being lifted above his head.

"You can come out now," whispered the captain, helping him unsteadily up to the poop deck. "I have made arrangements for you to make the journey in a cart with several others."

"How long will it take?"

"It's rather a slow wagon – so a couple of hours."

"Couldn't I rent a horse instead? It would be much quicker."

"That would make you too conspicuous. They're probably watching the roads around here. After all, they might guess that you arrived here by boat, and the obvious escape is into the city. Better to travel with a group – and keep your head down."

Fashang disembarked in company with his saviour, but found difficulty in walking after all the cramped inactivity of recent days. Gradually his muscles loosened up as he was led through the pre-dawn port to a large square. Several covered wagons were parked around the area, and passengers were climbing aboard. The captain then introduced him to one of the drivers of a large oxcart. Fashang paid the fare, thanked the barge-master profusely, and climbed into the vehicle.

His travelling companions formed a mixed bunch, initially not inclined to conversation. After a considerable wait, while the owner tried to squeeze as many people as possible into the confined space, they set off. For the first hour they rumbled through the outskirts of Suzhou, with the housing becoming increasingly stylish as they moved nearer to the town centre.

Periodically, a few jerky conversations took place, and Fashang tried to keep in the background for fear of his accent betraying him.

"Say, mate, where d'yer hail from?" was directed at him by a neighbour.

Slowly Fashang replied, "Hebei Province is my home, but I'm a long way from it now."

"So, why d'yer come here?"

"Harvest is bad up there – so I need to find work."

"What d'yer do?"

"I'm a stone mason."

Immediately, Fashang felt hot all over, and could sense the blood rushing to his face. He regretted his folly in giving away that nugget of information, and wondered if the common people were aware of the hunt for him. But his companion did not seem phased.

"That's a good job – plenty of work in Suzhou."

"By the way," interrupted a third man, "my uncle is a master mason, and always looking for help. Have you ever worked on jade?"

"Actually, I've done a few small jobs with that – very tricky material – can't afford to make a mistake."

"If you like, I'll take you to him. Mind you, you'd better be good."

Fashang accepted the offer, despite increasing his chances of detection. The ponderous progress continued, and eventually in the late forenoon the oxen came to a standstill.

"Everyone out – this is the end of the route."

They clambered down from the wagon, and then stood overawed by the sight of the bustling city before them. People, wheelbarrows, sedan chairs and animals crowded the streets. The air was warm and very humid, while the proximity to the Yangtze River resulted in a slightly unpleasant smell. Behind them, a parade of beautiful buildings was under construction.

Fashang's fellow-traveller had not forgotten his promise. He led the way along a lane that passed into the walled-city of Suzhou. In this warren of streets, he eventually knocked on the door of a fairly prosperous-looking business house. A servant answered, and ushered them inside. Entering a small reception room with brocaded curtains and settees, they were given small cups of tea, and asked to wait for the master of the house.

"My nephew, it is good to see you!" exclaimed an elderly, wispy-haired man as he entered. "And who is this with you?"

"My uncle, it is my joy to see you too, and this is an acquaintance of mine from Hebei. His name is... by the way, what is your esteemed name?"

"My humble name is Wu Fashang."

"A meaningful name indeed," observed the old man.

"My reason for coming, uncle, is that Mr Wu claims to be a stone mason in need of work. I thought you might be interested."

"Certainly I need craftsmen, but my standards are high. What is your experience, Mr Wu?"

This put Fashang on the horns of a dilemma. He needed to impress his possible employer, but also not to ignite any suspicions about his origins. So he tried to answer tactfully.

"I have worked on decorative inscriptions for gatehouses, and also tried my hand at small sculptures. If you wish, I will craft a jade miniature of one of the gods for your inspection."

"Maybe you do have some ability. You may sleep tonight in the dormitory of my workshop – and tomorrow you can demonstrate your skills."

The arrangement pleased Fashang, and he was directed to a large building near the town wall, where he found lodging with a dozen other employees of the master mason.

His fellow-artisans were pleasant to Fashang, and next morning, after a breakfast of congee and salted duck eggs, he was shown to the main workshop. To his surprise it was well-equipped with some of the latest sculpturing tools, and he was assigned a bench. While he was examining the implements on it, the owner appeared at his side.

"Now we will see what you are made of, Mr Wu! If your work pleases me, then I'll take you onto my work-team. If not, then you are back on the streets."

He placed on the bench a small painting of an old man with a small pointed moustache, wearing a lightly-striped cloak.

Fashang commented, "That's the Yu Huang, the Jade Emperor – sometimes called the Heavenly Grandfather."

"Quite right. Now, do you think you could carve a small figure of him in jade?"

"Depends on the material."

The master carver opened a small cupboard, and sorted through a collection of rocks, eventually holding one up for Fashang's inspection.

"Would this be suitable?"

Fashang took the green-grey stone to the window, and held it up to the light. Carefully examining the crystalline structure from several angles, he nodded.

"This piece is usable, except at the extreme end, where there is already a fracture plane. But it will take some time."

"Get to work, and I will see how you do! But remember that it's valuable. Don't spoil it."

Placing the slab of mineral on his bench, Fashang inked his writing brush, and then drew several lines on the surface of the stone. Clamping it into the wood-faced vice, he used a bow-saw to cut away several protrusions, and then very cautiously chiselled at the surface until the approximate shape could be seen. Knowing that further such action might shatter the stone, he turned to a simple hand drill whose metal bit was tipped with an embedded diamond. With this, he meticulously removed the unwanted material, ultimately producing the outline of the required shape. Then he utilised abrasive emery powder on blocks of quartz to smooth the surface, but he knew that the detailed finishing would require many more hours of drilling and polishing to complete the artefact.

He sensed somebody watching him, and turned to find the owner of the workshop following the proceedings intently.

"Not bad, Mr Wu - not bad at all! In fact, I can see you've been well trained, and you're experienced in this. I didn't know that there was such skill in Hebei, although I heard there were carvers of your standard in Shandong."

In confusion, Fashang muttered, "Well the two provinces are very close..."

Thus he was taken onto the workforce of the enterprise, and offered a substantial wage, reflecting the owner's delight at having found such a fine craftsman. For two days Fashang worked on the statue of the Jade Emperor. When that was finished to both his and the master's satisfaction, he looked around for the next task.

"Mr Wu, I have a special assignment for you. Have you ever carved the head of Kong Fuzi?"

"Yes, Master, I have done several busts of the sage."

"Then tomorrow morning I want you to come with me. It might be an exciting outing for you, anyway. Bring your writing materials."

The following day dawned bright and clear, with no sign of the ubiquitous mist which had shrouded the city until this time. Fashang and his boss boarded a small horse-drawn gharry, which took them out of the city's gate and towards the river. Before long, Fashang recognised the area as the waterfront that he had seen on arrival. But the clear weather had transformed the picture. Instead of a few misty islands, he now saw a mighty forest of tall, leafless trees stretching across the vista. As he focused more clearly, he perceived that he was looking at a vast armada of ships lying at anchor.

A sampan was hailed, and the two men reclined on its comfortable seats as they were rowed out to one of the ships. The size of the vessels was over-awing, and the one for which they were headed was particularly impressive.

"But what are all these ships?" Fashang asked in wonderment.

"This is the Imperial Navy, under the command of Admiral Zheng He. Already he has made history with his four voyages to remote places in the world. Now he is preparing to leave on another exploration of the Western Sea. There will be over three hundred ships in this squadron, and the Admiral hopes to go where no one has ever been. But I hear that he cannot find enough men to man the fleet."

"But why are we coming out here?"

"Straight ahead is the Admiral's flagship. He has particularly asked me, as the leading master mason in Suzhou, to install a statue of Kong Fuzi in his main stateroom. And I'm giving the job to you."

Soon the hull of the vessel loomed over them, and Fashang estimated that it was larger than the town hall in the main city of Shandong. Peering upward, he saw that everywhere there was bustle and hurry. Huge containers of food were being winched aboard by derricks, guns were being cleaned, and gangs of men were scrubbing and polishing the gunwales.

The sampan bumped alongside a pontoon next to an entry-port in the side of the ship. An armed guard demanded their business, and the master mason produced a scroll which was promptly scrutinised. Permission was given for them to pass, and the two men were taken by a soldier into a labyrinth of corridors and staircases. Their escort led the two visitors into a huge, sumptuous hall, abounding in expensive furniture. Apparently, this was the admiral's stateroom!

Pointing to a large alcove in the end wall, the master mason indicated that this was to be the location of the intended carving. Fashang carefully measured the aperture, and after inking his brush made several notes and drawings on his paper. Finally, he walked up and down the large saloon, considering the way that the light would fall on the carved cranium.

"I think I have enough information to proceed," he said in the end.

"You have three days before the fleet sails, and if I don't fulfil my commission, I'll be in trouble. And you too!"

Returning to the workshop, Fashang threw himself into the new project. Previous familiarity with this type of statuette assisted and encouraged him, so that the work proceeded quickly. This challenge especially thrilled him, by virtue of the fact that he was carving the head of one with the same family name as himself.

Meanwhile, he listened idly to the chatter of the other artisans as they worked on their tasks.

"I was down in the town centre this morning. Looked at all the notices on the board outside the city offices. There was one there offering a reward for a killer who was supposed to be lurking in Suzhou."

"Must be lot of those in this city…"

"Yes, but it said this was a stone mason – comes from Shandong."

"In that case, he would sound different from us, no doubt about it."

"Hey, I wonder…" said one, his voice dying to a whisper.

Fashang picked up a small mirror that he was using for his work. Without turning his head, he studied the other men in the room. He noticed that they were all looking in his direction and nodding. Most of them pretended to return to their work, while one of their number slipped quietly out of the door. Panic hit Fashang, as he realised once again that he was near to discovery. Within minutes, an officer would probably arrive, and he would be arrested. His feelings were in total flux, as he desperately sought a way out of what had now become a trap.

Carefully lifting a bowl that he had been using for his work, he made his way to the door, as though going for more water. Once out of the room, he ditched the bowl, and then ran down the corridor to the open street. Outside, he looked around, saw no one, and walked quickly in the direction of the most congested part of the town. In an area where a crowd of loungers was leaning or sitting, he surreptitiously found a place against a wall, while trying to marshal his thoughts. All his possessions were back in the masons' dormitory, and he had no money on his person. Certainly, his situation was dire. For several hours he sat, mused and fretted.

Suddenly there was a cry from one side of the area, followed by a great movement of humanity. The mass of indolent men abruptly came alive, and began to pour away down a lane with stricken looks on their faces. Fashang watched the fleeing figures with incredulity. One of the last ones called out to him.

"Better get moving, mate! The Press Gang is coming this way."

"What does that mean?"

"If you don't want to spend the rest of your life in the Emperor's navy, then start running!"

Fashang's first impulse was to get away with the throng, but then a strange idea hit him. If he were conscripted into the navy, it would certainly be a hard life, but there was a chance that the fleet would carry him away from China incognito. At least he stood a chance of survival. Grasping this straw, he remained seated on the ground. Shouts and screams reached his ears, and after half an hour a group of staff-wielding men rushed past, then stopped and looked down on him.

"He looks strong and healthy. Take him!" commanded the leader of the patrol.

Fashang made a pretence of trying to escape, but he was

grabbed roughly, and his hands secured behind him. Two men marched him through several streets, and then pushed him into a closed wagon already half-filled with frightened men. Soon the vehicle began to move, and after what seemed like eternity it finally stopped at the waterfront. The men were ordered out, and immediately put onto a large tender which was then rowed out towards the anchored fleet. Fashang struck up a conversation with one of the other unfortunates.

"And what will happen now, d'you think?"

"From what I hear, they'll first lock us below decks. When right out at sea, we'll be let out. And then they'll make us work. And it'll be tough work."

"But where will we go?"

"They say the Admiral wants to go further than any other voyage - even to a land that's hardly known to exist."

"And where is that?"

"It's called Africa."

Chapter 6

White Wedding

The confetti rained down, and so did the heavens. Despite the inclemency, the bridal pair emerged from the church doorway looking radiant. Ahead of them stretched a forest of umbrellas, which they negotiated until they were safely in the limousine. Then a short journey through the downpour across suburban south London brought them to the venue for the wedding reception. This Tudor-style hotel proclaimed the event to the world by the proudly-displayed sign "Alison and Alex" over the entrance portico.

Before the commencement of the lunch, the bridal pair circulated among the guests as they nursed their drinks. A quick survey of the faces soon revealed which were the relatives and friends of the bride or groom. The Zimbabwean roots of Alison's supporters were seen in their well-tanned complexions, despite their Caucasian origins. Her mother Corrie, fresh from the family farm in central Zimbabwe, was an imposing, matronly figure, her face a mass of freckles from the tropical sun. Alison's brother, Peter, was a rugged young man, who betrayed his outdoor interests in sport and hiking through his appearance. Next to him sat his arresting African wife, Rutiziro, a beautiful Shona young lady with dark, smooth skin. In contrast to these people, the extended family of Alex displayed a generally creamy whiteness, which bespoke life under the skies of Britain.

Corrie was chatting animatedly with Alex's mother about their offspring, as people do on such occasions. The bride's younger brother, Martin, was engaged in a technical conversation with Alex's father.

"I gather that you are studying electronic engineering, young man."

"That's right, sir, in the Faculty of Engineering at Cape Town University."

"And which area interests you most?"

"Definitely telecommunications. It's a wonderful mixture of advanced theory and practical applications. There's also a strong human element, since it's all about people sending messages to each other."

"Well, that is my field also. I joined British Telecom as a young graduate – and now, for some reason, find myself head of a division. By the way, I read a fascinating paper recently – about a clandestine radio system that was used about ten years ago in Zimbabwe, just before some election. Know anything about it?"

"I certainly do! It provided broadcasts across the country without the government being able to find the transmitter."

"I read about that. But where was this central unit that sent the signals up to the satellite?"

"Actually nobody knows. It was – and is – a well-kept secret, although the system has not been used for years. The funny thing is that my family smuggled that unit into Zimbabwe across Lake Kariba on our yacht."

"Well, that sounds like adventure. So, how is life in Zimbabwe now?"

"Ever since this new president, Reuben Madzingo, came to power, things have improved greatly. Lots of investment in the country, and emigres returning."

"What sort of chap is this Reuben?"

"Energetic, clear-thinking – and, above all, honest and transparent. In fact, our family knows him quite well. They worked with him six years ago in the run-up to the election which he won. Actually, he and my mother are on first name terms, and she sits on several social-welfare committees for government activities."

At that moment a bell rang, summoning the guests to the dining room, where they ate and conversed heartily. As the splendid lunch drew to a close with much banter, the master of ceremonies announced that several of the family and friends wished to make short speeches. Following a number of such contributions, the final speaker was introduced as Professor Horace Oatman from the University of Shorefield, where both the bride and groom worked. A squat elderly gentleman in bow-tie jumped nimbly to his feet, and launched into an enthusiastic peroration.

"Ladies and Gentleman. As you may know, I happen to be the boss of both the bride and the groom, which is why they are so well behaved today!" Pausing for laughter, he continued, "Alison came to us first as an undergraduate, fresh from the depths of Africa." Then, indicating Corrie, he added, "And I must say it's a pleasure to have her mother with us today from Zimbabwe. The bride is one of the smartest students that have passed through my department of Archaeology in a long time. Not only did she get her first and second degrees with ease, she has, as you all know, just passed her doctorate. So if any of you have questions to ask about the painted pottery of southern Africa, there's your expert!"

There was a buzz of comment, and a smattering of applause, before the speaker continued.

"I didn't know what to give them as a wedding present. I thought about a piece of painted pottery – from Stoke-on-Trent, of course," he joked. "But apart from that I was stumped. Then I remembered from my scant acquaintance with Zimbabwe that there was a place called the Elephant Hills Hotel, providing an incredibly luxurious standard of accommodation. Now, I think it's not a secret – I hope not, or I'll be in the doghouse – that the happy couple is going to Zimbabwe for the next few weeks. I know that this is partly to meet Alison's family, but also so that Alex can work on some research in the countryside there. What I cannot see is where a honeymoon fits into this schedule.

When I discovered that the Elephant Hills had a bridal suite second to none, I had found my answer.

With a formal bow he handed Alex an envelope. "These are vouchers for three nights in that bridal suite, overlooking Victoria Falls."

Amid the "oohs" and "ahs" there was much clapping, as the professor took his seat.

Following the meal there was animated conversation among the guests in the comfortable lounges of the hotel. Most people were reluctant to face the unappealing weather outside, and preferred to spend the afternoon more congenially indoors.

Peter sought out his new brother-in-law, with whom he was only slightly acquainted. Leaning on the bar in one of the reception rooms, they explored each others past and plans.

"So, I suppose that now my sister has got her Ph.D., you're going the same route. You can hardly be 'Mr. & Dr. Hampstead' for ever," Peter remarked with a grin.

"Quite true, Peter. In fact, I am registered already to work under Prof. Oatman. At the moment I am looking for a suitable area, and even something in Zimbabwe. After all, Alison has given me a strong attraction to the country."

"Have you considered Great Zimbabwe? Or has that site been worked over by archaeologists too much?"

"Actually, I've been looking at it. The African civilisation that built that great city five hundred years ago was widely linked to the rest of the world. They even found a Chinese bowl there."

"But I heard that it's believed the Arab traders brought that bowl up to the high veldt. Does anyone think the Chinese actually came to Great Zimbabwe?"

"No, of course not," Alex replied with a laugh. "It's an awfully long way from China."

"So what do you think there is left to find at the site?"

"Probably not much in terms of traditional archaeology – in fact Prof. Oatman is not sanguine about the idea. He wants me to do a dig in South America, on some Inca site. But I would like to try out some of my ideas in Zimbabwe. My special interest is the application of geomorphology to finding buried artefacts."

"Sounds pretty advanced. How does it work, Alex?"

"For my undergrad dissertation, I developed a computer program which could process successive satellite pictures in terms of the sun's shadows on the ground. By looking at the alteration of the shadows, especially near sunset, the software can determine the shape of the ground in some detail. If this is correlated against differential GPS measurements, one can sometimes spot non-natural humps or dips that might have archaeological value. In fact, my software package has flagged a particular feature at Great Zimbabwe, and I want a closer look."

"The best of luck with all this. No doubt we'll be seeing you in Zim fairly soon. You are flying this Saturday, I believe. We will stay another ten days, so that Rutiziro can see the UK – it's her first time over here. By the way, have you met Ru yet?"

"Not had the chance. You only flew in yesterday – and we've been rather busy!"

"Come on, Alex, I'll introduce you."

****

The next two days were full of preparations for the trip to Zimbabwe. Alison had not been back to her home for four years, and wondered what changes she would find. Alex had been reading widely to gain an overview of archaeological finds in the country, and hoped the trip would further his career, and establish himself in his academic field. He had also loaded his laptop with hundreds of satellite images of the Great Zimbabwe ruins, as well as results of his own image processing.

Although planning to spend several days at the family farm in central Zimbabwe as a sort of honeymoon, they were both delighted with Professor Oatman's gift of a few days in that romantic hotel setting. Thus they changed their plans, so that they could fly straight to the hotel at Victoria Falls, and then travel to the Robertson's homestead afterwards. From there it would be easy to reach the Great Zimbabwe ruins.

After packing and farewelling, they at last found themselves in the check-in area of Heathrow Airport. Clutching their boarding-passes, they were heading for the immigration desks, when a young woman approached the newly-weds. She looked around nervously for a moment.

"Are you Dr. Hampstead?" she enquired of Alison.

"That's me." responded Alison with a smile.

The girl thrust an envelope into Alison's hand, turned abruptly, and walked briskly away.

"Hey, who are you? What is this?" Alison shouted after her, but to no avail. The messenger vanished into the airport throng.

Opening the missive, they saw a single sheet of paper with three words written in an even hand: "BEWARE OF MWONZI".

"What is this? Some kind of wedding joke?" asked Alex. "Does it mean anything to you. Does it have significance in Zim?"

"Not to my knowledge – although it looks like a Shona word."

"Maybe it's a type of food. Might give one tummy trouble."

"Don't think so. It looks more like the name of a place or even a person's surname. Maybe it's just someone being silly. Anyway, it seems pretty trivial," Alison commented as she stuffed the scrap of paper into her handbag.

****

Slightly fuzzy from the long flights, yet feeling excited, the honeymoon couple stared across the African vista from their balcony high above the Zambezi River. The mile-wide stream glided slowly towards the frothing mass of the Victoria Falls, which plunged over the lip in five distinct sections. However, these were partly obscured by the towering clouds of spray rising above the waters.

"You know, there was a chap who went over those Falls in a barrel," Alison recounted, "sometime in the Victoria era."

"Should have had his head examined. Or was it a suicide?"

"I think it was some military guy – showing off to his friends!"

"Did he survive?"

"Amazing, but he did. In fact he became quite addicted to barrelling over the falls, and did it three times."

"Why did he stop?"

"The last time he was never found!"

The three days passed quickly in the ornate luxury of the Elephant Hills Hotel, which crowned a hilltop overlooking the river. Alison and Alex did all the obligatory activities, cruising up the river in the evening to watch the hippos, driving past the herds of elephant in the game park, and even braving bungee-jumping off the Zambezi bridge that linked Zimbabwe with Zambia. They thoroughly enjoyed every minute of it, and too quickly came the time to move on.

On the final evening of their stay, they were sitting on the stylish terrace of the hotel, enjoying the moonlit view of the mighty river, while watching a display of traditional dancing. A tall, athletic young African man approached, and addressed them politely.

"Excuse me interrupting, but are you Mr. and Mrs. Hampstead?" Looking a trifle embarrassed, he continued, "Pardon me. I mean Mister and Doctor Hampstead."

Alex looked up. "Yes, we are. Can we help you?"

"If I may sit down, I would like to introduce myself. My name is Daniel, and I am from the Department of Archaeology at the University of Zimbabwe."

Both Alison and Alex relaxed at hearing this news.

"You are very welcome, and obviously you know about us."

The visitor explained, "Our Head of Department has connections with Professor Oatman in the U.K., and heard that you were coming to Zimbabwe to do some research on the Great Zimbabwe site. We wanted to extend a hand of assistance to you, if possible. So, I was asked to fly over here from Harare, and meet you."

"That's very kind of you, Mr...?"

"Just call me Daniel."

"So, Daniel, what kind of cooperation were you envisaging?" Alex enquired.

"We've heard about your geomorphological software system, and wondered if you need further equipment for your field work."

Calling a waiter over, Alex ordered drinks all round. Soon they were settled with full glasses. Rapidly, the conversation turned technical, and Alex outlined the types of instruments that would be helpful in his ground survey of the proposed site. He was surprised at the range of resources possessed by the university, and the willingness of the academics there to loan the equipment. Finally, he mentioned one item that would be of real value during his project.

"For the detailed survey work, I would really like a TST, if you have one."

"You mean a Total Station Theodolite. Unfortunately our only one fell off a rock face recently."

"That's a pity, but can't be helped, I suppose."

"Our HOD anticipated you might need this device. So he has contacted some good friends in the University of Pretoria, and they are willing to lend one to you for the duration. You'll have to drive down to South Africa to get it. But they say it is the latest version, including GPS and remote robotic control."

Alison chimed in, "That shouldn't be a problem. We are planning to stay with my mother for a few days at her farm. And we could borrow the Land Rover to pop down to Pretoria."

"Well, in that case we'll set up the arrangements for you. Also, I hope that you will come to Harare to meet the departmental members. Perhaps you would give a lecture, Dr. Hampstead?"

"Alison, please."

"Yes, Alison. Some of your work would interest many people."

"Certainly I'll be happy to do that. And Alex needs as much local knowledge as he can get."

"Well, that's settled then. One more thing," Daniel said, producing a small wrapped package. "The department wants to send some specimens to a colleague in Pretoria, but they are a bit fragile. We thought you might be going, and hoped you could take them for us. The name is on the label."

"Of course, that'll be no trouble."

"It's getting late, and I'll be on the first plane to Harare, so I will bid you good night. And hope to see you at our university before long."

Alison and Alex thanked the young man, and assured him they would keep in contact.

"Oh, I nearly forgot. Here is my card," he said, handing one to Alex, and then disappearing into the hotel.

"What wonderful luck, meeting a chap like that!"

"It's all thanks to Oatman, actually."

"I didn't know he was familiar with Zimbabwe. Still, that makes things easier for us."

Turning the business card over in his hand, Alex read, "Lecturer in Archaeology, Dr. Daniel Mwonzi."

"Seemed a good fellow. Perhaps we'll get to know him better. Anyway, let's head for bed now. In the morning we fly to Gweru, where my mother will meet us. Then tomorrow night I'll be back at home. But no longer as Miss Robertson."

"Come on, then, Mrs Hampstead – or it is Dr. Hampstead," Alex replied playfully, and was rewarded with a punch.

Together they walked across the terrace towards their room. Suddenly Alison gave a little scream, and stood stock still.

"What's the matter, darling," Alex enquired anxiously.

Alison had turned rather pale. "What was the name on that card?" she asked hoarsely.

Alex examined it for a moment. "Daniel Mwonzi."

"I have a feeling that was the name on that piece of paper we got at the airport."

"Have you still got it?"

"Not here. But it must still be in my bag. Come on!"

In a changed frame of mind, they hurried to the suite of rooms that they occupied. After several minutes of searching, Alison held up the miniature document.

"As I thought!" she gasped. "It says: *Beware of Mwonzi.*"

Chapter 7

Uncomfortable Customs

Alex and Alison sat in the tiny departure room, hardly describable as a lounge, at the small airport outside Victoria Falls.

"So, what do we make of this Mwonzi fellow?" asked Alex.

"Very odd. He seemed such a transparent and helpful man. I really liked him. But what about that message?"

"Could be some sort of joke."

"In which case, it's not very funny."

"Perhaps someone doesn't like him – wants to tarnish his image."

"But we were given the paper in London – so it doesn't make sense."

"The important thing," concluded Alex, "is to decide what to do about it. We're bound to meet him again. He even seems keen to help with my research."

"Easy answer... Do nothing! We'll just deal with him in a normal fashion, but keep our eyes open at the same time."

The conversation was abruptly terminated by the roar of a small plane passing right over the building. Within a short distance, it had bounced onto the runway, and begun to taxi back.

"I see they are still using the Embraer jets for the domestic runs," observed Alison. "They're comfortable and take about fifty people – made in Brazil."

Soon they were airborne and passing over flat green

countryside, with a mixture of cultivated land and small woodlands. Several broad rivers could be seen winding through the area, all looking brown and sluggish.

"Of course, Alex, you are lucky to have your visit in the summer, when it's so verdant. In the winter months it's all brown and yellow – and the rivers either dry up or become trickles."

"Actually, it looks just like the Google Earth picture – so that must have been scanned in the summer. What's that town over there?"

"Our destination! Only half an hour by air, but a whole day by road. That's Gweru. The airport is to the east of the town - next to the Air Force base."

Twenty minutes later, they came out of the terminal into the arms of Corrie, who hugged and kissed both her daughter and son-in-law. They set off in the old, sturdy Land Rover, and several miles along the N1main road, they turned off along a narrow track leading to a pair of white pillars and a gateway. A sign announced "Acacia Farm". Following a twisting roadway, they rounded a bend and saw the farmhouse ahead.

"Say, is that your home, Alison?" Alex asked in delight, as he stared at the beauty of the classical black and white Cape Dutch architecture of the building.

"Sure, darling, we've arrived."

As they alighted from the vehicle, Alison looked in bafflement across the fields.

"But what are all those buildings over there? They weren't there when I left here."

Indicating the small settlement of brick and thatch houses, Corrie explained. "That is the project to provide skills for local people. Unemployment is so high, that we are running courses on practical subjects to equip young folk with the ability to make a life in this country. Much of the area is devoted to agricultural activities, teaching the use of modern methods to cope with drought and disease both on small plots and commercial farms. There's also a carpentry workshop, and a needlework school at the back there. We are planning some basic IT courses in the near future. It's called the Peace Training Centre – as you know, peace is what folk need these days."

"Very impressive, Mother. I didn't expect it to be so big."

"In fact, Reuben was down here last month, and is very excited by the idea."

"Reuben, by the way, is His Excellency the President, Reuben Madzingo," cut in Alison with a grin.

"I see, Mrs. Robertson," observed Alex dryly, "that you keep company with the high and mighty. First name terms with the President, and all!"

She laughed. "As Alison will tell you, he is a family friend. We worked together in those difficult years before he was elected, and now we still collaborate in facing the challenges of the new Zimbabwe."

"Mother, I'm roasting. Can we go inside?"

"Sorry, children, but I get carried away when I get onto this subject. Come on in!"

In the cool, large lounge of the farmhouse, they sipped drinks, while waiting for lunch.

"I am afraid you will have to put up with just me," said Corrie. "Peter and Ru are touring England for a while, and will be back for the new school term in a few days. Martin is going hiking in the Drakensberg."

"What a delight to have you all to ourselves," responded Alison, "although we're not really alone. There are 150 in the farm workers' compound, including their families. How many are there at the training centre?"

"About ninety – so we won't be lonely. And we do get visitors, like Paul Sibanda…"

Alison uttered a little cry of delight. "Paul, oh, he's a lovely man. I would like to see him again when he comes."

"Is this some former boy-friend of yours?" Alex asked roguishly.

"Paul is an old man. He's a pastor in Bulawayo, but often comes up here to minister to the workers here on the farm. He's got a great heart for the poor and sick. You'd really like him."

"In that case," Corrie volunteered, "I'll give you his mobile number."

That afternoon they toured the workshops and classrooms where African young men and women were enthusiastically studying and practising. Both Alex and Alison found the whole project very inspiring. As they walked back to the farmhouse, Corrie quietly made a suggestion.

"Would you like to look at the grave?"

"Certainly, Mother. I hoped you'd want to take us there."

They climbed a small kopje behind the house, and respectfully approached a large boulder near the top. Carved onto it in a beautiful script were the words:

William Robertson
Farmer, Friend and Father
At peace with the God he loved

Alison murmured to Alex, "As you've heard, he was killed in the violence before the election of Reuben. This lettering on the rock was carved by Mother herself. Took her two months."

"Very moving," was Alex's reverent response.

As they returned to the house, Alison explained their plans to her mother.

"Before Alex can start his work at Great Zimbabwe, there are several pieces of equipment he needs to get his hands on. UZ has offered most of what he wants, but there is one instrument that we have to borrow from Pretoria. Would it be all right to use the Land Rover to fetch it?"

"Can't see any objection. I can use one of the training centre cars if need be. When d'you want to go?"

"How about early tomorrow morning? We could get down there in about seven hours, spend the night with a friend, and return the next day."

"Sounds fine. You'd better get an early night."

****

Just as the inky blackness of night was becoming pale on the eastern horizon, Alex and Alison made their departure from the farm.

"Now go carefully, you two," cautioned Corrie, "and watch for animals on the road."

"Don't worry about us, Mother, "Alison replied, "I've done this trip many times. With luck, we should be in Pretoria by lunch-time, and then back here by midday tomorrow. Unless we have trouble at the border on the way back."

"No problem there now. The new President has tidied up that border post, thrown out the touts and made everyone wear official badges. The old bribery and inefficiency has pretty well gone."

"That's good news. Have a good day."

The happy couple joined the N1 road that took them through Gweru to Bulawayo. After passing Zimbabwe's second city, they began the long descent round the hairpin bends leading down the escarpment to the southern lowlands. Traffic was light, and the road surface good. The first couple of hours saw them passing through fertile land where crops of mealies and wheat were developing well. But after dropping to the lower altitude, they found the land more barren with rocky outcrops rising like miniature fortresses along the way. Soon the travellers began to perspire freely in the heat of the low-veldt, and were glad they had made such an early start. They were moving through an area of small Ndebele villages, where many of the houses had bright art-work painted on the walls. A constant watch was kept for cows or goats that had a propensity for suddenly crossing the road in front of vehicles.

Three hours later, they pulled into the Beitbridge border post, after which they would cross the Limpopo River into South Africa. Few people were queuing at the various counters in the offices, and soon the immigration and customs formalities were completed. Then they drove to the exit barrier and waited to be let out of the country. The gate man scrutinised their paperwork, and then grunted.

"I need to see what you have in the back."

"Okay," answered Alex cheerfully, "only some personal stuff for an overnight trip."

The man poked around the small amount of luggage in the back of the Land Rover, and then pulled out a small wrapped box.

"What is this?" he demanded in a somewhat altered tone.

"Only some items we're taking to a fellow in the university in Pretoria."

"Need to inspect. Park your car over there!"

A trifle mystified, they followed the man back into the customs office. As if on cue, four policemen materialised beside them. A beribboned senior African officer took the box to a table, and carefully cut away the packaging. When the receptacle was opened, he felt around in the mass of polystyrene chips, and then lifted out two small clay pots.

"As I said, just a couple of pots being taken to Pretoria," Alex offered lightly, although his feelings were slightly heavier than appeared.

"These might be ancient artefacts. Do you have a licence to export them?"

"This is nonsense!" exploded Alex. "We're just carrying something to help a friend. You can't make a fuss about that!"

Quietly, Alison murmured to him, "Cool it, Alex! Don't get excited. Best way is to keep calm, and keep a smile. These folk don't respond to anger."

"Since you do not appear to have a licence, I regret we must call an expert to evaluate these things. Since an offence may have been committed, you will have to await the decision at the local police station."

Immediately, the four constables closed in upon the couple, and taking their arms, escorted them out into the blazing sun, and into a black police car.

"What about our truck, and our luggage?" Alison expostulated.

"They will be looked after," was the noncommittal reply.

The vehicle was rapidly driven out of the border post area, and for several miles into the little town of Beitbridge. The detainees were then transferred into the charge office of the police station, where their situation was explained to them.

"You have not been formally arrested – but are being held on suspicion, while certain enquiries are being made."

"Can I phone for a lawyer?"

"Not until a formal charge has been made, and if that doesn't happen you will be free to go."

Fuming with exasperation and bewilderment, they were led to a small room containing several chairs. Following a request to wait there, the door was shut, and the lock clicked ominously.

"What's all this about?" Alex seethed, "Just some big mistake I suppose."

"Not so sure about that," Alison answered carefully. "We may have been set up."

"But how? And you are the one who knows about pottery. Couldn't you have told them they're not artefacts?"

"Trouble is... I did look at them... and it's possible they are of antique value. Did you notice that they were quite chipped, and one was cracked? One was a zoomorphic pot in the shape of a zebra without a head, and that's typical of Shona pottery. In the old days a wife would serve her husband beer from that – and it's called 'pfuko yaNevanji', the King's advisor's drinking pot.

"Such academic brilliance is hardly helpful in our present situation," bemoaned Alex. After a moment, he breathed a great sigh.

"I've got it! It all fits together? Remember our friend Daniel Mwonzi? He's the one who gave us the parcel to bring – and he's the one we were warned about at Heathrow."

"That makes a lot of sense – but why? We're only ordinary people. Why trap us like this?"

"Now I think about it, they did seem to be waiting for us at the border post. Those police guys moved in too jolly fast for it to be a coincidence."

"Agreed. This has been planned – but why?"

"And who is this Mwonzi fellow who's behind it?"

Their speculations petered out, and they both sat in silence, absorbed by their own thoughts and fears. Nothing happened for several hours, although two bottles of water were passed into the room at one point.

The heat in the cell was intense as the time moved into the afternoon. Both of them were feeling drowsy and a little nauseous, when a key was heard turning in the lock. A middle-aged man, dressed in a dark suit, entered the room, and sat down.

"My name is Detective-Inspector Charamba. Mr. and Mrs. Hampstead, I have to inform you that the items you were seeking to export to South Africa come under the category of restricted archaeological artefacts. It is illegal to take these across the border without a licence from the Department of Antiquities."

"But we knew nothing about what they were," exclaimed Alison.

"Well, usually, ignorance of the law is not a defence," intoned Charamba, "but that will be for a judge to decide. Putting it simply, we will have to charge you with smuggling. And this type of smuggling is taken seriously in Zimbabwe."

"So what happens to us now?"

"You will be kept in custody until you can be taken to court, probably tomorrow. A magistrate will take your plea and make a ruling, or perhaps refer it to the High Court in Bulawayo. I cannot tell which."

The detective rose, unsmiling, and left the room.

Stunned by this turn of events, the couple sat in confused silence for a while. The door opened, and two warders escorted them back to the charge office, where full details and fingerprints were taken. When Alex requested the use of the telephone to call for legal assistance, he was refused on the grounds that the phone lines were currently down. They were then conducted to another cell near the back of the building. It was damp and dark, lit by a single electric bulb. In one corner a well-worn toilet emitted an unpleasant aroma, and two decrepit metal beds completed the furnishings.

Sunk in depression, they lay down on the beds, but rapidly arose, when they found other occupants of the ancient mattresses. Slinging the offending bedding into a corner, they preferred to lie on the bare boards. At about seven o'clock in the evening, the door opened, and two metal trays were handed in. Recognising that this was meant to be their supper, they examined the soft white substance which was surrounded by a number of green beans.

"Welcome to Zimbabwe's traditional food, sadza!" Alison said without enthusiasm. "This doesn't look too good. Pity for your first experience. Our cook at the farm makes it excellently. Anyway, we'd better eat it to keep our strength up."

After a modicum of fortification from the victuals, they lapsed again into the depressive silence of their own thoughts.

Chapter 8

Confusing Clues

"I say, I've realised something!" Alison whispered suddenly in the gloom.

"What's that?" Alex asked dolefully.

"They forgot to take my mobile phone. Normally they check all one's possessions, and confiscate them."

"How come you know so much about being arrested?"

"Been in this country a while," she replied with a slight smile.

"So we can message your mother, and get out of here."

"I'm not so sure that is a good idea. Ever since my Dad died, she's been rather highly-strung. If she heard about this, she might go hysterical – and there's no one there to support her. Let me think…"

"Isn't there anyone in the law business you could contact?"

"Not that I remember… Ah, wait a minute, here's an idea. Mother gave me the number of Paul Sibanda. Perhaps he could help."

"That's the pastor who sometimes comes to your farm. What can he do, apart from praying?"

"There's more to his story than you think. He was a freedom fighter in the independence war of the seventies, did some horrible things, and then turned right around. Now he leads a church in Bulawayo. During the run-up to the famous election, he was a great help to Reuben Madzingo. In fact they were very close."

"D'you think he still has access to the President?"

"Don't know. But it's worth a try."

Realising the need for secrecy, Alison positioned herself to face away from the spy-hole in the door, and Alex stood behind her as she typed into her phone.

"Turn off the sound! Or the warders will be alerted."

"Okay."

At last the message was sent, but was followed by a long period of inactivity. Alex was in the middle of commenting that perhaps the pastor's phone was off, when Alison felt the instrument vibrating in her hand.

"Will see what I can do. Blessings. Paul" was the message on the little display.

Alex sighed again. "So maybe there's some hope."

With no alternative activity available, they lay down on the hard boards and sought sleep. After twisting and turning for hours, all they could do was to hope for the morning, although that was not a pleasing contemplation.

****

Sometime in the small hours, they heard the door being unlocked. The chief inspector of the station strode into the room with a puzzled smile on his face.

"You folks must have contacts among the top brass," he mused. "We've had an order from the Police Commissioner to release you immediately and unconditionally. Rumour is that it came from the President's office. Don't understand it. Anyway, all charges are quashed – you're free to go."

As he led them out of the cell, he added, "And there's a clerical gentleman waiting to see you."

At the entrance to the police station, Alison ran forward into the arms of a grey-haired African gentleman, and promptly burst into tears.

"Alright, alright, Alison! It's over now! And won't you introduce me to this young beau of yours?"

Recovering herself, Alison enabled Alex and Paul to get acquainted. The pastor spoke to the officer on duty, and soon arrangements were completed for the accused to be liberated. Leading them out to his battered car, Paul offered to take them back through the night to their Land Rover at the border post.

"But what did you do?" Alison asked with curiosity, once they were under way.

"I called an old friend of mine," he replied enigmatically. "One who owes me a favour."

"You mean the President?"

"I don't call him that – he's just my great pal Reuben," he replied chuckling. "And one word from him, and you're free, and all charges scrapped!"

Alex explained about the happenings of the last twenty-four hours, and Paul looked solemn.

"I'd say that you got mixed up with some sort of corporate crime. But what it is, I can't say."

"Do you know this chap Mwonzi at the university?"

"Never heard of him. But, of course, I'm in Bulawayo most of the time. Best just to keep your eyes and ears open. Although… I've heard rumours that there is some big racket going on across the border here."

"But why should we be targeted?" asked Alison.

"Perhaps you are in the way. Have you upset someone, or found some secret? If you had been convicted, they would most likely have expelled you from the country. Then it might have been hard to get back in again. Perhaps your enemies, whoever they are, wanted you out of Zim."

They arrived back at the border post in the early dawn, and the reception could not have been more different from that of the previous day. The immigration officer himself came out to meet them, and an atmosphere of obsequiousness prevailed.

"Mr. and Mrs. Hampstead, we are glad to see you again. I understand that the little difficulty has been overcome. You are free to cross the border now."

Their vehicle and luggage appeared to be intact, although there was no sign of the supposed artefacts that had caused all the trouble. The couple bade an emotional farewell to Paul Sibanda, and drove over the Limpopo Bridge into South Africa. Shortly afterwards, they travelled through the little town of Messina, and onto the highway for Pretoria. Alison texted her mother to say that all was well, despite some delays at the border. The details she kept to herself.

****

Five hours later, they arrived at the Archaeology Building of Pretoria University. They made their way to the office of Richard Dennison, their contact man for the required equipment. He was a warm person, who immediately insisted on taking them to lunch in the staff common room.

"I am actually the Senior Laboratory Technician for the surveying activities of several departments. This TST is one of the latest, with all the bells and whistles."

"Perhaps, Richard, you could explain this machine to me," Alison requested, "although I know that Alex is very familiar with it."

"Basically it's an electronic theodolite integrated with an electronic distance meter. To this has been added a very accurate GPS system, and a remote control facility. This means that single-handed one can set up the equipment, and then move a reflector up a slope while it records a complete profile of the ground."

"Sounds like just what you need, Alex."

"I'll give you a demo before you go," Richard offered. "But there is some paperwork here for you to sign. We have to be careful with these things changing countries. It's not getting it into Zimbabwe will be your problem – it'll be getting it back out again! They're getting very fussy at the border now, apparently because of some gang that is bringing things out."

"What sort of things?"

"From what I hear, much of it is to do with historical relics and artefacts. It seems there is a big market for such items overseas."

"But who would buy them? Surely they would be spotted by the police immediately," enquired Alex.

"Globally there are some rich people – not just rich, but mega-rich – who enjoy building up vast collections of priceless items from antiquity, even though they cannot show them to anyone. That's where these things are going."

Alex and Alison held their peace. But each wondered secretly into what sort of international conspiracy they had wandered.

Alison communicated with Corrie to say that they had decided to spend another night in Pretoria, and would hasten back the following day. The return journey was uneventful, and they crossed the border with a minimum of bureaucracy, even though it was necessary to register the temporary importation of the TST machine at the customs office.

****

In late afternoon they arrived back at Acacia Farm, where Corrie was pleased that the journey had gone so well. The young couple felt that they should not burden Alison's mother with the strange affair at Beitbridge.

"There've been some developments while you were away. I

got a call from Professor Mududzo at UZ. The equipment he promised to lend you was ready yesterday, and since one of his staff was passing through here, he dropped it off for you. It's in the store room at the back."

"That's splendid news – will save us a trip to Harare," enthused Alex. "And, by the way, who was the man who brought it?"

"A nice young chap... extremely polite and very friendly. Obviously knew his subject. His name was... Daniel... Daniel something."

"Was it Daniel Mwonzi, by chance?" asked Alison anxiously.

"Yes, that's it. Said he had met you at Vic Falls. Seems quite keen to work with you, Alex."

Neither made any comment, but covertly conjectured how much thicker the plot could get.

"Well, it follows that we can move on with the work on the ground. How about staying a couple of days, and then heading over to Great Zimbabwe?" proposed Alex.

"I'm easy," said Alison.

"Me too. Come and go as you like. I won't be around much for the next week. We have a convention on poverty alleviation in Harare," Corrie commented.

Chapter 9

Digging In

After travelling across the flat agricultural lands of commercial farms for two hours, the Hampsteads began to climb into a low range of hills.

"This is known as the Great Dyke, which runs diagonally across Zimbabwe, and is the source of most of the prolific minerals in the country," Alison said in her best guidebook voice.

Alex reflected on the map that he was studying. "We should soon be passing Masvingo, and then we are almost there."

"Keep watch for Lake Mutirikwi!"

They were now in an area of rugged hills, many with large boulders on their shoulders and heads. Suddenly the vista of a great sheet of water opened up before them. The distant shore was only vaguely visible through the tropical mist that lay over the surface. Their road followed the coast for several miles, until a sign directed them up a gully into the hills. After twisting round a series of prominences, the deteriorating track brought them out into a broad valley, guarded on each side by rocky outcrops.

On reaching a car park with several vehicles, including two large coaches, they donned boots and rucksacks. They waited in a short queue of tourists for a while, and then purchased admission tickets at the entrance kiosk.

"I suppose that if we start work seriously, we will get free passes." Alison soliloquised hopefully.

They set off down the valley, and walked for twenty minutes.

"This is Great Zimbabwe!" Alison suddenly exclaimed proudly.

"Well, I can't actually see much," retorted Alex, "except rocks."

"That's the wonder of the place, and why it's known as the House of Stone!"

Rounding a bend, Alex gasped, as he stared at an enormous circular wall surrounding a large area of trees and ruins.

"What's that?"

"It's the Great Enclosure, the capital of the Monomotapa Kingdom. That's where all the common people, traders and artisans lived."

"But it's huge."

"They reckon 20,000 people lived there in its heyday."

As they went closer, Alex recognised features from his previous studies of satellite data, and began to get his bearings. Entering the gateways through massive walls, he was amazed to find that the whole structure comprised dry-stone technology.

"These are the same techniques they use for farm walls in England. But the size is overwhelming."

"They estimate this place was made from over five thousand cubic metres of stones."

"Thank you, Mrs. Wikipedia!"

"No charge for information – but a tip would be appreciated!"

Alex's gratuity took the form of a firm embrace and long kiss.

"Follow me, and I'll show you an interesting secret passage," Alison declared, as she led the way to an inner wall running parallel with the massive outer ramparts. The space between the walls formed a narrow passageway which took them in a serpentine route through to an open area. Before them stood a tall conical tower of carefully interlocked rocks.

"What was this for?" Alex asked.

"No one is sure. Some think it's a watchtower, others that it had religious meaning, while the fact that it's shaped like a granary may mean a symbol of wealth. Still a mystery!"

After perusing the Great Enclosure for a while, Alex vented a question that had troubled him.

"You said the common people lived in this walled city. But what about the aristocracy and rulers?"

"That's where stage two of the tour takes place!"

Exiting through one of the several gateways of the enclosure, they stood looking across the valley at a boulder-strewn hillside.

"That is the king's palace. Look carefully at those rocks, and you will see that there are stone walls between them. It's been made into a series of terraces and rooms. We call it the Hill Complex."

Totally intrigued, Alex followed his wife up a little path that soon took them along a narrow corridor, and then up a steep staircase cut in the rock. After twenty minutes of exertion they came out on a platform surrounded by a stone wall. From there, other passageways diverged up the hill to further platforms.

"Originally these would have had thatched roofs and mud walls. This is where the king kept court, and where he lived with his wives and nobles."

Sinking onto a stone bench, Alex suggested plaintively, "How about lunch here?"

"Good idea."

As they munched the chicken legs and salad provided by the cook at Acacia Farm, they looked out towards the lower end of the valley.

"Now, if I'm right, the area that looked interesting on my

satellite scans is further down the valley."

"That's outside the area of all the previous digs. Why should somewhere so far away from the main city be significant?"

"Anyway, my software flagged it as worth looking at. There won't be time today to get all the equipment, so let's do it in the morning."

"Makes sense. We've got our bookings for the Jabulani Hotel – so we can head there now."

"Actually... where is this hotel?"

"Look at the skyline of that spur at the top of the valley. See anything?"

"Yes... I can see some thatched roofs."

****

Returning to the Land Rover, they drove the short distance to the hotel, and entered a large area of lawn enclosed by a set of straw-roofed African rondavels. On one side of the grass, a particularly smart structure obviously housed the restaurant, while on the other side a swimming pool could be seen. Alex turned into the car park, and then whistled.

"Now that is interesting! See that green car over there. What's painted on the side?"

"It's a coat of arms... and, yes, I can read the wording, 'University of Zimbabwe'. Must be one of the lecturers taking a holiday."

"Mmm... I wonder."

After collecting the key for their rondavel from the reception, they were walking towards the accommodation, when Alison grabbed her husband by the arm.

"Wait! Stay here a moment. We need to think. Look who's

over there!"

Seated at one of the tables on the verandah of the coffee shop was the unmistakable form of Daniel Mwonzi, chatting with one of the waiters.

"So – what do we do now?"

"The only way is to play it cool. We won't mention the trouble at the border, and see if he brings it up."

As they came into view, Daniel rose from his seat, and greeted them with a warm smile. He was dressed casually in a patterned shirt and jeans, appearing more like a vacationing stockbroker than an intense academic.

"Alison and Alex, it's a real pleasure to see you again. I must apologise if I'm gate-crashing, especially on newly-weds. But I just thought I might offer my services when Alex starts work here, although I really don't want to be in the way."

"Thank you, Daniel, but did you come down here just to see us?"

"Indeed. I had a few free days with no classes, and thought that if things start to move on your project, then a little local knowledge of procedures and bureaucracy might come in handy."

"Why don't we settle in, have a swim, and then meet for dinner in the restaurant?" suggested Alison.

"Perfect! See you later."

Refreshed, invigorated and hungry, they assembled at a table in the outdoor section of the restaurant, from which they could observe the stately parade of the brilliant stars across the sky.

"Is it true that the stars are brighter here than in Britain?" Alex queried.

"Probably the amount of light is the same – but here we have no background illumination. There are no towns nearby, and the atmosphere is so dry there would be no reflection. Mind you, that's only my theory," replied Daniel with a chuckle.

As the meal progressed, the conversation turned from the trivial to the more serious. Daniel asked what programme of work Alex was proposing, and whether he had particular areas that needed assistance. Still slightly perplexed by their uninvited visitor, Alex explained that he wanted to study the area further down the valley from the main archaeological site.

"Sounds very interesting, Alex, and I'd be happy to come with you, and help carry the equipment," offered Daniel. "In fact I'll call the site warden so that you can go in and out freely."

****

The next morning in the early light, the three of them drove as far as the car park, and then trekked onward to the area that had grabbed their interest. Each of them was well loaded with rucksacks containing the specialist equipment needed for the job. Eventually they found themselves in a broad, open area between two ridges. Alex consulted his many notes and computer printouts, before declaring that the gentle slope on the east showed signs of ancient human activity.

Having set up the Total Station Theodolite, they made several traverses across the slope, which indicated unexpected undulations. Alex then focused on a particular section of the hillside, and proposed that they use the Ultrasonic Time Domain Reflectometer. Alison was unfamiliar with this instrument, and asked for an explanation of it.

"Basically it sends a pulse vibration down into the ground and then waits for a reflected pulse to come back. From the time taken, the equipment can determine the sort of things that lie under the surface."

Alison commented that it sounded rather like a common radar system.

"Yes, in some senses," Alex elucidated, "but whereas radar identifies one object, like a plane or ship, the TDR gives us a profile of the material under the ground. We don't get just one pulse back, but a whole series of reflections, from which we can interpret the type of material - vegetation, soil, water, rock and suchlike."

The small electronic instrument was set on a tripod, and a laptop computer connected to it. After a few seconds an image appeared on the screen.

"As we might expect, we have loose sandy soil near the surface which becomes more compacted further down. There are also pieces of rock embedded in the ground. Now comes the tedious bit…"

As the sun rose and the researchers perspired, the measurements continued in straight lines in several directions across the small area. After a break for a brief lunch, the work continued. However, their painstaking attention was eventually rewarded, when in mid afternoon the UTDR showed some interesting results.

"It looks as though we have a layer of granite between one and two metres below the surface."

"May be just another piece of the general rock structure of the area." suggested Daniel.

"Yes, but the rock strata are all inclined at an angle around here," Alex said, taking out an inclinometer and sighting on the surrounding hills. "Mostly it's tipped by about 35 degrees. But this underground rock appears to be flat and horizontal. Might be of human origin."

"Certainly interesting," pondered Daniel. "I wonder if it's worth a little digging."

Alison interrupted harshly, "You of all people should know that you cannot disturb an area like this without a permit! And I guess it would take months to get permission."

"Quite right," Daniel responded, "but there is such a thing as a Trial Dig Permit."

"What's that?"

"Well, since so many archaeological digs in the country have taken a lot of administrative time, and then yielded no results, the government has made a concession. When it seems there might be artefacts below the surface, they will authorise a "trial dig", which must not go below two metres or cover an area of more than ten square metres."

"And how many committees does that have to pass through?" Alex asked caustically.

Daniel smiled. "Surprisingly, only one! It's a part of National Museums and Monuments of Zimbabwe." He paused before continuing, "And the chairman of that committee is my departmental head, Professor Mududzo. If you want a permit, I reckon I can get one for you tomorrow. It could be done by chairman's action."

Buoyed up by this unexpected opportunity, Alison and Alex accepted Daniel's offer to communicate a request to Harare for permission to dig. That evening the conversation at dinner centred on the practical details of an excavation at such short notice. Daniel's experience proved invaluable.

"Since I've been on digs here in the past, I have a few contacts. For example, there is a village over the hill where many of the men have worked as labourers for our department in the past. I could recruit a gang for you, if you wish."

"Please do."

"I doubt that we will get an answer before tomorrow evening. So we can have a day off!"

"D'you have any suggestions?"

"Here's one. A colleague of mine in the department owns a small yacht on the lake here. I'm sure he would lend it to us for the day – that's if you would like a sail."

Alison swiftly agreed to this idea. "That would be a great outing. Alex will be especially happy, because he was captain of the university sailing team in his undergraduate days."

After retiring for the night, the couple aired their bafflement about the presence of Daniel Mwonzi.

"He seems such a nice fellow, so helpful and experienced. Is he really a Trojan horse or something?"

"Certainly we could not go ahead without his know-how."

"But what about the warning, and the border fiasco?"

"Well, we must just make use of his help – but watch that we don't get drawn into anything."

****

As the sun came up with searing heat the following morning, the sailors rowed out from Kyle Sailing Club to a trim little yacht that lay moored offshore. Before long, the anchor was aweigh and the sails set. In a moderate westerly breeze, the small craft took off across the lake, and provided a splendid day's sailing amid dazzling views of sun-drenched granitic hills.

An e-mail awaited them on their return to the hotel that evening, to the effect that a short-term "trial dig permit" had been issued for them to excavate the site in the valley. The National Monuments warden had been informed, and they could proceed the next day. Alex could not believe that things had moved so fast, and hardly slept that night – partly from excitement and partly because of the mosquitoes.

The next day, the small party was met by the warden of Great Zimbabwe, who conducted them to the proposed dig site. Already assembled there was a gathering of African village men equipped with picks, hoes and shovels.

"These men have all been involved in previous digs. So they know how to clear away soil without damaging any antiquities." Daniel reassured Alex.

Work began on a two-metre square area which had been shown by the computer to be directly over the granite slab. At first the sandy soil yielded easily, but as the day wore on the labourers encountered heavy clay which slowed the work. Gradually a great bank of detritus from the hole arose around the site. Throughout the activity, Daniel kept a close eye on the progress. Although all conversation was in Shona, Alison was able to follow the drift of it from her years of growing up on a Zimbabwe farm.

After several hours, the leader of the diggers called Daniel to explain that they had reached a solid surface. Alex and Daniel climbed down into the shaft, and began to remove the earth carefully with small trowels and brushes. After an hour of meticulous effort, they revealed several flat slabs that had obviously been trimmed by hand. As more waste was removed, they saw indentations in the surface. Daniel called for water to wash away the mud, and to their surprise there were rows of marks running across the granite. Alex peered at these for a while, and announced his findings.

"I guess that this is Arabic writing. Perhaps we've hit on a tomb of one of the Arab traders who came up here."

Daniel bent lower into the hole, and stared for a long time.

"Alex, I don't think that is Arabic. I'm no expert in calligraphy, but I reckon this writing is Chinese."

Chapter 10

Treasure Fleet

Despite his distinctly uncomfortable position, Fashang kept his eyes open as the boat was rowed away from the dockside. Squeezed in among the crowd of detainees on the rough floorboards, with his hands secured behind him, he felt a strange mixture of exhilaration and desperation. He trusted that, at last, he had evaded his pursuers, while simultaneously being fearful of the life of toil that lay ahead.

Then another worrying thought struck him. Was it possible that someone on the ship might recognise him as the young stone mason who had taken measurements for a carving a few days earlier? With relief, he noted that the tender was not pointing towards the flagship, but was directed towards another vessel at the rear of the line. Even so, it was an impressive warship with nine masts and an abundance of reefed sail on the spars. Fashang's spirits rose a little at the thought of anonymity among the thousands of crew and soldiers in the massive fleet.

The conscripts were bundled up a gangway onto the main deck, where their hands were freed. Surrounded by menacing guards, they were forced down a hatchway into an empty hold – and the grating was locked above them. After several hours of intensely noisy activity above their heads, they felt the movement of the ship change – whereupon a number of his companions were promptly sick. The voyage had begun, and soon the floor was heeling with the motion of the craft in the strong wind.

As dusk was falling, a large pot containing rice, pork and vegetables was lowered through the hatchway. Surprised by the quality of the food, he commented to a neighbour.

"This is better than I would expect."

"One thing about the Admiral is that he believes in good victuals for his men. Says that it reduces his losses – particularly thinks veggies are good for men at sea."

****

After a sleepless night on the tossing planks, Fashang heard the hatchcover being removed, followed by a rough command for all men to come up. Blinking in the strong sunlight, they found themselves on the spacious deck, and all instinctively looked across the sea for sight of their homes. In the far distance a thin line of land could just be discerned on one side, while the empty sea stretched to the horizon on the others. The men were herded before a low platform, on which an officer in bright uniform was standing. With a cruel smile on his face, he addressed the company.

"If any of you feels like deserting, then now's your time! Just jump overboard, and swim for fifteen miles to the coast of China! We've invited a shoal of sharks to follow us – and they've not had breakfast yet!"

His face hardened. "You men are part of the Imperial Navy. You will take orders from the officers, and any laggardly behaviour will be severely punished."

The men were then divided into watches of twenty persons, each team with a particular name. Fashang was relieved to find that there was no interest in the individual names of the men, but he invented a nickname for himself, just in case of enquiry. The petty officer in charge of his watch was a small fellow with a loud voice and arrogant manner, coupled with a crooked nose that suggested a history of fighting. His first instruction shocked them.

"Now, you scum of the earth, breakfast will soon be served..." After a pause he added slyly, "...but only after every one of you has climbed the rigging from here to the top of the mast, and then come down on the other side. Any slackers will feel this!"

He produced from behind his back a stout bamboo cane, and struck one of the men heavily on the bottom.

"Now get moving, you animals!"

Fashang, being one of the younger and more agile of the group, led the way to the rope net between the shrouds that extended to the masthead. He began to climb, holding tightly every time the rolling ship dangled him out over the sea. The ropes had been liberally soaked in tar as a preservative, which made the ascent difficult. At times his feet lost their grip, and he hung by his hands until the swell of the ocean swung him back onto the netting. Far below, he heard some shouting, and looking down he saw a man absolutely frozen with fear partway up the net. The belligerent officer climbed up to his level, and then began beating him unmercifully with the bamboo. Suddenly the unfortunate released his grip, and plunged fifty feet into the sea. Fashang expected an immediate response and rescue operation, but the only result was a caustic shout from the officer, "Anyone else for a swim?"

Horrified by this unnerving experience, the remainder of the men climbed more vigorously up the slippery ropes. Having reached the highest point at last, they began the descent on the other side. This proved even more intimidating, as they tried to find footholds on the swaying rope mesh. Eventually they all made the safety of the deck, where several collapsed in a state of exhaustion and fear. Shortly afterwards, breakfast was served from a galley counter in the forward part of the ship, and the group was shown its quarters, which comprised a large bare cabin with crude plank bunks along the walls.

The watch was then assembled on deck, and Bent-Nose addressed his underlings.

"Now, listen, you bunch of fools. You're here to work – and work you will! Our watch will be on duty every day for eight hours – day or night. Some of you will be topside. That means furling or unfurling the sails – and even reefing in storms."

He looked around for a while, and then selected a number of men with the words, "You will be the topside party. The rest of you will be the deckhands, doing cleaning, stowing and rope-handling."

Looking directly at Fashang, he said, "You seemed to be the best climber, so you will be the lookout at the masthead!"

****

Fashang soon discovered that his daily occupation was to stand on an aerial platform that cavorted across the sky, as the ship heeled from side to side. A wooden voice-tube leading down the mast connected him with another member of his watch, so that information could be shouted between the deck and crow's nest. Throughout his eight-hour shifts, he was required to scan the horizon constantly for sight of significant vessels, rocks or land. However, the major danger was collision with the other three hundred ships of the fleet, as they sailed in convoy behind the flagship. Especially at night, he was kept busy detailing the positions and headings of neighbouring craft. From time to time, an unknown ship would come into sight, and he would report to the deck the description and course. Mostly, these were small trading junks and fishing boats, but he knew that every observation was being recorded by the senior officers.

Bent-Nose had indicated, with unpleasant oaths, that the penalty for a lookout who failed to be observant could be capital. Life was hard, and Fashang was perpetually tired, but he exulted in the fact that he seemed to be free of detection. For days the ship sailed along the coast of China, and the routine became fairly standard.

During his time off, Fashang began to make the acquaintance of other shipmates. Apart from the scores of sailors, there was also a contingent of soldiers on board ready for any hostile reception on the voyage. Soon he had made friends with a group of infantrymen, who were bored with the lengthy inactivity at sea. From them he learned a great deal about the modern weapons carried by the fleet. His days as a stone mason in Shandong had taught him about making gunpowder for quarry blasting, and so he understood the basic concept of firearms. He was intrigued by the "nest-of-bees", which was a multi-barrelled rocket battery consisting of many hexagonal tubes filled with arrows. Charges of gunpowder behind the arrows could be fired to launch the projectiles at high speed over long distances. Fashang was awed when his military friends showed him the workings of the great cannons along the bulwarks of the ship. All this time, he was avidly memorising details of these devices, being fully aware that some day he might part from the fleet, and have to fend for himself. Another piece of armament that he studied carefully was the iron grenade, which could explode with terrifying results.

"Of course we don't use that stuff very much," laughed one of the soldiers.

"Why's that?"

"Mostly we use firecrackers to frighten the local people into submission in these primitive places. That way no one gets hurt, and they quickly surrender."

"Yes, we have lots of them. Kept in a bunker just aft of the third mast," another added.

Fashang tucked all these details away in his mind.

****

After several days of fast sailing in a strong north-westerly wind, the fleet began to bear westward, following the China coastline and then skirting the land of the Malay peoples. To do this, the ships had to tack repeatedly, using the special fore-and-aft sails instead of the square rigs. Consequently, the members of the fleet were often out of sight of each other, as they made long legs to windward. This made the lookout duty more onerous, since the captain was concerned not to lose contact with the main fleet. Fashang was warned to be particularly attentive as they rounded Lion Island, known in the local dialect as Singapura, because its inhabitants had a bad reputation.

By this time their ship was well behind the main fleet, partly due to a couple of storms that they had encountered. Late one afternoon, the captain was trying to make up time by crossing a large bay fairly close to shore. A headland blocked the wind, and the ship's way began to fall off, until it was barely moving. From the masthead, Fashang was looking at the peaceful scene of the palm-fringed beaches, backed by mangrove swamps and thick jungle. Then a slight movement caught his eye. From a small river mouth, a series of black dots appeared to be issuing. Lifting his sighting-tube, he examined them. They were moving fast, and heading towards him. Then into focus came the image of scores of long canoes with high prows carrying figureheads, paddled vigorously by dark-skinned men. From descriptions he had heard, he recognised that these were the notorious Malay "prahus", used as war-canoes by pirates. He also saw the glint of steel, which galvanised him into action with his voice-tube.

"Attention deck! Canoes approaching from the shore on starboard bow! Moving fast!"

"Captain says: How many?" was the reply.

"Estimate about fifteen."

"Captain can deal with them."

While holding this brief conversation, Fashang had failed to continue his survey of the sea. Then, looking astern he was aghast to see a vast swarm of canoes racing towards the ship from that direction.

"Attention, deck! Large number of war-canoes astern of us."

At once a great gong started to beat from the bridge of the ship, and men scurried to their action stations. From his vantage point above, Fashang saw the huge cannons being primed and loaded. On the high stern of the vessel, men were manoeuvring a nest-of-bees into position, while along the gunwales soldiers stood ready with swords and spears. At a command, the nest-of-bees launched its deadly shower of arrows in a cloud of blue smoke, and Fashang saw many of the paddlers in the canoes fall backwards or into the water. Meanwhile, a cannon was fired from the bow, its ball slicing through the rowers of one canoe and upsetting another.

The gunners manning the nest-of-bees struggled hastily to refill the tubes with gunpowder and fit new arrows. But time was not on their side, and some of the surviving canoes managed to reach the safety of the high overhanging stern of the ship. It was only a few seconds before black figures appeared on the poop, each waving a "kris", the short wave-shaped sword favoured by the Malays. The boarders were immediately tackled by soldiers rushed from the middle deck. In the ensuing melee several Chinese were downed by the swords and daggers of the Malay pirates, as they advanced towards the bridge.

Looking forward, Fashang could see that the other flotilla of canoes had nearly reached the bow of the ship. Then he saw an officer on the foredeck whirling a slingshot containing an object about the size of an orange. The device flew through the air, and landed in the middle of a canoe, whose occupants eyed it suspiciously. Without warning, it exploded, casting shards of metal for dozens of metres all around. Seven canoes disappeared completely, and the remainder began to sink, or turned for home.

The battle on the stern was going badly, and the captain was barricaded in the bridge, which would soon fall to the assailants. With the removal of the threat up forward, the soldiers were transferred aft, and formed disciplined ranks along the deck. Gradually they pushed the Malays back, until realising that all was lost, the intruders dived over the side into the sea. As they tried to regain their canoes, the Chinese militia poured volleys of arrows onto them.

All of a sudden, a command was given to stop firing. The soldiers obeyed, looking puzzled. A senior officer walked to the side and pointed into the sea. Soon ropes were lowered, and a man was hauled up onto the deck. Fashang could see that he was Chinese, and assumed it to be one of the defenders. But as he squinted more closely, he became conscious of the fact that the man's dress, colouring and hairstyle were quite alien. It appeared that he had been one of the pirates. Much mystified, Fashang waited for the end of his watch to descend to the deck, to find out the truth about this strange man. Meanwhile he watched the work details clean the dried blood from the decks, and prepare the fallen crew members for sea-burial.

****

At the end of the watch, Fashang climbed down the netting, keen to hear details of the engagement. Almost at once, one of his watch-members called to him.

"Can you understand this bloke? He speaks like you."

The man was pointing to the Chinese who had been rescued from the sea, and Fashang was immediately cautious lest the fellow was from north China, and would give him away. Speaking slowly, he asked the man who he was, but received a torrent of verbiage in return. It was certainly not the dialect of Shandong. Try as he might, Fashang could not communicate with the newcomer. Then an idea hit him. Perhaps this man was literate, and if so they could write to each other, since the Chinese characters were the same across the country, despite differences in speech. He decided to ask the man's name. Taking a piece of burnt firewood, he dipped it in water and then wrote the characters for "Gui xing?" on the dry planking. Immediately the man seized the improvised pen, and began to write in the same way, indicating his name. Although the process was slow, the man soon conveyed the fact that he was a native of Guangdong in south China. He was a trader, expeditioning into the Malay jungle in search of medicinal plants. While there, he had been attacked and captured by a band of local warriors. After being taken to a nearby kampong, he was forced to work for the Malay chief of the area for over a year. Subsequently he was drafted into the crew of a prahu, and compelled to participate in several pirate raids.

This information was passed to the captain, who ordered the liberated man to be added to the same watch as Fashang, replacing a seaman killed in the brawl with the pirates. Thus the southerner was initiated into the life of a naval conscript under the supervision of the obnoxious Bent-Nose. Gradually Fashang's new friend learned to converse in the standard language of the northern plains, but Fashang never managed to grasp the intricate sounds of Cantonese. Fashang discovered that in the south of China it was traditional to use a person's surname with the prefix "Ah" - and so his new companion became known as Ah-Wang. The two men were drawn together, because both had different origins from the majority of the sailors, who came mostly from the Suzhou region.

****

Following the debacle with the pirates, the ship rejoined the main squadron, and proceeded towards the town of Malacca. As the fleet anchored in orderly rows offshore, the crew and military men were allowed a brief spell ashore, after the weeks at sea. Fashang and Ah-Wang wandered through the port, surprised at the strange combination of Chinese and Malay cultures in the buildings, clothes and food that they found. They learned that the Sultan and Sultana of Malacca had already visited China, and that strong ties linked the two places. Already, in his mind, Fashang was speculating about his chances of deserting the ship in a port such as this, and setting up as a mason in some secluded area. But Malacca was too small for him to hide, and he reluctantly reboarded his ship with the rest of the crew.

As they journeyed out into the great ocean to the west, Fashang fell into conversation with an army corporal who seemed quite knowledgeable.

"But why is this called the Treasure Fleet?"

"You see, this is the fifth expedition by Admiral Zheng He. I've been on three of them, and each time he goes a bit further – finds some new lands. When he returns to China he brings masses of stuff - gold, wood, ivory, and even animals. It's truly a treasure chest that he brings back to the Emperor!" the seasoned traveller replied.

"So are we looking for more treasure this time?"

"Actually the purpose this time is to take back the ambassadors that went to Beijing on the last trip. They have all sworn allegiance to our Emperor, and are being returned home in style."

"Are they travelling on the flagship?"

"No, they are dispersed among the fleet. This is why we will be splitting up to go to separate lands, and then rendezvousing at certain points. There are nineteen of these emissaries, and we have one on board."

"Who is that?"

"We are carrying a prince of the royal house of Aden. He was ordered by the Sultan to take gifts to our Emperor. A lot of gold and porcelain was sent, and even some animals."

"That must have made the Dragon Emperor happy," Fashang commented.

"The fleet is dividing up. Several ships are heading for Sumatra and Java, but we will probably stop at Calicut in the south of India, and then go straight across to Aden."

Chapter 11

Arab Experience

One morning Fashang noticed a distinctive group of men leaning on the gunwale. They were obviously not Chinese, having swarthier skin and each wearing a long tunic down to the knees, over which a light cloak was thrown. Their heads were covered with turbans wound from lengths of cloth. Intrigued, Fashang greeted them in Chinese, but with little response. Then one of the group came forward and spoke haltingly in the language of Beijing. Soon Fashang discovered that these men were retainers of the Arab prince that was returning to Aden. They were evidently bored with the long voyage, and glad of a new acquaintance. Gradually the conversation began to flow more meaningfully, and Fashang found them a welcome change from the largely uneducated sailors with whom he worked. He introduced them to Ah-Wang, who appreciated the association.

Thus began a ritual. Whenever the Arabs were off-duty they would gather at a point amidships on the middle deck, and Fashang and Ah-Wang, if free, would socialise with them. One outcome of this was that the two Chinese began to pick up Arabic, and after a couple of weeks of monotonous sailing they achieved a usable level of fluency.

****

Ultimately, after making long tacks out into the great ocean because of contrary wind directions, the ship made a landfall at the large city of Calicut. The vessel was berthed in the spacious harbour against a stout stone jetty, and Fashang saw his chance for a change of life-style. Confiding his ideas to Ah-Wang, he discovered that his companion was of the same mind, and that both of them would like to escape into the conurbation that stretched several miles inland from the shore.

Despite being a cosmopolitan city on the tip of the Indian continent, with a huge range of religions and cultures, it was surprising to find a strong Arab influence there. Beautiful mosques abounded, and Arabic was widely spoken in the streets and markets. For several days the members of Bent-Nose's watch were sent ashore to transport large containers of water to the ship, and then to collect ropes for replacement of the ship's rigging. All this gave Fashang and Ah-Wang the chance to reconnoitre for suitable places into which to fade when they deserted the navy. To their surprise, their limited fluency in Arabic did allow them to communicate with the local people, many of whom were also second-language speakers. As sailors on the ship, they had only been paid a pittance by the captain. But this had accrued sufficiently for the prospective escapees to envisage surviving for a few days, until they could find work.

Behind the port lay a warren of unpaved and unplanned paths leading to a mass of shanties of dubious repute. Fashang's illicit excursions into the area led him to select a small reed-roofed building that was obviously some kind of doss-house for peasant workers, tucked away among a selection of shebeens, drug-dens and brothels. Although the proprietor of the establishment was an Indian, he had sufficient Arabic for Fashang to enquire the daily fee, which he found to be within their means for at least a few nights. Returning to the ship, he made plans with Ah-Wang.

After the next morning muster, the two men were assigned to a shore detail to collect repaired sails. Secretively carrying some possessions, they joined the work squad. At a suitable point in the afternoon, they slipped away down an alley, and slunk through the town to their hideout in the hinterland. Having booked in with the Indian owner, they were allocated spaces in a large, dirty dormitory. Immediately they began to look for employment opportunities.

Fashang soon discovered that there was a thriving industry making small stone carvings of Hindu gods, and his enquiries met with positive responses from several artisans in the narrow streets. Ah-Wang also was successful, since with his hunting experience he could handle meat. One of the butchery stalls in the nearby market offered to take him on the following day.

Buoyed up with these initial encouragements, they looked forward to a new and different life. As they returned to their lodging, they made plans about how they would move to a better area, once they were financially autonomous. Their fantasies even stretched to a proposed extensive tour of southern India. But it was not to be.

****

Fashang led the way through the door back into the dormitory, and was instantly felled by a blow to the back of his head. Momentarily he was stunned as he lay on the floor, and when his vision cleared, he looked up into the leering face of petty officer Bent-Nose. Despite his ringing head, he saw the nasty grin and heard the words.

"Thought you'd just leave us, you two rats, did you?" he snarled. "Without even saying goodbye! Well, you'll regret this. People who desert the Emperor's navy find themselves dancing on the end of a rope."

Unceremoniously, four soldiers from the ship lifted Fashang and Ah-Wang, who were too dazed to resist. They were carried bodily through the streets to the dockside. As they were taken aboard, the sides of the ship were lined with crew and soldiers witnessing the return of the deserters. The captain stood on a platform in front of the bridge, and the recalcitrants were thrown onto the deck before him.

"You know the penalty for being absent without leave. It is death! But I cannot give the order without the Admiral's confirmation. So, you will be confined, until we meet up with the flagship again."

He turned, and added, "But give them twenty 'chi' first!"

Obediently, Bent-Nose gave a command. "Strip off their clothes. Tie their hands to those two halyards, and haul!"

Soon Fashang and Ah-Wang found themselves hanging by their hands half a metre above the deck. While they struggled with the awful strain on their wrists, Bent-Nose gave an order. Suddenly Fashang felt a searing pain across his shoulder blades, followed almost immediately by the same sensation across his naked buttocks. Glancing down, he saw a soldier brandishing a long thin bamboo cane, and preparing for the next stroke. The torture continued, with Bent-Nose counting each blow, as Fashang's back and legs were lacerated by the cane. He could feel the warm blood running down his torso, and dripping off his feet. The pain became so intense that his consciousness became foggy. Vaguely he heard the voice of Bent-Nose call out the final number, and stop the beating. What Fashang did not see was the sailor who drew a bucket of sea-water up onto the deck. Next moment the brine was poured over Fashang's back. He screamed, and fainted.

****

When he came to, Fashang found himself on the floor of a small room in intense pain. A pungent miasma assailed his nostrils, and after a while he realised that it came from the pool of blood in which he was lying.

"It's better if you lie on your front," came a croaky voice that he recognised as belonging to Ah-Wang. "Thank the gods that we're alive – even if only just."

Fashang moved to a slightly less painful posture, and looked across at a bloody mass of meat, which he comprehended with horror as being his good friend.

"Do you think we'll die?" Fashang asked tremulously.

"No, we'll make it. The seawater they threw over us will help the healing. Just lie still, if you can."

As Fashang lay there, throbbing and sore, he was overcome with a great cloud of depression. His will to live departed, and he sunk into despondency. His world seemed to have collapsed, and now he was nearing the end of it all. Then, like a shaft of light, his memory recalled the words of the sage, "Our greatest glory is not in never falling, but in rising every time we fall." Once again, his determination seeped back, and he resolved to keep strong against all odds and expectations.

"What is this place?" he asked Ah-Wang.

"It seems to be a punishment cell below decks. It can't be too far down, since there are a couple of drain holes to let water out."

From his prone position Fashang could see two large scuppers at floor level. Although not wide enough to allow passage of a man, they provided some illumination in their jail, and permitted a limited view of the outside world. They could see the far shore of the Calicut dock line, which assured them that the ship had not yet put to sea.

"If we had water, we could clean up this mess."

"It seems there are buckets along the wall," said Ah-Wang rising stiffly with great difficulty. "Yes, two with water, and one empty."

"I suppose that one is the latrine."

"The others will give us a chance to drink and wash. Oh, now I can see our clothes in a heap by the door."

After several more hours, the two prisoners felt able to move more freely, and used some of the water to wash the sticky floor, and their many wounds. Dressing was painful but necessary, they felt, to preserve some measure of hygiene.

From then on, life became a monotonously sparse routine. The days passed, with the only events being the morning and evening opening of the door to let out the soil bucket and receive food and water. The fare was surprisingly nutritious, even if only rice and vegetables, and Fashang commented on this.

"The captain wants us in fine fettle when we reach the gallows," offered Ah-Wang with a grim chuckle.

****

After a couple of days, the rolling and pitching of the ship indicated that they were under way again. From their little scupper spy-holes the two men watched the land recede, and for several days after that they observed only the empty horizon.

Late one afternoon, Fashang sensed that the ship had come up into the wind, and soon a sharp jerk suggested that they had anchored. At first there was nothing but sea visible. But as the vessel swung to its mooring, they glimpsed a coastline with square white houses along it. A city of domes and minarets came into view, silhouetted against rows of sand dunes. After several hours of watching, they were rewarded with the sight of a richly decorated dhow putting out from the shore. This elaborate craft sailed out of their vision, and they heard sounds of trumpets and gongs ringing out.

"My guess is that this is Aden, and the royal prince is being welcomed home."

"Sounds very likely," agreed Ah-Wang, "and looks like a sumptuous place to live."

"Perhaps we should have deserted here," joked Fashang. "We could have hidden in the desert!"

The ship did not approach the city, but remained at anchor well offshore. Lighters were continually being rowed between the ship and harbour, evidently for reprovisioning, and to provide shore leave for the ship's company. In all their observations the two incarcerated friends did not catch sight of another Chinese warship, and deduced that they had separated from the main Treasure Fleet to deliver the ambassador to Aden. Two days later, the ship put out to sea again.

****

The weary life of bondage continued for another week, at the end of which the door of the cell was suddenly thrown open, with a command to come out. Stumbling into the sunshine, the inmates were met by a squat figure that they did not at first recognise. It was only when they perceived the crooked nose, that they realised it was petty officer Bent-Nose. He looked small and hunched, his skin was grey, and his voice was a whisper.

"But, sir, what has happened?" Fashang asked in astonishment, looking around at the empty deck.

"A few days after we left that dratted Aden, a great pox hit the ship. We think it was a sickness from the city there, or from its gods. Almost everyone who had been ashore had the fever, with vomiting and headaches. I'm sorry we went to that hellish place. It was steaming hot, and the mosquitoes were biting all the time."

"But how about the captain?"

"He would not set foot on land there – believed that the air was bad. So, he and the senior officers did not get sick."

Fashang looked around with incredulity. High in the rigging he could see a few sailors, and on the foredeck was a small gathering of soldiers. Otherwise the ship looked desolate.

Bent-Nose continued, "A third of the men have died, and the rest are very weak. We need hands to man the ship. The Captain has pardoned you two, so that you can get back to work."

Just at that moment, an officer came up to Bent-Nose. He asked if he could find a man with experience of steering to replace the helmsman, who had been struck down. Bent-Nose looked doubtful about finding such a substitute, and Fashang seized his chance.

"Pardon me, sir, but I have experience steering a river barge."

"Well, that's better than nothing," the officer said, "Come up to the bridge with me!"

And thus it was that Fashang became a steersman on one of China's great treasure ships.

Chapter 12

Remote Rendezvous

Fashang soon discovered that helming a twenty-thousand ton man-o-war on the ocean was a far cry from steering a barge along the inland waters of China. As he was escorted to the bridge deck, he was astounded by the size of the tiller, about eleven metres in length. It was made from a great tree trunk, and far too heavy for a man to handle. Therefore a system of ropes and pulleys was used to move this huge beam, which was connected directly onto the ship's rudder. Fashang was inducted into the helmsman's art by the first mate, and began to wonder if his forwardness had been wise.

Unlike following a canal which had visible boundaries, ocean navigation proceeded by the use of charts and celestial observations. Thus the captain and officers would plot courses, and then send directional headings to the steersman. This was all completely new to Fashang, and he puzzled over the bowl of water fixed in a bronze stand just forward of the steering position. His instructor enlightened him.

"That is a South-Pointing Fish."

"And what does it do?"

"Look carefully!" he said pointing into the middle of the bowl. Fashang saw a thin strip of metal, shaped like a fish floating on the water.

"But why doesn't it sink?"

"It is so thin that it floats on the top of the water, like on a skin. Now watch carefully while I change the direction of the ship!"

The mate pulled hard on one of the tiller ropes, and Fashang felt the ship heel slightly and change direction. As he watched the floating fish, he saw that it moved in such a way that it continued pointing in the original direction. At once a shout came from the officer of the watch.

"Take care of your direction, helmsman!"

"I'm just showing the new man, sir. Will be back on course at once," the mate replied.

Readjusting the tiller ropes, he pointed at the basin.

"Now when you're steering, you must keep that fish pointing at one of those characters."

Fashang now noticed that engraved round the edge of the instrument were twenty-four Chinese characters.

"The officer on duty will tell you which heading he wants. If you deviate by more than two characters from that, you will be severely punished."

"But how does the fish know to move?"

"Our scholars call it 'magnetism', whatever that is. But the fish always looks to the south, wherever we are."

Fashang nodded with apparent understanding, while secretly wishing he had opted for a more mundane task. However, he soon became accustomed to the position, and found that his powers of concentration enabled him to steer for many hours on any given compass heading. Life improved, and he began to enjoy the experience and power of his important role. He was one of three helmsmen, and took an eight-hour watch each day. The officers on the bridge still treated him with some disdain, but he could tell they were not unimpressed with his performance.

****

One advantage of his position at the tiller was that he heard the conversations between the master and his officers. From these he gleaned that their voyage would take them down the east coast of the newly-discovered land of Africa. They were required to call at an island called Kilwa, which was the capital of a vast empire stretching along the coast. It was ruled by an Arab sultan, who had sworn allegiance to the Chinese emperor on a previous voyage of the Treasure Fleet, but had since reneged on payment of promised dues.

The captain had orders to sail to Kilwa, and collect the taxes that were owed to the court of Beijing. Fashang had mixed feelings of excitement and apprehension as the small island came in sight. Then a large harbour at the head of a bay slid into view, with a city of blindingly white buildings on the hill behind it. The captain set his course towards the port, while Fashang paid close attention to the small changes of heading shouted to him by the senior navigator. With an acquired dexterity, he worked the tiller ropes, as they entered Kilwa harbour under a fresh breeze.

Suddenly, without warning, a flash of fire and a spurt of smoke erupted from a high tower in the city. Within a few seconds a cannon ball flew across their bows and splashed into the sea.

"Stupid idiots! Don't they know who we are?" shouted the captain in high dudgeon. "Wear ship - immediately!"

By now Fashang had learned that this was the most dangerous of sailing manoeuvres in a strong wind. On hearing the command, sailors rushed to the sheets in preparation for jibing the vessel round from one tack to the other. Fashang knew that a slight fault on his part could do much damage to the sails and rigging, and possibly bring down a mast. Pulling with force and precision on the tiller ropes, he waited until the fore-and-aft sails were sheeted in hard before putting the ship onto its new course. The combination of his skill, and the efforts of the seamen on the ropes, produced a smooth turn away from the threatening harbour.

"Not bad, helmsman," the captain murmured.

Taking the ship out to sea, the captain then ordered battle stations. When the cannons were positioned and primed, he sailed back into Kilwa harbour. Swinging broadside onto the city, he ordered the gunners to fire. An ear-splitting crash resulted, accompanied by thick black smoke which hid the land from sight. As the air cleared, they could see that several buildings had been damaged, and part of the sea wall breached.

While preparing for another cannonade, the captain saw several white flags appearing in the town, and held his fire. Before long a dhow was seen sailing towards the Chinese vessel. The captain ordered the ship to be hove-to, and Fashang obeyed by swinging the vessel onto a beam reach. By deft adjustment of the headsail sheets and by backing the square sails slightly, the captain brought the great ship to a virtual standstill. Fashang lashed the tiller into position, so that they remained almost stationary on the water.

****

As the small sailing craft approached, Fashang was able to study it. He realised that the rigging of the Arab dhow was completely different from that on Chinese ships. Instead of the broad sails with bamboo battens across them, the dhow had one triangular sail hanging from a long wooden yard mounted at an angle to the single mast. There were no battens, and the mass of canvas was loose-footed, controlled by a single sheet attached to the bottom corner. This lateen sail enabled the boat to sail well to windward, a fact that was now evidenced by the rapid advance of the Arab craft towards the ship. A man in the bow was vigorously waving a strip of white cloth.

In view of the hostile reception that they had received, the captain did not greet the newcomers at the entry port, or take them to his stateroom for refreshments. Instead, he had the delegation escorted to the bridge, which had the advantage for Fashang that he could hear the exchange.

It was soon apparent that the captain had a good command of Arabic, and throughout the ensuing conversation he maintained a grim and unsmiling mien. Four expensively-dressed Arab gentlemen were led onto the bridge, where they were confronted by the senior officers of the ship.

"And what is the meaning of this? You have fired on us without cause!" demanded the captain.

All four men fell to their knees.

"We humbly beg your forgiveness, Effendim. It was a great mistake, and we crave your indulgence."

"This is an act of war by a tributary nation!"

The heads dropped lower, until only a few centimetres from the deck.

"It was a misunderstanding with the gunners, Effendim, and they will be severely punished."

"Now, what about the tribute that is due to the Dragon Emperor. Why has that not been sent to Calicut as agreed?"

"Effendim, it is not our fault, nor that of the Sultan. The ships were loaded and ready to sail, but a great storm came, and all were wrecked."

"I don't believe a word of it, and intend to destroy your city and take your Sultan to Beijing in chains."

At this pronouncement, a great wailing arose from the noble gentlemen.

"Have mercy, excellent Effendim! We will give you the tribute now. In fact we will double it, and add valuable gifts as well."

"I don't want it doubled. You can give me four times the amount, and I will spare your city. And send your presents as well!"

"You are indeed kind, wise, generous, merciful, sensitive, honourable..."

"Enough! Now I want that cargo transferred out here as quickly as possible."

"But, Effendim, may we suggest that you come alongside the dock. It will be so much faster, and we have prepared a suitable welcome for you and your crew."

"I wonder what he means by a suitable welcome," surmised the captain, switching his speech into Chinese. "I don't trust them at all, and neither do we want more sickness because of the bad air in there."

Reverting to Arabic, he replied, "No, we will anchor in the lee of that headland, and you will bring everything out to my ship within two days."

With many salaams and insincere expressions of gratitude, the delegation left the ship, and sailed back to the city. Very soon sails were being hosted on a fleet of dhows, which rapidly came alongside the anchored ship. As loaded baskets were swung aboard, the officers made detailed inventories of everything. Since Fashang was temporarily relieved of his duties on the bridge, he enjoyed watching the arrival of all the tribute items. Among these were bars of gold and silver, delicate porcelain basins and statues, and great bolts of expensive silk.

****

On the second afternoon, Fashang was looking idly across the sea, when he saw a substantial barge, without a sail, being rowed out from the harbour. As it came nearer, he could see a tall, thin statue amidships, and assumed that an idol of one of the local gods was being donated. This surprised him, because he had heard that the Muslim religion banned such images. The boat was carefully brought alongside, and Fashang saw that the statue had been painted in a mottled combination of light and dark brown paint. The head was long with two little protrusions on the crown. Suddenly Fashang jumped spontaneously – he thought he saw one eye of the statue blink! As he gaped, astounded, the whole head rotated towards him, revealing the most unusual animal he had ever seen.

"What is that down there?" he shouted to the inventory-taker.

"Don't you know? That's a Long-Necked-Deer. They roam the grasslands of Africa, and are quite harmless. The Emperor specially wants to see one – so he'll be happy with this gift."

Carefully the giraffe was hoisted aboard, and a wooden cage hastily constructed on the deck for him. Fashang never tired of watching this strangely peaceful animal throughout the rest of the voyage.

The captain finally showed satisfaction with the quality and quantity of goods sent out from the port. With severe warnings to the Sultan about failure to make future payments, he set sail.

****

The following day, two other ships of the Treasure Fleet came in sight, heading in the same direction. Fashang inferred from the bridge conversation that they were approaching a rendezvous point for the whole fleet - at a place called Sofala.

After another couple of days of sailing, with the African jungle coast to starboard, they saw a substantial town on flat land in the delta of a wide river. But their attention was drawn away from it to the sight of hundreds of masts offshore, betokening the whole of Admiral Zheng He's fleet at anchor. Fashang sensed the captain and officers becoming apprehensive, as they closed with the long lines of anchored warships. Coloured pennants were hoisted on the signal mast, and corresponding signals returned from the flagship, instructing the captain as to where to anchor in the mass of shipping.

"File five, position twelve," the signals officer read from the distant flags.

"Won't be too easy," commented the captain, "but at least the wind is blowing across the fleet, so we can sail right up to the mooring."

The great vessel cruised along the outside of the huge rectangle of anchored craft.

"That's file five. Helmsman, don't use the compass now – it's too imprecise. The first officer will give you tiller instructions. And keep on your toes!"

"Hao de, Captain," Fashang acknowledged.

As the ship entered the specified lane between the moored vessels, Fashang was amazed at how narrow the corridor was.

"The Admiral's not given us much room," complained the captain testily.

By now, they were proceeding along the constricted fairway, desperately trying to prevent collision with the vessels on either side. Their point of sailing was a close reach, but their speed was dangerously high.

"Furl the square sails," came the order to the deck, which was followed by a great scrambling of men up the shrouds. "Leave the sprit sails and mizzen!"

Soon the huge rectangles of cloth were being hauled up and tied to the upper spars. This made the ship more manageable, as the fore-and-aft sails were trimmed carefully by gangs of sailors straining on the sheets. Every member of the crew was sweating profusely in the hot sun, but it was also the innate danger of their situation that motivated them.

The first officer rapped out a series of commands, to which Fashang feverishly adjusted the positions of the great tiller.

"Zou… zhong… zuo yi diar… zhong… you… zhong… port… amidships… port a little… amidships… starboard… amidships…"

After a while, the captain identified a space in the line of ships as being their designated berth.

"Helm, prepare to come up into the wind. Steady… Hard a starboard!"

At this, the great warship swung diagonally across the space between the neighbouring vessels.

"Loose all sheets!" was met with the raucous flapping of canvas, as the ship slowed its pace. But its enormous momentum carried it forward towards the upwind vessel, whose crew looked fearfully over the stern. Fashang held his breath, expecting an imminent impact. However, the captain's seamanship proved adequate, and they came to a halt just a few metres from the poop which rose before them.

"Let go anchor! Tiller hard a-starboard!"

With a mighty rattling of chain the huge steel grapnel plunged to the sea bed. The wind forced the ship backwards, while the tiller turned it into line with the rest of the flotilla.

"Snub the chain!"

With a jolt, the anchor warp came tight, and after a short time of dragging, it held in the subterranean mud. With a sigh, the captain collapsed onto a seat.

"That was a close thing," he gasped.

"Perhaps the Admiral chose this berth as a test of our skills," offered one of the officers.

"More than likely," agreed the exhausted master. "Now put out a stern anchor!"

****

Once the vessel was securely moored, a small sampan sailed alongside. An official, in an imposing uniform, came aboard, and went straight to the bridge to meet the captain.

"The Admiral sends his compliments, Captain. We trust you had a successful voyage."

"Indeed, I have sought to carry out the Admiral's orders to the best of my humble ability."

"I have come to issue an invitation for you dine with the Admiral and other commanders tomorrow night. Dress uniform of course."

"Thank you. Please inform the Admiral of my pleasure in accepting his invitation."

Throughout this conversation, Fashang was within earshot of the speakers, while he coiled the ropes and checked the locking of the tiller.

"And by the way, Captain, there is one other little matter. It seems a fast ship has come from Suzhou with a report that a murderer may have joined the fleet somewhere."

"Do you refer to that case of the Shandong landlord who was killed? I heard about it before sailing."

"That's the one. The chief eunuch is still on the man's trail. Anyway, you are asked to check all members of your crew tomorrow morning. This fellow speaks with a Shandong accent, and also has a long scar on his left thigh."

Fashang's heart nearly stopped. His mind went back to the day, several years before, when he had been working on a temple in his home area. A stone had slipped, and he had gashed his upper left leg with a chisel. The wound was now well healed, but the scar was there. But how did they know about it?

"Just parade your whole crew naked, Captain, and if anyone fits this description, send him to the flagship in irons."

"Certainly, sir."

Slipping from the bridge, Fashang found a spot just behind the serene giraffe's cage to sit and recover from the shock. Once again, he had that gut-wrenching feeling of being hunted. On the canal and in Suzhou, he had been close to discovery, and here he was again in the same predicament. His nerve failed him, and he toyed with the idea of throwing himself over the side to the waiting sharks.

Chapter 13

Foreign Shore

Gradually Fashang's panic subsided, and he became more rational. He considered his various options - which amounted to only one. If he were to avoid being dragged back to Beijing as a felon, the only chance lay in reaching the nearby shore, and hoping he could survive there. But the coast was a long way off, across water infested with man-eaters. Anyway, he was not a strong swimmer.

An idea flashed into his mind, as he remembered that whenever the ship was at anchor, several small sampans were left moored to the stern to allow officers and messengers to cross to other ships. But then his slight elation was dampened by the realisation that rowing a sampan with a single oar required a definite skill, which he did not possess. About to abandon this embryonic plan, his thoughts turned to Ah-Wang. Since his friend had grown up in a fishing village on the Guangdong coast, there was no doubt that he could scull a sampan without difficulty. The problem lay in whether he should confide in Ah-Wang, and what his response would be. Both men were still stiff and sore after their last attempt at desertion, and he doubted that they could endure another beating of that nature. Deciding that there was nothing to be lost, he sought out Ah-Wang in a quiet corner of the deck.

"I've got a problem, Ah-Wang," he explained

"And what's that, my friend? Must say you look terrible. What's on your mind?"

"Something that I've never told you. You see, I'm on the run..."

Ah-Wang regarded him quizzically. "Running from whom?"

"In fact, from the law. I've been accused of murder – though I did not do it. Now it seems they are about to catch up with me. I am planning to get to land, and look for safety. Will you come with me?"

Ah-Wang chuckled briefly, "It seems we have both been keeping secrets. I, too, am on the run!"

Aghast, Fashang questioned him, "But who is looking for you. Is it the Jinyiwei?"

"No, in my case I fell foul of the local secret society, the White Lotus. I refused to cooperate with an extortion racket, but I knew too much. They sent a contract-killer after me. That's why I fled into Malaya to make a new home there."

"Yes, I understand," Fashang said thoughtfully. "Those societies are powerful and vicious. So I suppose you can't go back."

"Afraid not. They'd get me as soon as I surfaced in south China. So I've nothing to lose by trying to desert again. But what's your idea?"

Together the conspirators talked through the details of an escape that very night. They were encouraged by the fact that, after the great sickness, the number of crew on guard duty was very small. Casually, they strolled to the stern of the ship, and looked down onto the small sampans tethered there. Ah-Wang confirmed that he had rowed that type of boat for many years since childhood.

As darkness fell, there was much merriment from the crews of the cluster of ships all around. This helped to drown the sound of the two escapees, as they moved their possessions and some food into hiding on the poop deck. It appeared that the officers were taking their rest after the exertions of the previous days, meaning that Fashang and Ah-Wang were able to move freely and furtively about the ship. Fashang broke open one of the gunpowder bins, and scooped a quantity into a bag. Remembering the comment of one of the soldiers, he found the locker where the firecrackers were stored, and armed himself with a supply of these. However, he knew that this ammunition would be of little value without a means to make fire. After searching through several lockers, they found a waxed bag containing a large number of short sticks. Carefully examining them, Fashang perceived that each had been dipped in sulphur and allowed to dry.

"I've found a supply of fire-sticks," he whispered to Ah-Wang.

****

Sometime after midnight, Ah-Wang climbed down the rope ladder over the stern, and stepped into one of the moored sampans. Gingerly, Fashang handed the bundle of combustible and explosive materials down to him, followed by their simple baggage and victuals. Casting off quietly, they drifted away from the ship.

At this point, Ah-Wang showed his prowess as a boatman. Lifting the long single oar, he placed it over the stern, and aligned the small indentation half way along it with an iron nail protruding from the transom of the boat. Fashang thought that the oar would not stay balanced on the pivot for long. But, using his practiced expertise, Ah-Wang swung the oar to one side while rotating it to keep the nail in the hole. At the end of the stroke, he reversed the force on the oar and rotated it appropriately. In this way, he began to propel the small craft across the water at a considerable speed. Fashang watched in wonderment at the dexterity of his friend.

"Which way shall we go?" whispered Ah-Wang.

"The shore to the right is heavily forested. Let's go that way."

As they distanced themselves from the ships, and began to navigate parallel to the shoreline, Fashang voiced his concern.

"How long can you keep going like this?"

"Don't worry, good friend. In my young days I would row like this all night when we were fishing. I'm accustomed to it – and can carry on for several hours."

****

Fashang kept watch as they paddled on through the darkness. There was no moon to help them, and so they navigated by keeping a constant distance from the faint white line of the surf breaking on the shore. Imperceptibly, the sky lightened as they travelled slowly along the seaboard of Africa, revealing white beaches backed by thick jungle. Ah-Wang showed no sign of tiring, as he swung in a rhythmic movement to the oscillation of the oar.

"How far shall we go?" he asked.

"Maybe till sunup. That's when they'll call muster on the ship – and then they'll be after us!"

"But we need to look for some habitation. We can't exist in the jungle by ourselves."

"Good thought! Let's watch for any sign of human activity."

In the far distance, Fashang spied a wisp of smoke rising behind the dense mass of trees.

"There's someone over there. Can we land near here?"

"No problem," Ah-Wang assured him, as he turned the sampan towards the shore. But as they neared the beach, they found that the surf was pounding upon it more fiercely than they had anticipated. Soon the little craft was being carried up to the crests of big waves, before plunging down waterfalls of water into the troughs. Each time the sampan reached the bottom of a valley, Ah-Wang sculled the long oar vigorously in an effort to keep ahead of the following wave, which threatened to break right over them. If that had occurred, then the cockleshell would doubtless have rapidly been swamped and sunk. While holding on grimly with one hand, Fashang was fully occupied in baling out the water that was building up in the bilges. After twenty minutes, seeming like an hour in this watery mayhem, they looked down from the crest of a wave, and saw a sandy beach ahead. That itself was consoling, since they had no desire to be wrecked on a rocky coast. Finally, Ah-Wang managed to keep the boat balanced on the top of a wave as it broke onto the beach, crashing them onto the sand in a tumult of foam.

Ah-Wang leapt ashore, grabbing the bow of the sampan. He shouted to Fashang to hold the boat firmly, as the receding wave tried to pull it back to the sea. Struggling with the wooden craft, they managed to drag it several metres up the beach, before collapsing with exhaustion.

"That was a great bit of steering," panted Fashang.

"At least we are on land. But we shouldn't hang about for long. They may send a fast junk along the coast to find us. I don't fancy another beating, d'you?"

Fashang shivered.

****

Climbing to the top of a ridge of sand dunes, they saw that a large area of mangrove swamp lay between them and the edge of the thick jungle.

"Now, how do we find a way through that?" Fashang mused.

"What's that over there? Looks like a couple of tree trunks," Ah-Wang exclaimed, as he led the way along the dunes.

"Yes, as I guessed," he said pointing. "Those are dugout canoes. There must be a way through the marsh."

Inspecting the ground carefully, Fashang reported, "There's a small path on the solid ground through the swamp. Let's get our stuff, and see if we can find people."

Returning to the boat, they loaded themselves up with the cargo. Ah-Wang carried most of the food, clothing and general items, while Fashang struggled along with the various packages of pyrotechnic material. They took the little path that led towards the forest edge.

"Pity about the boat," Ah-Wang complained. "The search party will probably find it, and know where we've gone."

"Can't be helped. There's no way we can hide it – or sink it."

The path entered the vegetation, and it was immediately obvious that, without the narrow track, the jungle would be impenetrable. Although the trees were not tall, they had limbs projecting at weird angles, festooned with vines and lianas. Plants with huge leaves rose from the ground, and the whole place had a damp, earthy smell. The humidity was intense, and the two Chinese were soon running with sweat, and beating off myriads of flies, large and small. There was evidence that someone had cleared the track, and on occasion they saw footprints in the mud.

Eventually the forest gave way to an open valley. It appeared to have once been part of the jungle, but the presence of burned tree trunks suggested it had been cleared for agriculture and settlement. Indeed, several fields could be seen, and a flock of goats was browsing at one end of the dale. On the far side, a collection of thatched huts nestled against the forest wall.

"I wonder how we can make ourselves known to the locals," Ah-Wang queried.

But they need not have worried about becoming conspicuous, as the events of the next few minutes demonstrated.

Fashang had stopped to retie his bundle of materials, with the result that his companion was several hundred metres ahead of him, striding along the path into the valley. At one point he was passing a small clump of low bushes. Suddenly, to Fashang's horror, a tall black figure stepped out behind Ah-Wang, dwarfing the short Chinese. The African must have moved silently, for his victim seemed totally unaware. Raising a long wooden club, with a large block on the end, he brought it down on Ah-Wang's skull with great force. This prostrated him immediately, and was the signal for a dozen other warriors to leap out of the cover to dance around the fallen man.

Fashang could hardly keep his eyes on the scene, as short spears were brandished, and then plunged into the body of his friend. After that, the men grouped together for a discussion. They turned, pointing in Fashang's direction. He knew what lay in store for him. Steadily the men began to march up the hill, their shiny spearhead's slick with blood.

Terror seemed to energise Fashang's survival instinct. Almost without thinking, he found himself tearing open his bundle, and grabbing a firecracker. A quick search located the packet of fire-sticks. He grabbed two of them, and began to rub them briskly together. A small amount of smoke was emitted, which died away. In consternation Fashang remembered that these matches were intended for dry climates, and often malfunctioned in damp environments. Seizing two more, he rubbed them smartly against each other. This time he was successful, and one of the sticks burst into flame.

Looking up, he saw that the head warrior was only a few metres from him, and increasing his grip on the shaft of his club. Frantically applying the burning match to the fuse of a firecracker, he threw it forward. But he was too late. The great block of wood came sailing down onto him. Quickly rolling sideways, he avoided his executioner, who grunted and raised his weapon over Fashang for a final blow.

Even Fashang's eardrums were shot with pain at the explosion that followed, and the effect on his assailants was electric. The leader jumped a metre in the air, hit the ground, screamed, leapt up, and ran at full speed down the hill. Some of his henchmen were even quicker.

Shocked by the experience, Fashang sat dazed on the hillside. A loud cackling alerted him to a vulture flying inquisitively overhead. He saw the bird swoop down onto the corpse of Ah-Wang, and then take off to call his carrion brothers and cousins to the feast. Fashang averted his eyes from the scene, and promptly vomited onto the ground.

As he tried to analyse his situation, he grasped that he was in a real predicament. Behind him Chinese soldiers were possibly searching the shore, while in front lay hostile African villagers. He predicted that his surprise use of the firecracker would hold them at bay for a while, but doubted that he would be safe once darkness had fallen. Having no choice, he lay back on the hillside, while keeping a keen eye all around for movement. In the far distance, he could see groups of people in the village, and vaguely discerned some sounds of chanting.

****

Towards evening, as his apprehension escalated, he was astonished to see a group of men walking up from the valley. Most surprising was the fact that the leader was not African – in fact, judging by his white robes, he was an Arab. Seeing Fashang, the man stopped, stared, and then threw back his head and roared with laughter.

"Do you speak Arabic?" he asked, between convulsions.

"Indeed, I do, sir. And I'm mighty glad to see you," replied the puzzled Fashang.

"So you're not a Tokolosh, after all. You're a Chinese. And I guess I know who you are!"

The man and his attendants sat down on the ground, and Fashang asked for clarification.

"Please could you tell me what is going on?"

"Certainly, my young friend. It makes good telling! You see, I live in the next valley – I'm a trader, by the way. This morning, my workers came with a story that a tokolosh had been seen over here."

"What's a tokolosh?"

"A demon – according to local superstition. And sometimes quite powerful, they say. Of course I don't believe all their nonsense. But if there was a chance to see a tokolosh, I wanted to meet it! You've made a name for yourself already, it seems. The story is that when they tried to attack you, the whole hill rose up and the sky dropped down onto them. They are bragging about their bravery!"

Fashang glanced nervously down into the valley. Seeing this, the Arab reassured him.

"Don't worry about that village. Those folk are nasty. They're pirates and murderers. Even the local chiefs can't control them properly."

"Are you not afraid of them?"

"Certainly not – in fact the other way round. I've had a few run-ins with them, and now they respect me," he said, brazenly fingering the jewelled dagger in his belt.

"Did you say you know who I am?"

"Well, let's say I put two and two together. First thing this morning, I heard a rumour from Sofala that the Chinese had landed, and were searching the town for two deserters. Then the story of a tokolosh – and I suspected it was a deserting tokolosh!" he explained, with more guffaws of merriment.

He then looked puzzled. "Where is your companion, by the way?"

Fashang nodded wordlessly in the direction of the squawking mass of birds below.

"I'm sorry," said the man, "but I'm happy to offer you shelter in my home, if you wish."

"I would greatly appreciate that, and my name is Fashang."

The large Arab stood up, and salaamed. "Ibrahim Bin Sharif at your service, my friend."

Chapter 14

Inland Expedition

Greatly relieved at his unexpected salvation, Fashang accompanied the Arab through the valley and along several jungle paths, emerging finally on a hilltop. Crowning the crest was a white building, similar in style to those of Kilwa and Aden. His host invited him inside, and conducted him to a large guest room overlooking a broad river. Water was brought by African servants for his ablutions, and a fresh set of Arab-style clothes was provided for him.

Refreshed and relaxed, he sat down to a splendid meal of Arab delicacies and local fruit. Ibrahim Bin Sharif was a generous man, and explained that he was a native of Sofala. His grandfather had come from the Yemen, when the Arabs first colonised that section of the African coast. The family had built up a network of trading connections with the interior of the continent, and consequently were able to live in substantial affluence. He asked Fashang about his story, and the young Chinese man frankly described the events since the fateful day of his sister's wedding.

"I pride myself on being a good judge of men," Bin Sharif said rather grandly, "and I think your narrative is true. But what are your plans now?"

"Obviously, sir, I have none. I am at a dead end."

"Exactly. But you cannot stay around here for too long, or the Chinese authorities will track you down. And I don't want to be in trouble with them."

"But I am ignorant of this country and its people..."

Leaning closer, the Arab began to speak more confidentially.

"Perhaps I can help you – and you can help me."

"Anything you suggest," Fashang remarked hopefully.

"I have a base up in the central plateau between the two great rivers that flow out along this coast. It's the capital of the Monomotapa Kingdom, a thriving commercial region, run by Africans of the Karanga tribe. We import and export a large range of goods between that place and Sofala all the time."

"Sounds like an interesting city."

"Well, I've been thinking of establishing an agent up there – to look after my interests, and to do the book-keeping. Maybe you are the answer to my prayers."

"Is it safe - and what about language?"

"It's a peaceful place, because the king wields absolute authority – and we are on good terms with him. A number of the officials speak Arabic to some degree – it's not a problem."

Fashang saw this as a heaven-sent opportunity to detach himself from any contact with the Treasure Fleet, and readily agreed to enter Bin Sharif's employment. Late into the evening, they discussed details of the extensive import/export business run by the family, and of the role that Fashang would play in the enterprise.

Bin Sharif was planning a trading expedition to his base in the high veldt of Africa, and suggested that Fashang should accompany him to take up his new appointment there.

That night as he lay abed in the luxury of the Arab's home, he experienced a galaxy of emotions. Delayed shock hit him, as he thought of the dramatic events of the day. A visceral fear gripped him, when he recalled how near to death he had been over recent weeks. Underlying all this was a deep sense of grief at the loss of his Cantonese comrade, with whom he had formed such a close bond. He acknowledged that without Ah-Wang's incredible feat of rowing the sampan through the night, they would not have reached safety. Again, he faced an unknown future – in a new land, with a novel culture and new races of people. He wondered momentarily whether his psyche could stand this kaleidoscope of experiences. Finally, he took to wondering about where Meili and her husband were at that time, and what their life was like. With such thoughts he drifted off to sleep.

****

For several days, Fashang remained as a guest in Bin Sharif's home, while preparations were made for the journey into the interior. Fashang was outfitted with the necessary clothing for living at the higher altitude, and acquired appropriate medication to combat the sicknesses of the humid forests and plains. The journey would cover about three hundred miles, and Bin Sharif would take a hundred porters to carry the supplies, tentage and trade items. It was estimated they could reach the Monomotapa capital in about two weeks.

On the morning of departure, they made their way down the hill to the broad landing-stage on the river below Bin Sharif's house.

Indicating a swarm of long canoes tied to the pontoon, he said, "This is the Buzi River. We can travel up it for four or five days across the coastal plain. Then we'll come to the mountains, and from there onward it will be trekking."

With much shouting and apparent confusion, the boats were loaded, and the long procession of canoes began to move upstream. Fashang and Bin Sharif rode in a specially constructed craft with an awning amidships under which they reclined on soft mattresses. The crew of this canoe was heavily armed with daggers and knives, from which Fashang surmised that these men constituted the bodyguard for the trader.

At first the waterway was wide with small villages on the banks. Gradually it became more constricted, and the increased current taxed the energy of the paddlers. The shore was lined with hot, humid jungle, and clouds of mosquitoes hovered over the water. One afternoon they heard a warning shout from one of the leading canoes, and shortly afterwards saw a disturbance in the water. A large brown back appeared on the surface, and then disappeared, followed by another. Fashang was suddenly surprised to see a huge head break the surface, and an enormous mouth open wide towards the sky.

"Do you know what that is?" asked Bin Sharif.

"I've heard about that animal, but never seen one. In Chinese we call it a River-Horse."

"Well, it's much the same idea in Arabic. Over there is a pod of them, which means that it's a family group. We're keeping ourselves well clear. If a boat goes between a mother and her young, then they will often capsize it. Once you're in the water with them, you don't stand much chance."

Each night the great expedition camped on the fields near a village. It was obvious that the local people were familiar with Bin Sharif's trading activities, and he was welcomed by the communities where they stopped. He had instituted a disciplined procedure which worked well. The tents and cooking equipment were carried in some of the leading canoes, so that by the time the Arab himself arrived at the campsite, it would be all set up and running. Fashang was somewhat amused by the way in which, once they had landed, they were conducted straight to a luxurious tent furnished with tables, chairs, beds and ornaments. Each evening they were then served coffee and Arab sweetmeats while waiting for the evening repast. He was struck by the incongruity of Bin Sharif and Fashang living in such peripatetic opulence, while the workers endured a frugal and simple existence. However, he had noticed that the Arab was a fair man, who treated his employers as human beings.

Two days up the river, they heard the sound of roaring water ahead.

"Now comes the hard part," said Bin Sharif wearily, "since we have to portage around these rapids."

Fashang could see ahead a foaming mass of water pouring down through jagged rocks. The fleet of canoes pulled into a grassy area below the turbulence, and everything in the boats was unloaded onto land. Then the crews lifted the heavy vessels from the water, and carried them along a steep path that by-passed the obstruction. The cargoes were laboriously lugged up as well, and then the boats were launched again and reloaded. After several hours of exertion, the flotilla paddled onward up the river.

One evening Fashang was sitting by the river bank, swatting the flies and mosquitoes that plagued him. He noticed several large logs in the mud at the water's edge. One of the kitchen workers walked down to the river with a bucket in his hand. Abruptly, one of the logs came alive. A long mouth opened wide, and with unbelievable speed a monstrous crocodile ran at the man. Within the blink of an eye, the prey was in the vast jaws, and being carried screaming into the water. With a splash, both disappeared out of sight. Bin Sharif had witnessed the incident, and came over to Fashang.

"A bad business. But that man should have been aware of the danger."

"Any chance he will survive?"

"None at all. The croc will hold him under water till he drowns. After several days, the meat will be tender enough for the monster to eat."

"Sounds horrible!"

****

After some days of battling with heat, flies and rapids, they reached the head of navigation on the Buzi River. The cargo was unloaded and distributed among the porters, who would use wooden frames on their backs to carry it to the destination. A small group of tough fellows remained to guard the canoes, and the main expedition began to trek further up the valley.

Although they were following a well-used trade route, the vegetation grew back so quickly that the vanguard was constantly employed with machetes in clearing the path. From previous visits, Bin Sharif knew the various camping places along the route, as well as communities where fresh produce could be obtained. The long line of porters stretched away into the jungle, and only occasionally could Fashang spot the leaders when they came out onto some high promontory.

Imperceptibly, the forest began to thin, and the thick mass of foliage gave way to smaller trees and bushes as the group climbed higher. After a week of trudging upward, the terrain began to level out into open grassland. Small thatched rondavels stood beside plots of farmland, where crops of corn and vegetables could be seen. The whole area seemed fertile, and the frequent rainstorms suggested it was well watered. Bin Sharif pointed out herds of wildebeest and zebra grazing on the pasture, or fleeing swiftly from predators. Large eland, tiny duiker, galloping giraffe and belligerent buffalo frequently came into sight as the line of weary men trekked on.

"We are now on the highlands, and still have several ranges and valleys to cross. But the toughest part is over," explained Bin Sharif.

Fashang rubbed his eyes when he saw a most unusual tree. It had a huge trunk, out of the top of which some thin bare strands were growing, with no sign of leaves. He expressed his surprise to Bin Sharif.

"Yes, they are very strange indeed. The local people call them Upside-Down Trees, but they do have value in that their fruit is good for medicine."

One morning Fashang noticed a column of people coming towards them down a hillside on the same path. As the leaders came in sight of each other, there were exuberant shouts of greeting. The head of the other group was an Arab, dressed similarly to Bin Sharif. Instead of salaaming to each other, they rushed forward and embraced.

"Fashang, I would like you to meet my brother, Yacob," said Bin Sharif, introducing the other man. Fashang could see the similarity of features, although the brother seemed to have a harder expression and manner. He greeted Fashang courteously, and then the two siblings began an animated conversation, which the Chinese young man could not follow. After a short while, they parted with the intimation that the other expedition was heading down to the coast.

Bin Sharif ordered his men to pull aside, thus allowing his brother's column to pass. As they did so, Fashang was appalled to see a long line of African men tied together in pairs by wooden yokes round their necks. Further along the column, there were women and children in the same state of bondage.

"Are these slaves – and where are they going?" he asked Bin Sharif.

"Yes, there is a regular trade from the highlands to Sofala. Then they are taken across to Arabia. It's a sad business."

"So you don't approve?"

"In fact, it's a cause of major disagreement between me and my brother. I believe that our holy Quran says that the freeing of slaves is a meritorious act. Therefore slave-trading is wrong. But not many of my countrymen agree with me. I certainly will never take slaves – all my men get a return for their work."

Fashang's admiration for the Arab grew.

****

For several more days they crossed the savannah of the African highlands. At times, this involved negotiating mountain ridges and following tortuous valleys. There were plentiful routes across the area, and the rural inhabitants seemed contented and industrious.

A fortnight after leaving Sofala, the weary file of porters

turned into a long gentle plain that sloped upwards between two rocky ridges. People were scurrying everywhere, and it was obviously a centre of trade. Fashang watched everything with great interest, and then his attention was taken with a lofty stone rampart at the head of the valley. Following his gaze, Bin Sharif explained.

"Welcome to the House of Stone. In the local language, they call it Zimbabwe!"

Chapter 15

Cryptic Characters

Alison and Alex stared at Daniel Mwonzi, and then peered at the bottom of the gaping hole in the ground.

"What did you say, Daniel?" Alex asked.

"Simply that it's my guess those marks on the granite slabs could be Chinese."

Alex examined the surface for a while. Then he remarked, "By Jove, I think he may be right!"

"But how could Chinese writing have been done at Great Zimbabwe? Perhaps these slabs were imported from abroad," Alison offered.

"It would be a mighty job to carry them all the way from the Indian Ocean," objected Daniel, "so the chances are that they were carved here."

"If I may make an observation, Dr. Hampstead," said the National Monuments warden, "I think it would be wise to dismiss the workers at this point."

Daniel readily agreed, and after the village men had departed with the assurance of remuneration the following day, he explained. "We have found in the past that it is best to avoid early publicity. After all, we don't know what we've got here. Best to keep it to ourselves till we're sure, and then make a proper press announcement."

"That makes sense," said Alison with approval. "After all, if it is Chinese, it may still turn out to be useless – perhaps just a list of names or places... or furniture!"

"This means the important thing is to find someone to verify if this is Chinese – and what it means. But how can we find a literate Chinese person in Zim without making it public?"

The group was thoughtful for a while, until Alison uttered an exclamation.

"I've an idea!"

"Let's hear it then!"

"My brother and his wife are teaching at a school near Harare. It's Riverhead School…"

"Riverhead School?" tittered Daniel.

"Yes, why do you react?"

"Only because I was a boy at that place, quite a while ago," laughed Daniel. "Very good school, mind you. Sorry. But what has it to do with this matter?"

"Peter told me that they had a Chinese lady there, teaching music. Part of some exchange scheme with China. Perhaps we could persuade her to come down here and tell us what this writing means."

At this point the African warden broke in. "Sounds a very adequate solution, if you can achieve it. From now on, I will have to protect the site. I will use a security company, but keep it low key until we know what we have found."

"Good for you, my Alison, always full of bright ideas!" Alex added, putting his arm round her shoulders.

"I'll call Peter now, and tell him we'll come up tomorrow," she said, reaching in her bag for her phone.

"A word of warning, if I may…" whispered Daniel. "Don't tell your brother the real reason on the phone. Wait till you see him before spilling the beans. I will stay here, in case people get too inquisitive."

****

Early the next morning the Land Rover started out from the Jabulani Hotel, and was soon on the A4 trunk road for Harare. Three hours later, on the outskirts of the capital, Alison directed them onto a minor road which ran through open bush country for a while. Before long, they entered a tree lined thoroughfare, and came to a sign announcing "Riverhead School".

"Don't be surprised if this is not quite like your typical South London secondary school," Alison said enigmatically.

"What d'you mean, love?" Alex asked.

"Wait and see!"

The drive led up to a large park-like area surrounded by flowering trees, and containing a whole village of low buildings constructed in brown brick with thatched roofs.

"This is a beautiful place," enthused Alex. "But look at those boys over there. Are they in fancy dress?"

"That's the school uniform of red and white blazers and boaters."

"Wow! But where do we go?"

"No idea. Ask one of the boys!"

"Hey, boy, can you help us?" Alex shouted.

An African boy detached himself from a group, and approached the car. Raising his hat with great politeness, he deferentially greeted them.

"Good day to you, Sir and Madam. In what way can I be of assistance to you?"

"We are looking for the staff housing – in fact for Mr Robertson."

"That will not be difficult, sir. Follow this roadway until you reach the squash courts, and then turn right along the side of the rugby field. The teachers' accommodation lies directly ahead."

"Thanks a lot."

"The pleasure is entirely mine, sir," he concluded, tipping his boater again.

"Gosh!" exclaimed Alex, as the car moved on. "Do people really speak like that in the twenty-first century?"

"In Zimbabwe they do."

"Sounds like Eton School in 1850."

The directions were accurate, and they soon found a trim little bungalow with a nameplate on the gate saying "Mr & Mrs P. Robertson". As they came to a halt, a young dazzlingly attractive black lady ran out of the house in great excitement.

"So you've come! This is wonderful. You've made my day!"

When both of them had been thoroughly hugged by their hostess, she led them inside, talking non-stop.

"I hoped you'd come and see us here before too long... that time at your wedding was too short... have you had anything to eat? Peter will be back in half-an-hour... he's running a tutorial..."

Alison cut her short. "Thanks so much, Rutiziro. We do appreciate your welcome – and your hospitality."

"This is an incredible school," observed Alex.

"Yes, just like something out of 'Fifth Form at St Dominics'. Do you know that book?"

Alex looked blank.

"Never mind. I'd forgotten you are scientists!" bantered Rutiziro. "Not fully educated!"

"I like that!" Alex responded in mock dudgeon. "You tell me the Second Law of Thermodynamics, then!"

"Heat is work, and work is heat – and ever more will be so!" she threw back at him.

"Not bad. But that's the First Law, actually! Touche!"

"Stop it, you two!" Alison commanded. "And do you think we could sit down, Ru?"

"Oh, I'm so sorry. Come out onto the stoep! I'll get drinks."

Soon they were settled into comfortable sofas on the large porch that looked out onto the rear garden. Two sides of it were bordered with rhododendrons, while a large swimming pool occupied a far corner. The remainder was tastefully landscaped as lawns and flower beds.

"Did you do the garden yourself, Ru?" enquired Alison.

"Yes, it's been a new experience for me. At my home in Harare we had a gardener, but I wanted to try for myself. I'm really enjoying it, though I don't get much time between all my classes."

At that moment a bicycle whirled into the garden, and skidded to a stop.

"Hi everyone. So you've come!" beamed Peter, looking tanned and athletic.

Having kissed his wife and sister, and pumped Alex's arm, he enquired about lunch. Rutiziro announced that it was ready, and they adjourned to a table and chairs set out under a msasa tree. After the usual small talk, Peter asked Alex about his research project.

"That's exactly why we've come," he answered.

Immediately, Alison took up the tale, and described their experiences since flying in from London. When, at last, she reached the discovery of the granite slab, Peter whistled.

"This is quite a story! How d'you manage such excitement in so short a time – while we just plod on here?"

"Now's the time for you to get involved. We want to confirm whether the writing is Chinese, and what it's about. Apparently you have a Chinese lady teaching here..."

"You mean Meili. She's a real sweetie!" gushed Rutiziro.

"So you think she might be willing to help us?" queried Alex.

"I'm sure she'll be excited too. She only lives a few houses from us. I'll go and call her now!"

"Wait till we've finished lunch, please," implored Peter.

Shortly afterwards, Rutiziro disappeared out of the front door, and rapidly returned with the Chinese lady. Alex was rather stunned to see her. Expecting a stout middle-aged Asian school teacher, he was bowled over when a young girl with an elfin face, framed by long black hair, was introduced to them. He estimated that she was about sixteen years old, but once she began to converse, he revised his figure upwards by about ten years.

"Good afternoon, my name is Pang Meili," she announced in slightly accented English.

Peter introduced his sister and brother-in-law.

"I'm sorry, but I missed your name," Alex apologised.

"As you probably know, in China we put our family name first. Mine is Pang. Then comes the personal name. You can call me Meili."

Sitting under the trees, they began to explain what they were doing.

"Just a moment," Meili said politely, "but I'm not familiar with that word. "Please say it again," she asked, holding up her smartphone in front of Alison.

"Arch-ae-ol-ogy," Alison enunciated slowly.

Glancing at her phone, Meili nodded. "Kao gu xue. Yes, I understand. A very advanced subject, I believe."

Alex explained that they wished to identify the writing, and before he could appeal to Meili, she had responded with alacrity.

"Could I come and see this? I'd love to be part of your project. I had no idea that there was anything Chinese at Great Zimbabwe."

Peter looked at his watch. "You would need to get permission from the Head to take Meili away for a day. I think the Old Man is still in his office. Shall I go over and beard him in his den?"

Peter vanished on his bike like a whirlwind, while the others remained and chatted animatedly. Meili explained something of her background.

"I studied music at Shandong University, which is not far from my home. Then I taught for a year. When I saw the advert for an exchange position in Africa, I jumped at it. My contract is about to finish here."

Becoming more serious, she added, "But I must warn you I am not a literary or calligraphy person. In fact, I may not even recognise the writing, if it's too old. You see, we only learn the simplified characters in China today. The classical ones have many more strokes – so you may find I'm not much use."

"Don't worry, Meili. I'm sure you can give us a valuable insight," Alison encouraged her. "Incidentally I took a few shots of the site, but the light was very poor."

Producing her phone, she displayed a series of photos, which Meili studied with fascination for a while.

With a tone of relief in her voice, she reported, "Happily they appear to be standard classical characters. I was afraid the writing would use something like 'oracle bone script', but that is extremely ancient."

At that moment, Rutiziro's mobile phone rang. After listening for a while, she smiled.

"The headmaster would like to see Alex and Alison in his office now. Peter says he is quite fired up with the idea."

Following directions from Rutiziro, they walked through the manicured, colourful lanes between the school buildings until they reached the central administration block. This was a large black and white structure in the Cape Dutch style. Peter showed them to a grand, book-lined office, where the school principal greeted them. He was an avuncular African gentleman.

"Welcome to my school, Mr. Hampstead and Dr. Hampstead!" he said cordially. "Come and explain what Mr. Robertson has been talking about."

After a further recital of the events at Great Zimbabwe, the headmaster smiled broadly.

"As a loyal Zimbabwean, I'm greatly interested in anything that points to the true history of G.Z. You have my full support in this, and I can do some rescheduling to allow Miss Pang a day off tomorrow, if that is what you want."

They thanked him for his understanding, and began to leave. Alison turned back to the headmaster with a question.

"Do you remember a pupil here by the name of Daniel Mwonzi?"

After a moment, he replied, "Yes, of course. He was a bright lad, and went on to do well. Teaches at the university now. But in some ways, he was a dark horse."

Alison thanked him, and followed the others out. Back at the bungalow, they felt buoyed up by this turn of events, and started to make plans for taking Meili to the ruins the next day. Unfortunately, the headmaster's permission did not extend to Peter and Rutiziro, who, to their chagrin, would have to remain in their classrooms.

****

Making an early start, the three of them headed back down the main road away from Harare. Meili was particularly enlivened by the whole idea, and could not stop talking.

"I've been to Great Zimbabwe twice already, and found the history marvellous. But I never knew that I had any links to the place."

By mid morning, they were driving along the narrow road into the historical site. To their surprise, the car park was jammed with vehicles, and they had difficulty finding a space. As they walked through to the ruins, they were stopped by a uniformed security guard.

"Sorry, sir, but access is restricted today. You can go up the hill complex, but the lower valley is in use for other purposes."

"My name is Dr. Hampstead – and I'm associated with the excavations down there!" announced Alison assertively. "These are my assistants."

The guard looked slightly overawed by her tone, and reluctantly allowed them to pass. Alex felt somewhat miffed at being demoted from project leader to assistant.

On reaching the lower valley, they saw a crowd of about twenty people round the excavated hole. Several tents had been erected, and red tape strung on poles to keep the working area clear. Out of the crowd, Daniel Mwonzi came running.

"Alex and Alison! So you've made it. And is this the Chinese lady? Greetings to you, madam! Sorry about this great horde, but someone must have let the secret out. We've got chaps from the ministry, some media guys - and even my head of department got wind of it, and hurried down this morning."

At this juncture, a large grey-haired gentleman came confidently towards them, and announced in a loud voice, "I think I have the pleasure of meeting Mr. Hampstead."

Rapidly, Daniel stepped forward, and made the introductions, "This is Professor Mududzo, Head of the Archaeology Department at UZ."

"Thank you, Professor, for the loan of all that equipment for my work," Alex interjected quickly.

"Delighted to be of help, my boy. Good to see that you've found something interesting. It's not every day we find Chinese influence in this country!"

Passing through the red tape, they stood at the edge of the hole, and Meili looked down mesmerised. The curator approached them. In guarded tones, he suggested that Meili should write down her findings on a clip-board, rather than announce them to all the straining ears behind the red tape. She agreed, and then she and Alex jumped carefully down into the hole.

Kneeling on the muddy slab of stone, she fingered the incised wording on the granite. It was apparent that her exhilaration overflowed.

"This is really old!"

"How old?" asked Alex.

"A hundred years, maybe two. I've really no idea."

"Which way does it read?"

"All ancient Chinese was written in columns starting from the right. See, here is the first word in the top right corner."

"Can you read it?"

"Some of the characters - yes. But others are too classical for me. Oh, I can see the beginning. It looks like 'My name is Kong Jinwei' and then further on it says 'from the province of Shandong. Ai-ya, this is astonishing! I cannot believe it!"

"Why's that?"

"I will tell you later – it's rather complicated."

After studying the script for several minutes, she shook her head. "I'm sorry, but I can only get a very general idea. Many of the characters I don't recognise – and also the grammar seems a bit different, more poetic and lyrical. I think you will have to find a calligraphy expert for this."

"You've done a great job! We now know it's Chinese and antique. Let's get out and clean up."

"Wait a moment – I can work out something else. Let me write it down to be sure. If this is really true, then I misled you just now."

After Meili had made several notes on her board, they climbed out of the pit.

"Is there somewhere that we can go to sit and talk," Meili asked eagerly.

"How about back to the hotel on the hill?"

"Sounds fine – because we may have found something to take our breath away!"

****

The great metal antenna dish, which stood on a hillside north of Harare, carried terabytes of data every hour to the outside world. The Mazowe Satellite Earth Station was the main conduit of information from all the computers and phones in Zimbabwe.

On that particular evening, a brief email message passed out of the country, saying:

"They have found some Chinese artefacts. Start preparations for us to get our hands on them. M."

Chapter 16

Ancient Chronicle

The inner circle, comprising Meili, Alex, Alison and Daniel, gathered for refreshments in a comfortable room at the Jabulani Hotel. Alison was a little unhappy about the presence of the last member of the group, but had to admit that without Daniel's help they would not have got thus far.

Most of them were refreshing and refilling themselves from the table, but Meili was too agitated to eat, and brimful with enthusiasm to share her finds.

"Right, Meili! What did you read in the hole?" said Alex, indicating that the floor was hers.

"Well, two remarkable facts about this man, Kong Jinwei. First is that he came from Shandong."

"Why is that place special?"

"It was the home of Kong Fuzi!"

When they looked bemused, Meili opened her phone, and typed briefly.

"In English, you call him Confucius. His surname is Kong. And it is believed that everybody named Kong today is in some way remotely connected to Confucius's family."

"Does that mean that this Kong man was descended from Confucius," asked Alex wonderingly.

"Not necessarily a direct descendant – but certainly part of that family through some earlier common ancestor. For me, this is especially interesting. You see, I come from Shandong province too. My home is only about a hundred miles from that of Confucius."

"Wow, that really is something! The genes of Confucius found in Africa. I can see the newspaper headlines!" enthused Alex.

"Hold your horses, Alex! We've only found some slabs of rock, so far," Alison counselled. "But what was the second wonder?"

"In the text, I noticed the expression '...*the sixteenth year of Emperor Yongle's reign...*' Now he was the most powerful of the Ming Dynasty rulers. I've just checked with Google that he became king in about 1402 CE on the western calendar."

Turning to Alex, she said, "And so I was wrong in saying a couple of hundred years. This writing is talking about seven hundred years!"

"Gosh!" he replied. "This is truly a remarkable artefact."

"If I may have an input," Daniel offered politely, "it seems to me that we need to get an expert opinion and translation of that text. One way would be to lift the slabs, and move them to a laboratory. But there is a problem. While you were away, there was a long discussion between Prof. Mududzo, the minister for artefacts and the G.Z. site warden. To dig further down would require the permission of a committee, involving all the stakeholders both inside Zim and internationally. The next meeting will take place in three months."

"Golly, three months!" expostulated Alison. "We can't wait that long! Here we are on the verge of a major discovery, and we are hamstrung by a committee!"

"All I can suggest," offered Daniel soothingly, "is that we bring up some strong lighting, and then photograph the slabs in detail. Perhaps we can find somewhere to get a translation done from the pictures."

Alex chipped in. "I reckon that Professor Oatman in the U.K., who is my supervisor anyway, could look for a Chinese department with the skill to do that."

"Okay, Alex, why don't you sound him out?"

****

Having returned Meili to her school, with firm promises to keep her fully in the picture, the Hampsteads drove back to the Jabulani Hotel. The next day proved that Daniel did not let grass grow under his feet. He called for them early to accompany him to the dig.

This time, the security was even tighter, and the public was kept further back. Articles in newspapers had tentatively publicised the find, drawing more inquisitive faces into the valley. However, the lack of detailed information prevented it becoming a media circus.

When the three archaeologists arrived at the excavation, they discovered two mobile light towers standing beside the working. Using metal halide lamps, they were illuminating the granite slabs in dazzling whiteness. A professional camera on a robot arm was moving over the pit, taking pictures of each section of the carefully-chiselled writing.

That evening, back at the hotel, Alex opened his e-mail inbox to discover two interesting messages. The first was a reply from Professor Oatman at Shorefield to the effect that he had contacted the Department of Asian Studies. They had a lecturer specialising in Ming language and writing, who would be happy to translate the text from the photographs. Oatman also sent his congratulations that the project had advanced so quickly. The other message was from a professional photographic company, and included a large number of attachments. These turned out to be the photos taken that day in the pit. Alex opened a few of the pictures, and found them to be in sharp focus and contrast. He then attached them to another e-mail, which he promptly sent back to his supervisor in England.

Late that night, Daniel called their hotel room to say that word of their find had reached State House. His Excellency the President was planning to tour the site the following morning.

****

After a comfortable night, Alex and Alison hurried down to the ruins, to be on hand for the official visit. The whole area had been taken over by the Zimbabwean National Army, and only those with appropriate credentials were being allowed anywhere near the excavation. Jeeps were parked at various points in the valley, with soldiers in abundance along the whole route. Alex spotted sharp-shooters on the wall of the Great Enclosure and at the top of some of the granite peaks. The Hampsteads were placed with other dignitaries in a row just behind the dig.

Shortly after eleven o'clock, the sound of police sirens could be heard, but did not draw nearer. Soon the rumour passed around that the President had requested to walk the last mile down the valley, to see the archaeological site in its proper perspective. After another long wait in the sun, a group of men, sweltering in suits and ties, came rapidly towards the reception party. Walking in the middle of them with a springy stride was a tall figure that everyone recognised. As decorum demanded, he started at the head of the line of dignitaries, shaking hands and chatting with each of the important people.

Eventually, he reached Alison, who was introduced by the protocol officer.

"Your Excellency, this is Dr. Alison Hampstead."

Alison curtsied, and murmured, "Your Excellency."

The President laughed. "When did you become so docile, Alison? You were always such a firebrand! Anyway, you must tell me all about this business, when these formalities are completed. By the way, I saw your mother yesterday. She sends her greetings, and says stay out of trouble!"

The President then began an informal tour of the site. Flanked by security men, President Madzingo called Alex and Alison to explain what had been found. He was obviously passionate about the history of the country, and asked many detailed questions.

"That is a great piece of research, Alex, and we are indebted to you for adding this page to our national story. When will you lift those slabs, so we can find what's underneath?"

Alex looked downcast. "It seems there is a problem – something to do with a committee or suchlike."

"Really? How can that be?" Madzingo asked, before striding across to a group of government ministers.

Alex could hear a lively discussion in progress, although not registering the details. He only caught Madzingo's final words.

"Thank you, gentlemen. This is a matter of national interest – proceed with it!"

Shortly afterwards, Daniel came over to the Hampsteads, his face beaming.

"Problem solved! The big boss has over-ridden the committee's authority. He will issue a Presidential Decree authorising the excavation to continue at once."

"What wonderful news," rejoiced Alison. "And when will they lift the slabs."

"It must be done very carefully, very professionally. Our department has been given the job, but we have to bring in specialist lifting equipment. Then we will transport the stones to an air-conditioned laboratory at the university. It will be several days before we can start the operation."

"In that case, why don't we go back to your mother's place for a break," Alex suggested to his wife. "I have a lot of writing to do about all that's happened – reports to Oatman, and even some preliminary papers to prepare for publication."

"Sounds fine to me. Mother's ears must be itching to hear all about it." Addressing Daniel, she said, "And you will let us know as soon as the lifting process begins, won't you?"

Daniel nodded.

****

Corrie was delighted to see her daughter and son-in-law drive up the track to the farmhouse.

"It's wonderful to see you again! There are all sorts of stories flying about. Even Reuben cancelled a meeting yesterday to go to Great Zimbabwe. Come in, and tell me all about it!"

The next few hours were pleasant and vibrant, as the saga of the discovery was rehearsed, repeated and analysed. Corrie wanted every detail, and they could hardly prevent her rushing out to her car and driving over the hills.

Over a leisurely alfresco lunch on the stoep, with the backdrop of the purple hills, they discussed the next step.

"I really have to do some paperwork on all this," said Alex, "and wait for some developments at the dig site. This is such a calm place, that I feel I can unwind for a while after all the recent action."

"I was thinking," suggested Corrie, "of inviting Peter and Rutiziro down for a few days, now that their term has ended."

"It won't be a calm place if Ru comes!" Alison giggled, "but only joking! It would be lovely to have them here."

Alex thought for a moment. "Would it be all right to ask Meili, the Chinese girl as well? She's very much part of the story now. Anyway, I think her contract at the school has ended. So she will be returning to China soon."

"Certainly!" Corrie agreed.

Two days later that farm became a livelier place, with banter and laughter throughout the day. Corrie appreciated the boisterous atmosphere, which helped to relieve her persistently nagging grief at becoming a widow a few years earlier. The family spent days hiking in the hills, swimming in the dams, and bird-watching on the wooded kopjes. Meili had never experienced a Zimbabwean farm, and loved every aspect of life there.

On the evening of the fourth day, Alex announced that an email had been received from Professor Oatman. It contained two attachments, and they crowded round his laptop as he opened them. The first took them by surprise, since it was entirely in Chinese.

"Marvellous!" exclaimed Meili, as she looked at the first paragraph. "They have transcribed the text into simplified characters – so now I can read it properly."

Corrie offered to print the whole thing out on paper, if that would be of help to Meili, and the offer was accepted. The second attachment proved to be an English translation of the text from the slab, and was extremely lengthy.

Meili laughed. "People don't realise that Chinese characters are a very succinct way of writing down information."

Following this windfall of data, they agreed to separately read the documents, and then compare notes. The Hampsteads settled onto a sofa on the stoep with the laptop, while Meili sat in the tastefully furnished lounge of the farmhouse with her pile of paper.

Hardly had ten minutes passed, when Meili came screaming out onto the verandah.

"It's unbelievable! It's miraculous! How can it be true?"

"What is it?" Alison asked.

"That this Kong Jinwei had a sister with the same name as me! She was also Meili! I almost feel he was my brother!"

"Quite remarkable. Only the surname is different?"

"Yes. She was Kong Meili, and I'm Pang Meili. Wow, I'm excited."

Calming down slightly, she offered the comment, "Of course, it's not an unusual name in China. Both the characters 'mei' and 'li' mean beautiful – so parents often choose it for their daughters."

"You certainly deserve it," murmured Alex.

As the two versions of the ancient story were read, the atmosphere grew more solemn. They followed the trail of a fugitive across the world, and despite the seven centuries that separated them, they all began to feel quite emotional.

Long after midnight they concluded their study of the early narrative.

"Gosh, that is the most incredible piece of writing," enthused Alex.

"What a fantastic man to have survived all those ordeals."

"He must have been tempted to throw in the towel many times."

"Unfortunately, we don't know the end," Meili said in a sad voice. "The writing finishes with his arrival at Zimbabwe city. How long he lived here, and what he did – we have no idea. Even whether he was allowed to settle…"

"Or whether he found happiness in his troubled life. He deserved that after all he'd been through," observed Alison.

Each with their own thoughts and feelings, they retired for the night.

****

A strange, harsh noise woke the sleepers at about 7 o'clock the next morning. Groggy, from the late night, Alex fumbled his way to the ringing phone in the farm kitchen.

"Hello, Acacia Farm."

"Alex, this is Daniel. I've been trying your cellphones, but you seem to be out of range. The fact is that we are ready to lift the stones today. We've brought in a special mobile crane from Bulawayo, and the whole UZ team from the Archaeology Department is here – ready and waiting."

"How long can you wait? We're on our way!"

"I'll give you till 11 o'clock."

"We'll be there!"

Routing Alison and Meili out of their beds, he asked for a packed breakfast to be made quickly. Corrie herself was thrilled by this step forward, and provided them with sustenance for the journey.

The drive was totally unlike the previous journey over the hills, in which they had sedately enjoyed the view. This time, the Land Rover roared across the plains, and along the twisting highway through the mountains. As they travelled, they ate. Three hours later, the steaming vehicle pulled into the car park at the ruins.

"You qualify for Formula One!" Alison said to Alex approvingly.

The appearance of the dig had changed considerably since their departure. Many more tents had been erected, and a large lorry and caravan were parked nearby. Alex noticed that the latter was a mobile laboratory from the university. A team of professionals was waiting, and Professor Mududzo was very much in charge.

"Mr. and Dr. Hampstead, we are glad you have come. This is really your baby. Now we can commence."

At a signal, several African technicians began to loop cables under the exposed ends of one of the slabs in the pit. Alex noticed that the hole had been widened significantly to allow access to the underside of the granite block.   These lines were then led up to the jib of a crane overhanging the excavation.

"Now start lifting – very gently. And pray that it doesn't crack," ordered Mududzo.

Eyes strained downwards as the granite sheet trembled slightly, but did not move.

"Sorry sir, but we are at the limit of the crane's lifting force," called the winch operator.

"Try attaching to one end only!"

The alternative technique was more successful, and slowly the rectangle of stone rotated upwards. A slipway of baulks of timber was then built into the pit, and after much experimentation the slab was persuaded to slide up the ramp to the surface. It was immediately apparent that it was more massive than expected, being a regular thirty centimetres in thickness. Preparations then began for loading the artefact onto the lorry, after it had been carefully wrapped in sacking and plastic.

By this time, Alison and Meili were feeling the effects of the early start and exposure to the harsh sunshine.

"It will be some time before all the slabs are out. Why don't we go back to the hotel for some refreshment, and come back when the rocks are cleared?" proposed Alison.

Alex and Meili agreed, and left the university party at the site. The professor promised to inform them of progress.

After a prolonged cool-off in the palm-surrounded pool at the hotel, the three of them relaxed on the sun-beds to discuss the events of the morning.

"I suppose that once the slabs are in the laboratory in Harare, we will be able to study the material and techniques used to make them," commented Alex.

"Personally, I am more interested in what lies underneath," was Alison's observation.

Late in the afternoon, Alex's mobile rang. It was Mududzo

from the ruins.

"Mr Hampstead, we've got all the slabs out. And believe it or not, underneath we've found a skeleton!"

Chapter 17

House of Stone

"Tian!" exclaimed Fashang, involuntarily slipping into Chinese. "That is the most staggering city!"

He gazed up the valley to the enormous granite walls, and was overawed by the grandeur of the scene. On either side, rocky hills towered upward, often crowned with large rounded boulders. The combination of the grey stone, verdant grass and cobalt sky etched an image into his memory, which would remain for ever. His reverie was broken by Bin Sharif's hearty voice booming in Arabic.

"Well done, my Chinese friend! Who knows? Maybe you are the first of your race to reach the heights of Africa."

Fashang noticed that the dusty track they had been following suddenly metamorphosed into a firm roadway of carefully-trimmed granite blocks. Soon they arrived at a palisade of sharp stakes, extending across the valley. A guarded entrance stood at the middle, and the newcomers joined the lengthy queue of people waiting for admission.

On reaching the access point, they were confronted by a group of six muscular African men, all carrying knives and short spears. They demanded something of Bin Sharif in a language unintelligible to Fashang. In response, the Arab reached inside his cloak, and produced a small oval piece of stone with a motif carved on it. When the warriors saw this, they relaxed and asked another question. Bin Sharif turned and pointed to the long line of porters stretching behind him. The guards nodded, and allowed the expedition to pass.

Marching towards the great city, Fashang was amazed at the huge amount of activity in the wide valley. People with a wide variety of dress, physiognomy and age crowded along the various pathways through the area. Fashang noticed many other stone structures filling the space between the city and the hills. Some of these were round in shape, like miniatures of the main city itself, and scattered among them were thatched huts by the myriad.

The wall of the city fascinated Fashang from a professional point of view. Coming from a background where stonework was securely fixed together with mortar, he was startled to find that the stones had been assembled without any adhesive. Looking more carefully, he detected that the granite blocks were carefully shaped so that they fitted closely against their neighbours, and that an interlocking pattern made the whole configuration extremely robust. An intriguing feature caught his eye, when he spied a part of the surface, where the flat blocks had been arranged in a chevron pattern to form a frieze. Another section was made up of blocks in a herringbone format. While wondering at the expertise of these African craftsman, he found that they had almost reached the main gate of the city, and he looked forward eagerly to seeing the interior. But it was not to be.

"The Great Circle is reserved for the city officials and the citizens of Monomotapa. Foreigners and visitors have to live in the Little Circles."

"Will I never see inside the great city?"

"Oh, certainly! We may go inside to trade and visit. But we may not live there."

Abruptly, Bin Sharif turned left just before the portal, and led his men along a small paved path skirting the city wall. A short distance further on they came to another circular enclosure, with walls much lower and thinner than the city itself.

"Since I am a frequent trader here, I've been assigned this circle ahead."

He led the way through a narrow opening in the wall, revealing a large compound with many huts. Along one side were open-sided structures that appeared to be for storage. Another thatched area seemed to be a kitchen.

"This is my empire!" the Arab announced, with feigned hubris. "That covered area is the import department, while the other is the export zone! The porters and workers live in the huts at the back."

"And what about you?"

"That rondavel is my private apartment," Bin Sharif responded with a laugh. "And that is the visitors' accommodation – which you can occupy."

Fashang approached his new quarters cautiously, not being over-enthralled at having to live in the squalor of a mud hut. But, on entry, his misgivings were chased away. The floor had been beaten hard, and treated with some type of wax. Upon it stood a table, chair and a bed, all made from a variety of wood that he had never seen. The place was clean and had a sweet smell, which he only discovered subsequently to be that of dried cow-dung.

Ibrahim Bin Sharif invited him to his own hut, which was appointed in even more luxurious style. Persian carpets covered the floor, and coloured curtains festooned the walls. The two men reclined on couches, while a servant proffered tea and delicacies. Fashang began to think that he could enjoy life there. The Arab explained that he kept a permanent staff in the enclosure to cook meals, run errands and maintain security.

Hearing the sounds of activity outside, Bin Sharif insisted that they should supervise. They found that the porters were already depositing and unpacking their loads into the "import department". A first consignment was disappointing, being entirely large blocks of salt.

"Don't despise that," the Arab cautioned. "In this climate, it's often worth more than gold. Salt is almost a form of currency in the middle of Africa."

Further packages were opened, and some of the contents

surprised Fashang. Tears welled up in his eyes, as a set of Chinese bowls in the striking blue of the Ming dynasty was unpacked. This was followed by several cases of grey-green celadon pottery, of a standard only rarely glimpsed in the best houses of China. The treasures continued to appear, including huge rolls of silk and several boxes of glass beads of Persian origin. All these items were stacked on shelves under the shelter of the thatched roof.

"This is also our display showroom," declared Bin Sharif, "and the traders from the city are free to come and browse. The actual bartering takes place in the Great Circle on certain days."

"But it looks awfully unsafe," put in Fashang. "Don't you find that some of the stuff is stolen? It must be a great temptation."

"Look carefully at those men at the back. They live and work there as the guards. Everyone knows that if any person crosses the line of poles at the front, then they've taken their last breath!" Chuckling, he added, "And so we have never lost a thing. Those guys are actually thugs and murderers from various African kingdoms around. They obey me implicitly as the price for their freedom."

Fashang winced.

Moving to the other storage area, the Arab looked inside with eagerness. "Let's see what we have been offered this time. Not bad! A good pile of gold ingots, and some animal skins, but not of great quality. By the way, Fashang, d'you know what those things are, stacked at the back?"

He looked at the great yellow and white pile. "Surely they're not elephants' tusks. There are so many."

"Quite correct. That ivory will find its way to your country, as well as India and Arabia."

"You are obviously a very rich man," Fashang said astounded.

"But I have to work for it."

****

Over the next few days, Fashang was introduced to the culture and customs of Zimbabwe. He visited the Great Circle, and saw the market place where trading occurred every ten days, under the watchful eye of a city official. The costumes of the local people intrigued him. The peasants often wore only a loin cloth while at work, but the general populace was dressed in clothing made from animal skins. This trend was accentuated in the upper classes where the men sported carefully sewn leopard-pelt coats of elaborate design. Occasionally he saw a man wearing a hat, but it appeared that is was a badge of status, rather than a protection from the elements. The addition of feathers to headgear seemed to be a sign of special distinction.

Outside the dominating grey walls of the Great Circle, Fashang found a host of craft workers making jewellery from gold or copper, carving in wood, and weaving locally-grown cotton into fine cloth. It was a society of great industriousness, and consequently the inhabitants of this large area lived well above the poverty line.

Two questions dogged his thinking, as he learned more of the foreign environment into which he had come. He solicited answers from Bin Sharif.

"Why is it that I have not seen a palace in the city? Where is it? Surely the king lives in splendour!"

"Look up, young man!" Bin Sharif replied jovially, pointing at a rocky mountain that dominated the valley. "There's your palace!"

Straining his eyes, Fashang observed that, among the mass of rocky outcrops and huge boulders on the hillside, there were walls, terraces and thatched roofs. In fact the whole mountain looked like a warren of passages and stairways.

"So that's where the king keeps court. What's it like up there?"

"No one knows. Very few people are allowed access, and there are all sorts of taboos and rules about it. The king is called the Mambo, but I've never met anyone who's seen him."

With a chuckle he concluded, "He doesn't seem to invite folk to his place very often!"

Fashang thought for a moment.

"By the way, there's something else that puzzles me. I haven't seen any carvings of their gods – but they must worship something. In China we have god-idols everywhere."

Bin Sharif laughed. "In some ways, these people are like us Muslims. They believe in one god, whom they call Mwari. He is the one who created the world. They also believe that the ancestors have influence on the world."

"Just as we do in China…"

"There are also some spiritual messengers between Mwari and the people, but I've never understood how that works."

Very soon Fashang's induction into the economics of African trading began. Being required to keep careful documentation of all transactions, he was flummoxed for a while by the language problem. Although having mastered spoken Arabic quite well, there was no way in which he could learn to write in a short time. Bin Sharif had provided a copious supply of paper, reed-pens and ink for the keeping of accounts. Eventually, a compromise was reached in which Fashang learned the Arabic counting method. To his surprise the system was also based on the number ten, and he soon became familiar with converting the Chinese numerals to their Arabic equivalents. Describing the merchandise proved more of a problem, but when they realised that the range of commodities was quite small, a system of symbols was devised to cover the items.

An important person on the trade scene was the "shambadzi", an African who acted as the middle-man in any business deal. Bin Sharif employed a young man, named Simba, in this role as his go-between. Although a native of Zimbabwe, he had travelled with one of the trade expeditions to Sofala several years previously, and spent some time at the coast. Consequently, he was familiar with the relevant commercial procedures, and spoke both Arabic and the local Shona language with ease. In age he was close to Fashang. Owing to the similar temperaments of the two men, they soon became good friends, despite their diverse backgrounds. Often they could be found spending time together in Fashang's hut, conversing, eating and drinking.

One day, Bin Sharif informed Fashang that a recently-arrived expedition from Sofala had reported that the Chinese fleet had returned to its homeland. This put Fashang's mind greatly at ease, with the realisation that finally he had escaped his pursuers.

****

A fortnight after their arrival, Bin Sharif formed up his porters, and departed for Sofala, taking with him the vast assortment of purchases he had made. This left Fashang to carry on the business in Zimbabwe, and he soon settled into a routine. Every ten days, he would go with Simba, the shambadzi, to the central market in the Great Circle, and engage in negotiations for items being offered or desired. There was no system of currency in use, and so equivalents had to be agreed in terms of relative quantities of items to be exchanged.

As an added measure of security for his merchandise, Fashang adopted a practice from the world of Chinese commerce. Selecting a small piece of stone, he fashioned it into the form of a cylinder. Then, painstakingly, he incised the flat end with the Chinese character for Kong, but formed it as a reflection. This became his personal chop, which remained with him at all times. Whenever a consignment of gold, ivory or other bulk material was sold, he would ink the chop and stamp his personal signature on all the items. The guards in his compound were instructed to let nothing out of the gate without this distinguishing mark.

While carving his original family name, he was overcome with a feeling of wistfulness. How long was it since he had been Kong Jinwei? How was his family doing now? Above all, he wondered about whether his sister Meili was enjoying marriage – or even whether by this time he had a nephew or niece. Deep inside, he longed to settle down into a family environment again, but he could see no way this could happen. Shaking himself out of his soliloquy, he returned to the demands of the present.

Although the position was one of responsibility, it was not excessively time-consuming. Thus Fashang began to study the rocks lying in such abundance in the valley and on the hillside. His trained eye soon picked out several specimens that would be suitable for sculpture. Locating some iron tools in the market, he began to rejuvenate his skills in handling stone.

In an empty hut on his compound he constructed a workshop with the necessary tools for his work. At first he made small statues of animals, which he took to the rudimentary bazaar in the Great Circle. To his pleasurable surprise, there was a wave of interest in these products, and he saw a number of sales. Broadening his spectrum of styles, he produced larger sculptures, which became popular with the aristocracy of the city. As an alternative to granite, he began to use the ubiquitous soapstone of the area. Its softness made carving that much easier, especially for intricate designs. In his early days in Shandong, he had used this material for many of his figurines, and loved the range of green-blue patinas on the finished surface.

Lacking a system of coinage, Fashang would frequently find that his remuneration took the form of two chickens, a bag of corn or a large bundle of vegetables. On one occasion he was paid in terms of a piece of ivory. Before long his prestige rose, and he was generally addressed with the honorific Baba Fashang.

During this period, Fashang began to pick up the local language. Although totally different from his own mother tongue, he quickly adapted to the novel grammatical forms, and to the long words that contrasted with the single syllables of Chinese. He was slightly amused to discover that objects were grouped into categories, which affected the grammar - not totally dissimilar to Chinese. Tutored by his friend Simba, he soon found himself able to talk freely in the city, on all except the most complex of topics.

While touring the nearby hills in search of raw materials for his carvings, he stumbled across a valley in which thousands of young men were engaged in a variety of gymnastic activities. Watching carefully, he concluded that this was a moderate-sized army, which was being given clandestine training. Whereas he had sensed a peaceful milieu in the city itself, he realised that the Monomotapa state was actually prepared to defend itself in case of aggression. His presence in the valley did not seem to disturb the military leaders, and so he was able to examine the weapons being wielded. Many of these were made of bronze, while the use of wood was common. Spears, knobkerries, swords, bows and arrows were all in evidence.

One afternoon when leaving the Great Circle with Simba, he was concerned to see his friend in a state of mild agitation. Grabbing Fashang's arm, his companion drew him quickly into the shadow of a large rock, and appeared to be hiding.

"Hezvo! Keep out of sight!"

"But why? What is the danger?"

"Not really a danger, but it's best to keep out of his way!"

"Who?"

"The Mhondoro – over there," replied Simba with a tremor in his voice, pointing along the roadway.

Fashang goggled at an amazing sight. A tall, slender individual was walking slowly towards the city gate, with people all either turning away or averting their eyes. He was splendidly dressed in a long cloak made of a combination of leopard and pangolin skins. The latter animal Fashang recognised from north China, and knew it to be a rare creature. The Mhondoro had a colourful ornamental head-dress, and his arms and ankle bore bangles, which produced a musical sound as he walked.

"Is that the king?"

"No! In some ways he's more powerful than the king. The Mhondoro is the spirit-medium, who bears the authority of Mwari."

"Why are you so frightened of him?"

"If you cross his path, he can have you killed at once. Best to keep out of his way."

Adding that information to his store of local lore, Fashang resolved to avoid the shaman whenever possible.

****

Unexpectedly, Simba appeared at Fashang's lodging one morning, to announce that a delegation of the city administrators wished to speak with him. Going out to meet the fabulously-dressed gentlemen, he invited them to take seats under a tree within his courtyard.

With the linguistic assistance of Simba at certain points, he learned that the representatives had come regarding an important matter.

"Honoured elders, I greet you!" said Fashang in welcome.

"Baba Fashang, we greet you!" responded the leading man.

"I trust that you are all in good health and spirits."

"And we trust that you are in good health and spirits."

Eventually the obligatory greetings were completed, and they got down to business.

"Baba Fashang, we come to you on a professional matter. It has not escaped our notice that you are a stone mason of considerable experience."

"It will be my pleasure and privilege to assist in any way I can," Fashang offered.

"One of the gateways into the Great Circle has become damaged. You are requested to see whether a repair can be made."

After a further exchange of information, the delegation led Fashang and Simba to a rear entrance of the main city. A pile of stones in the entryway indicated a structural collapse. Looking up, Fashang saw that the supporting lintel had snapped, bringing down a portion of the block work above it. Studying the fractured granite cross-member in detail, he gave his diagnosis.

"It seems to me that there was always a small flaw in that lintel. Because of the extremes of heat and cold in this place, the fault has gradually enlarged over the centuries – and now the member has failed."

"But, Baba Fashang, what would you suggest as a remedy."

"We should look for a suitable piece of well textured, crack-free granite on the hills, and make a replacement."

"If we gave you sufficient men, would you be able to undertake this repair? There would be compensation, of course."

"Certainly I am willing to try, although replacing a lintel with that weight of wall above it will be a tricky business." Then he added quizzically, "But I am puzzled that you do not have masons here to do this."

"Unfortunately, over the time since Zimbabwe was built, the expertise for this type of construction has been lost. We now have no one who could handle a project of this magnitude."

So it was that Fashang became a master mason again. His first task was to find a suitable stratum of granite in the boulders of the surrounding area. For several days he tapped rock faces, and studied the colours and lines of stone outcrops. After a while, he found a suitable section that could be exfoliated from a boulder on a remote hillside. The local men set to work separating the strip of rock from its parent, using a long-established traditional technique. First, a series of fires were built along the seam where it was intended to make the break. After allowing the rock to become very hot, cold water was poured into the appropriate area. Rapid contraction caused a number of sharp sounds, but the boulder did not split. The procedure was repeated again and again, but the section of granite proved very resilient. After several unsuccessful days, Fashang confided to Simba that he was not very sanguine about success.

"Their method will not give me the large section that I need. But I do have an alternative…"

"So what is that? We only know the use of fire and water to crack rocks."

Fashang was reluctant to expose his secret, but decided that it would improve his status in the community if he did so. Next morning he carried a bag of powder over the hills to the worksite. After instructing the labourers to chisel a number of small holes along the line of the intended fracture, he carefully packed them with gunpowder from his precious Chinese supply. Improvising with the use of some dried creepers, he made fuses of equal length leading to the charges. Then he tied the ends of the fuses together at a suitable point some distance from the rock face.

"Now, Simba, please impress on the men that they must retreat downhill, and then hide behind the rocks in the bottom of the valley. They are to lie flat on the ground – otherwise they will be hurt. Warn them that there'll be a loud noise."

Satisfied that the workers were in safety, Fashang lit the end of the fuse. It sparked and smoked, but to his consternation spread along the fibres much faster than he expected. In panic, he ran across the hillside, and threw himself down behind a large lump of rock. Almost instantly, the whole mountain heaved up in a great convulsion, with a vivid flash. A rumble, much louder than thunder, echoed among the crags. For a while everything was obscured by blue smoke and raining granite particles. As the scene cleared, Fashang noted that his improvised blasting operation had succeeded. A long length of granite had been blown halfway down the hill, and he saw that it was the piece he had chosen for the new lintel. Instinctively he turned his eyes down the hill to check on the safety of his workers. On seeing the immobile bodies lying across the grass, he feared that the shockwave had killed them. But then he noticed that they were very much alive, yet lying on their stomachs and chanting in unison.

Simba came back up the hill, and explained the strange behaviour.

"They are all worshipping you! To them it's obvious you are a magic-man of great power. Just listen to them! They are calling you the Great-Wizard-Fashang!"

From the valley came the synchronised chant of "N'anga Huru Fashang, N'anga Huru Fashang…"

He tried to persuade the labourers that his achievement was based on chemistry rather than metaphysics, but they persisted in the view that he was possessed of special powers. Before long, the workmen recovered from the shock of finding that they were supervised by a near-deity, and put all their energies into the project. Using hammers and chisels, the huge block was trimmed to the shape required for the gateway. A large wooden sledge was constructed after felling a dozen trees, and the slab of rock was manhandled on-board. Recruiting more labour from the main city, he ordered the loaded vehicle to be dragged over the hills to the collapsed doorway.

Already Fashang had set men to work shoring up the

stonework around the gate, and using thick timbers to support the massive weight of the upper wall. When the replacement lintel arrived, he used a series of levers to lift the stone onto scaffolding at the appropriate height. Then, very gradually, it was coerced into the space left by the fractured beam. After many anxious hours, he proclaimed that the position was correct, and work began to fill the space above the lintel with shaped blocks to reinforce the upper wall.

When the task was completed, the city elders came to give their approval. Such was their admiration for Fashang's work, that they proclaimed a celebration feast several days later. Fashang secretly suspected that this was actually more of an excuse for festivity, than an acknowledgement of his contribution. The whole valley came alive with preparations for the event, as great quantities of beer were brewed, animals were butchered and dishes of vegetable and fruit cooked.

For two days the citizens and invited guests of the Monomotapa capital feasted and roistered. Long into the night, the earth shook with the thunder of the drums and the dancing feet. At the place of honour in all this sat Fashang. He had finally established himself in the community.

Chapter 18

Broken Beak

Consternation began to develop throughout the great city of Zimbabwe, which housed and fed something like twenty thousand people. As the months of that year went by, eyes were constantly turned to the skies. The uniform blue dome, untarnished by clouds, stared back at them. But in the fields the lack of rain was causing the slow death of the corn and mealie harvest, upon which the populace depended.

Fashang himself began to feel the effects of the drought. His servants reported that the stream, running through the top of the valley, was drying up. Everyone was talking dolefully about the prospect of starvation in the coming year if the harvest failed. One day, Simba explained what measures the community was taking to combat this adversity.

"I hear that the Mambo himself is very worried about the failure of the rains. Another fortnight and the crops will be irreversibly ruined. The mealie cobs need a lot of water very quickly. So they have called for a 'muwerere'."

"What's that?"

"A special spiritual ceremony to open the skies."

"Well, what happens?"

"For several days now, a group of women have been brewing beer under a tree just outside the city wall."

"So, are they having a party?" Fashang said lightly.

"Aiwa! It's no joking matter," his friend replied seriously. "The beer is made from very special millet, according to a strict procedure. Its fermentation is symbolic of the growth of crops. The actual rite will be performed tomorrow. I will take you to see it."

The following day, the two friends joined hundreds of people around the sacred tree, where pots of beer stood in readiness. After a considerable wait, a murmur like a soft breeze wafted through the assembly, and everyone sank to their knees. Fashang watched with great interest as a lone figure approached from the direction of the holy hill. It was the fearsome personage of the Mhondoro, but over his colourful clothing a black cloak had been thrown.

"The black symbolises the dark rain clouds that we want," Simba whispered.

Approaching the tree in the centre of the gathering, the spirit-medium began to chant in a high cackling voice. Pausing, he poured a little of the beer into a copper bowl, which he lifted high. The formula was then repeated several times, after which the sinister priest strode away towards the hill bearing his beer-filled bowl.

"Where's he going?" Fashang asked.

"To the sanctuary, which is somewhere in the sacred hill. He will pour out the beer before the holy messengers, beseeching them to intervene in our weather."

Throughout that day, and the next, people looked hopefully upwards. A few wispy clouds drifted across the cobalt, raising expectations, but then dissipated completely. Gloom settled on the valley.

Just before dawn on the third morning after the muwerere, Fashang was startled to hear Simba calling him urgently from his hut.

"Fashang, you are wanted. Come, at once!" the frightened voice commanded.

On exit from the gate of his enclosure, he was immediately met by the intimidating presence of no less a person than the Mhondoro himself. Falling to his knees, which seemed an appropriate gesture, Fashang heard the cackling sound of the man's speech. Barely understanding, he was glad of Simba's interpretive skills.

"The Mhondoro says that you are to come to the sacred hill. The spirits have work for you there."

Totally mystified, Fashang nodded.

"Come!"

Under a lightening sky, Simba and Fashang followed the strange person across the fields of the valley towards the sacred complex on the hill. At a narrow point on the path, they came to a strip of solid granite, across which an intrusive vein of quartz formed a low, narrow ridge.

"This is the threshold to the sacred space," cackled their guide. Pointing at Simba, he commanded, "You will remain here!"

Taking Fashang by the arm, he led him to the transverse ridge of rock. Gradually, Fashang found that he could understand the gist of the old man's speech.

"First we must open the way. Follow what I do!"

Taking up a small stone from the ground, he tapped it along the length of the translucent bar, while Fashang copied his actions. After they had stepped over the obstruction, the priest repeated the tapping operation in reverse.

"We must do this to shut the door now, to keep out the evil spirits," he explained.

Walking at a fast pace, the Mhondoro conducted the young Chinese up the hillside, through a mass of towering boulders, mysterious shelters and mazelike passages. All this time, they were climbing higher and higher, but at last came out into a vast chamber. It was basically a terrace with decorated side walls and thatched roof. One side was open to the vista. Fashang was enthralled by the view towards the rising sun, showing range upon range of brown hills receding into the distance.

Leading him forward, the Mhondoro instructed him quietly, "On your face!"

The two men prostrated themselves, and then began to wiggle their way across the tiled floor. In a pleading voice the older man began to beg.

"Oh, holy messengers, forgive our intrusion! Do not blast us with the fury of your power. We come in peace. I have brought one who can restore the lost dignity of your brother."

By this time, Fashang could not contain himself any longer, and curiosity lifted his head. Before him stretched a high rock face in front of which stood six slender columns. The top of each was crowned with a beautiful carving of a bird, and he recognised at once that the material was soapstone. Each bird was of a different design, and he guessed that some represented eagles, while others looked similar to falcons.

Satisfied that the birds had accepted their presence, the Mhondoro rose to his feet, and indicated one of the carvings.

"You will see that the beak of this one has been broken off. Some months ago, a thunder storm caused a rock to crash through the roof here, damaging this sacred messenger. It has been revealed to me, that this injury is causing the skies to hold back their moisture."

The stone mason inspected the fracture on the bird carefully. It was obviously a clean break, resulting from a sharp impact.

"Young man, are you able to heal him – in such a way that the break is invisible?"

"Yes," Fashang replied thoughtfully, "but I will have to search carefully to find a good match of colour and texture. I would need to make several visits to this place to complete the work."

"In that case, I give you permission to ascend whenever you wish. The messengers here will understand that you come for their good, and will not harm you."

Fashang could not really comprehend how the inanimate avian creatures could harm him, but keeping his own counsel, he agreed to undertake the repair. He then tried to commit the particular hue of the bird's head to memory, in order to get an exact colour match for a new beak.

On descending through the labyrinth of stairways and passages, he realised that armed guards had been secreted in alcoves along the way. To each one, the Mhondoro explained that the stone mason was to be allowed unrestricted access to the sanctuary chamber.

Returning to the main valley, after respecting the necessary rituals of passage, Fashang swiftly made for an area where quarrying of soapstone had been in progress. After searching for a while, he acquired a selection of about a dozen stones of similar colours. Then he retraced his steps to the sacred hill, where he was allowed access both by the armed guards and the resident spirits. Climbing quickly to the sanctuary with his bag of sample stones, he was surprised to find it deserted. The midday sun was shining directly into the chamber, illuminating the six mounted birds.

Carefully holding up each of the coloured stones, he rotated it alongside the broken bill of the damaged image. Watching the play of the light on the surface, and repeatedly polishing it with a soft cloth, he sought to find the best match.

Hearing only the soughing of the wind through the rocks and bushes, he continued his intensive study. Soon he realised that one of his samples was close enough in texture and colour to make a suitable substitute beak.

Against the soft background of natural sounds, he heard the scraping sound of a pebble being moved. Looking around for visitors, he still found that he was alone in the sanctuary. A little later, he heard a stifled cough, and became conscious of another person nearby. Treading warily, he moved around the terrace. Coming to a cleft between two boulders, he was shocked to find himself gaping into an African face.

Jumping back, he looked again. And his gaze became locked. Confronting him was a young woman with a confident smile, who sidled out of her hiding place. He was captivated by her face, her skin being light brown and smooth as soapstone. Large dark eyes twinkled at him, and her smile revealed a set of pure white teeth. He noted that she was about the same height as himself.

"Why are you here?" he stammered.

"I'm watching you." was the cheeky reply, coupled with a mischievous smirk.

"But are you not afraid to be in this sacred place?"

"Not at all! It's very quiet here, so I come quite often."

"But the sacred birds…"

"Oh, them," she replied with a shrug, "I do like them – but they're only bits of stone really."

"They are the messengers of the ancestors, so I hear."

"I don't believe in the ancestors. They have had their time, and now are dead and gone." Lowering her voice, she continued, "They're just stories made up by the Mhondoro to frighten people."

Although the direction of the conversation was totally unexpected, Fashang found his concentration focussed upon the lovely female before him. Realising that he might say or do something foolish, he attempted to terminate the encounter.

"It has been my pleasure to meet you," he concluded in a slightly dismissive tone.

"And mine too, Baba Magic-Maker! The one who makes the mountains jump."

"So you've heard about that! I am not really a magic man, you know."

"I know that you aren't."

"What do you mean?"

She jerked her head up, and stared him full in the face. "When I was much younger, I had a tutor. He was an old sekuru, and full of wisdom. Many people did not believe him, and laughed at him – but I listened to his words."

"Well?"

"He told me that the ancients used to collect certain rocks, and crush them to powder. Then they blended that with other powders from deep underground, and heated the mixture over a slow fire. Finally they added salt and other granules. The result was a powder that would respond to a flame with a loud noise and force. My sekuru told me that the art had been lost. But I think in your country they still know it."

"You are a very intelligent young woman."

"Thank you," she replied coquettishly. "But although you are not a magician, you are very clever Chinese man."

She concluded the conversation. "Don't let me stop your important work!"

With a final broad smile and a wink, she glided out of the sanctuary.

Fashang stood for a moment, nonplussed. He could not shake the image of the girl from his mind, and as he descended from the hill complex, he stumbled a few times in distraction. Reaching his own workshop, he cut the chosen piece of soapstone into roughly the correct size for the sacred beak. Then he took his callipers, ruler, paper and reed-pen, and ascended the sacred mount for the third time that day.

Try as he would to dispel the rising emotion within him, he hoped that the alluring girl would be present again. But once more the sanctuary was empty, and since nightfall approached, the holy chamber was lit by burning oil lamps. Making careful measurements of the damaged bird, he noted them on his paper, and finally drew around the truncated end of the bird's bill to record the exact shape. He then copied the outlines of the other birds to provide a reference.

"What is that you are doing with the reed?" uttered a familiar voice behind him.

Turning to his visitor, he saw that the soft illumination of the lamps made her look more appealing than ever.

"Have you been here all day?" he asked.

"No! But I kept watch till I saw you coming up the hill."

"Please, may I know your name?"

"I am called Gamuchirai."

He racked his brains for the meaning of the word, and then it came to him.

"That comes from the verb 'kugamuchira', which means to receive a gift."

"You clever man! But did you know that in our culture, you must always receive a gift with both hands? Like this…"

Seizing both his hands in hers, she held tightly, and refused to release him. Drawing her arms back, she pulled him close to her, until they made contact. Fashang felt an entirely new feeling, as his whole body began to tingle. He sensed, rather than saw, the beautiful face drawing closer to his, and in no time her lips touched his. Time seemed to halt - and at last she let go of him.

"Did you like that?" she said gently.

Fashang could not speak.

On recovering his voice, he croaked, "You are a very unusual girl."

The bantering style returned. "Yes, I know. My father keeps

telling me that."

"Does your father work here on the hill?"

She grinned. "Yes, you might say that."

Fashang suddenly grasped that time was moving on. He had much to do if his repair work on the bird was to be completed the next day. Reluctantly taking leave of the smiling apparition, he returned to his dwelling in the valley.

That night, when Simba came to discuss business and socialise, Fashang made an enquiry of him.

"Do you know a girl by the name of Gamuchirai?"

"Well, yes, it's quite a common name for females."

"One that lives up on the sacred hill?"

"Oh, are you referring to the Princess Gamuchirai?"

Fashang inhaled hard. "Yes, possibly. What d'you know about her?"

"There are lots of rumours from the palace servants when they come off-duty. They say that she is a strange one, and the Mambo has tried to marry her off to local rulers, but without success."

"Why is that?"

"Firstly, she is quite short in stature – and most kings want tall, slender women to look like impressive queens. Then, so they say, she refuses to revere the ancestors, and has unconventional ideas about the spirits. Anyway, why do you ask?"

"While working up there, I met her."

"Wow, did she speak to you?"

"Yes." was all that Fashang was prepared to divulge about their encounter.

****

Late into the night, Fashang toiled in his workshop, cutting, grinding and polishing. At length, he was satisfied that the new beak resembled his drawing sufficiently accurately to replace the lost portion. Next on his list of activities was the preparation of a special adhesive, which would cement the stone pieces together, as well as making the joint less visible.

Early the following day, he left his home carrying an assortment of materials and tools. As he walked through the myriad of huts in the valley, an old woman shouted to him.

"Baba Fashang, can you not help us! We have food now – but in a few weeks there will be nothing. Don't you have power over the rains!"

"Sorry, Ambuya, but I am simply a stone mason," Fashang replied, thinking sorrowfully that the people would not be able to eat the gold and ivory in his warehouse. The apprehension of an impending human tragedy in the coming months depressed him, as he walked through fields where crops were making their last gasps of life.

Making his way up the now-familiar stone stairways, he arrived at the sanctuary, to be greeted by the Mhondoro himself. He came forward with a frowning face.

"Baba Fashang, the future is bleak. The people are in despair. If the rain does not come, there will be a year of starvation ahead. Unless you repair the bird quickly, all will be lost."

"Revered Mhondoro. Rest assured that I will exert all my efforts to finish the task today."

Grumbling and cackling to himself, the spirit-medium retired into a dark corner, from which chants, songs and smells began to emanate. Fashang commenced putting the finishing touches to the new beak, thus ensuring that it fitted snugly to its parent. He took the prepared cement, and glued the new appendage in place. After holding it for several minutes, he stood back and observed it critically. He felt confident that when the join was properly concealed, the bird would be indistinguishable from its brothers.

It would need about an hour for the adhesive to bond sufficiently. After that he would be able to sand and polish the joint. Feeling the need for a short rest, he moved to the wide edge of the platform that opened onto the view of miles of hills and valleys. The whole countryside was a dull sandy colour, punctuated by the grey masses of rocks. Not a speck of green could be seen. He knew that, in normal years, the people should be reaping their harvests by now. Relaxing there, he noticed a black line on the horizon, and could not at first explain it. After several minutes it had thickened, and become more irregular. As the distant transformation continued, he perceived that he was looking at a bank of black clouds racing towards him.

By this time, the sacred bird was ready for the final sanding and polishing, which would fully renew it. Working carefully, he completed the work with a sense of satisfaction.

Approaching the Mhondoro in the midst of his incantations, Fashang coughed gently, and quietly addressed the old man.

"Honoured sir, I believe that the injury has been healed."

"Then I will come and see for myself," murmured the priest, as he scrambled up, and stood before the row of birds.

"By the ancestors," he said with vigour, "I cannot tell which is the broken one. You have done an excellent..."

His final words were lost in a mighty rush of air, which swirled through the sanctuary, flapping his cloak up over his head. Simultaneously, a mighty crack of thunder echoed and re-echoed through the chamber. The Mhondoro collapsed, looking totally bewildered. When the sound turned to the rushing of mighty waters, his expression converted to delight.

The rain poured down on the thatched roof of the sanctuary, spilled over onto the rocks below, and progressed into a deafening waterfall that fell into the valley. Running to the exposed edge of the terrace, the two men could see nothing but a blanket of water before their eyes.

The tension, the effort, the hunger and the fear of the last few days suddenly reached Fashang, and he dropped onto the sacred floor, and fell fast asleep.

****

The massive downpour itself did not last for more than an hour, and was replaced by a steady drizzle that was ideal for agriculture. This continued for several days. The delight of the inhabitants of Zimbabwe at the long-awaited rain was accompanied by the endless retelling of the story of the broken beak. If Baba Fashang was well respected before, he was now promoted to the role of national hero.

With the return of precipitation, the people were able to drink and wash. Within a few days the sagging staple crops moved towards maturity. The prospect of a good harvest lifted the spirits and songs of the populace.

Chapter 19

Royal Reward

Fashang decided that it was useless to swim against the current of popular opinion that gave such praise to him. In retrospect, he realised that from his hilltop vantage point looking eastward, he was probably the only person to have seen the approach of the rain clouds. So he contented himself with humbly accepting the accolades showered upon him. Periodically, he still heard shouts of "N'anga Fashang" as he passed by.

Three days later, a group of city elders arrived at his compound, dressed in all their finery. They looked serious.

"Baba Fashang, we greet you!"

"Honoured elders, I greet you!"

"We have come to bring a command..."

"From whom, may I ask?"

"From His Majesty, the Mambo." At the mention of this name they all made a slight obeisance.

"What does His Majesty, the Mambo, desire?"

"That you should present yourself for an audience this afternoon. We will accompany you as far as the spirit gate."

Understanding that this was not an invitation, but an order, Fashang concurred. Choosing the best clothing from the wardrobe left by Bin Sharif, he made himself as presentable as possible in the Arab style. Having heard tales of these African despots, he felt a certain foreboding about the forthcoming interview.

After tapping his way across the quartz ridge at the sacred threshold, he left the party of elders on the other side. At once a cadaverous man stepped forward, and introduced himself as the king's vizier. He led Fashang along a different route to the base of the hill, which he assumed to be the entry to the palace itself. In single file, they ascended a very narrow set of stone-cut steps between two towering boulders. The passage was so restricted that on occasion Fashang had to turn his body sideways to edge through. A solid door blocked the head of the stairway. As they approached, a small window opened in the wall to one side. The unfriendly face of a warrior looked out, demanding the reason for their presence. The vizier explained, and the door swung open.

As they continued to climb, Fashang saw that the whole hillside comprised stone platforms bearing groups of huts. Women were gathered round fires or working at food preparation, but there was little sign of male presence. Children ran and shrieked among the dwellings and rocks. Slowly, the vizier became more communicative.

"Each of these terraces belongs to a different wife of the Mambo."

"But… how many wives does he have?"

The guide looked surprised at the question. "By custom, the Mambo must always have ten wives. If any die, or are sent away, he must find a replacement."

The obvious question rose to Fashang's lips. "And so, how many children does he have?"

"Thirty seven – of whom twenty are boys, and the rest girls."

By this time, they had reached a wide level area surrounded by rocks, over which hung a solid roof. The hall had little natural illumination, but lamps burned brightly around the stone walls. Shields adorned the surfaces, and the glint of gold came from many points. Richly-embroidered carpets covered the floor. The place was well-filled with people in costly dress, mostly sitting at the sides of the open area. But the riveting feature of the scene was a huge wooden chair with an occupant. Fashang stared hard, as his eyes became accustomed to the low light, and could not believe what he saw. Without doubt he was observing the Mambo himself. The man was like a mountain of African muscle and sinew, and dominated the assembly by his sheer size and weight. Fashang mused that the reason he was not seen in public might be that he could never squeeze down the entry staircase!

The vizier had already primed Fashang about the etiquette of the court, and so he promptly fell to his knees, and shuffled slowly forward. His companion did the same, and began an oration.

"Great Mambo, Lord of Zimbabwe, King of Monomotapa, ruler of the lands between Zambezi and Limpopo, owner of ten thousand cattle, master of..."

The huge man cut him off loudly. "Thank you! Proceed with the introduction of this person that you have brought before me."

"Your Majesty, may I have the honour to present Baba Fashang."

"Oh, it is you, is it?" the king bellowed. "Come nearer that I may see you."

As Fashang crawled on his aching knees, the Mambo peered at him with interest.

"So this is the Chinese man from across the world - the one who was sent by Mwari to save our city. You are not like these Arabs who come here. Maybe you are from the world of spirits!"

"Great Lord, I assure you I am a mere human. I only wish to serve your Majesty."

"Whatever! But the truth is that you have been a saviour to my people. It will never be said that the Mambo of Zimbabwe does not reward those who please him."

"I need no recompense, Mighty One," Fashang responded humbly.

The king ignored this remark, but clapped his hands. "Begin now!"

At this summons, a train of servants appeared, carrying a strange assortment of goods. The first bore a magnificent garment of fine cloth, which he presented for Fashang's inspection. Interwoven into the fabric, he recognised an intricate pattern of gold thread. The next man carried a carved wooden chair in a material with a strong, pleasant odour. As the queue moved past him, Fashang realised that these were all gifts for him. Ivory in various shapes, carpets, statues, gold and several unrecognisable objects passed before his gaze.

When the procession of riches came to an end, the Mambo announced authoritatively, "And our deeply respected servant, Baba Fashang, shall receive five hundred head of cattle from my prime herd."

Fashang quaked a little at this generosity, not knowing where he could put such a number of animals.

"And for the keeping of them, I bestow on him ten thousand acres of pastureland by the Sabi River."

"Great Mambo, this is too much. You have rewarded me excessively."

"Silence! None will say the Mambo skimps on honouring the hero."

For the first time a slight smile crept onto the great face. "In fact Baba Fashang, destroyer of mountains, healer of birds - my munificence has not ended yet."

He followed this enigmatic statement with a sharp bang on a gong at his side. Immediately, a large group of servants entered from an archway, and drew near slowly. By their pace, Fashang guessed that they were carrying something heavy in the middle of the phalanx. They formed up before the young

Chinese, and then parted to reveal, not an object, but a person standing at the centre. It was a woman in a richly-decorated long garment, her head covered with a veil. Fashang's heart nearly burst out of his chest – but he cautioned himself against wild hopes.

With a great roar of laughter, the Mambo cried, "You shall remain single no longer. I am giving you one of my daughters to wife!"

It was customary that the courtiers followed their master in everything he did, and so an explosion of laughter followed.

Fashang's head reeled. For a moment he expected to awake from a dream at any moment, and find it was all fantasy. How many daughters did the king have? Seventeen, or was it eighteen?

Leaping up from his throne with unexpected alacrity for such a colossal frame, the king strode vigorously across the hall. He towered above the other members of his court, and dwarfed the young Chinese. Standing beside the woman, he drew the veil gently off her head and shoulders. She slowly raised her eyes, and Fashang found he was looking into the face of Gamuchirai.

"I too have my spies," boomed the Mambo.

Chapter 20

African Family

For several days the sole topic of conversation among the thousands living in the great valley, was the impending marriage of the Princess Gamuchirai to the Chinese hero. The matter was discussed from all angles, and opinions were as many as the sand grains below their feet.

"In my view, it's got the Mambo out of a difficult corner. After all, no local ruler wants to marry that girl."

"Nxa, but Baba Fashang has saved our city. He deserves great honour."

"From what I hear, they are very much in love. It sounds like a fable from the past."

"Any other husband would have been forced to pay a huge lobola for her - probably hundreds of cows. But here the Mambo is giving presents to the bridegroom. It's all back to front!"

"There's not even a munyai to make the negotiations between the two families. Truly it is a strange thing!"

"At least they can look each other in the eye – they're about the same height!"

Unaware of the inconsequential chatter in the huts, Fashang continued to walk on clouds. Although not permitted further contact with his intended, he lived in a trance as he waited for the great day.

The grand vizier became a frequent visitor to Fashang's enclosure. He explained in detail the formalities of the ceremony, and the king's intentions for the bridal couple.

"His Majesty has set aside a suite of rooms in the upper levels of the palace for your married accommodation. He wishes to keep you near him, that you may become one of his advisors."

"He is both wise and generous."

"Unfortunately the wedding ceremony cannot take place for several weeks. Now that the rains have come, we are in the 'month of the goat', Mwedzi weMbudzi," the vizier explained rather apologetically.

"And what does that mean?"

"In our thinking, this period is a sabbatical for the ancestors. We are not allowed to perform any significant spiritual events during this time."

"Then I'll just have to be patient a bit longer!"

The monarch had ordered that the wedding ceremony should take place in a large plaza in the Great Circle. This would accommodate the thousands of invited guests and the great feast that would extend for several days. The Mhondoro consulted the spirits, and set the most auspicious date in the following month for the event. At once, the city leapt into life with preparations. Huge volumes of beer were brewed, and food delicacies of all types were cooked. The Circle was decorated and thoroughly swept.

Throughout this period, Fashang continued to live in his compound, prior to moving to the hill-top palace, when wed. He experienced a sense of deja-vu, as he witnessed the intensity of the measures taken to make the day really special. His mind carried him back to another auspicious date - on another continent - in another culture – with another bride. The face of his sister Meili swam before his eyes, and he tried to envisage her response to the news that he was betrothed to an African princess. But he knew that his whole remarkable story would one day be lost. He would be remembered, if at all, as the hunted criminal who had disappeared from sight in north China. The thought saddened him.

Suddenly the words of the sage came back to him, that when

one falls, then one must rise again. Surely his life history exemplified that motto, and a fierce determination grew inside him that his legend should not be lost to the world. He would make a permanent record of his life, so that following generations would know the chronicle of Kong Jinwei. Thus he decided to use his calligraphic and carving skills to leave his life-story somewhere on a rock.

The day dawned, like most in that idyllic country, bright and fair. Musical instruments could be heard on all sides, as young and old streamed into the plaza, to await the arrival of the bride. Beer was dispensed and consumed liberally, to the accompaniment of much animated repartee and chitchat. Fashang held pride of place at the centre, although the imposing presence of the Mambo on a high throne was the ultimate authority. The bridegroom suppressed a chuckle about the report that a special rope system had been installed on the palace hillside, in order to lower the bulky monarch to the valley. In one area of the alfresco auditorium, the royal family sat on cushions under the protective eyes of several guards. Each of the king's wives was encircled by a horde of offspring and grandchildren.

As tradition dictated, the arrival of the bride would take place unexpectedly, at a time of her own choosing. Knowing Gamuchirai's mischievous nature, Fashang suspected that she might keep them waiting till the next day. However, he was not subjected to such extended torture. Late in the afternoon, drums and gongs were heard from the direction of the palace hill. After a while, a long procession of African women in vivid, multi-coloured dress entered the arena. Gamuchirai led the pageant of female beauty, outshining all the others with her gorgeous attractiveness. With slight anxiety, she looked around the vast assembly. Then, lighting upon her beloved, her face was transformed to a radiant smile.

She was dressed in white, with a long multi-hued bridal train, whose colours matched the clothing of her female companions. Round her neck was a hoop of plaited grass, covered in tinted beads. Copper and brass rings around arms and legs indicated the strength of her commitment to her lover, although slowing her movements a trifle. Her hair was carefully styled, and covered with an ornate head-dress.

Women ululated with shrill cries, men cheered, and an orchestra of mbiras summoned the spirits. Fashang and his bride positioned themselves before the throne, and turned to watch as the Mhondoro and his assistants led a complaining cow into the centre. The bride closed her eyes as the animal was despatched with short spears, to loud acclamation from the crowd.

The spirit-medium then stood forth to make what appeared to be a benediction, but to Fashang's ears it sounded only like a prolonged, high-pitched cackle. However, the audience understood sufficiently to infer that the marriage bond had been secured. Shouts, songs, ululations and mad stamping of feet greeted this proclamation, and a crowd of young girls poured into the area to perform a dynamic dance. This was followed by a troupe of young warriors who acted out a stylistic version of a lion hunt. All the while, meat was being roasted and served in one part of the plaza, and the event became steadily more raucous.

Darkness having well and truly fallen, the revels continued by the light of bonfires around the square, as well as flaming torches along the walls. The bride and groom were thoroughly exhausted by all the activity and thankful when the Mambo indicated that he, and they, should withdraw.

As part of the royal entourage, Fashang and Gamuchirai entered the palace precincts. Separating from the others, they climbed the labyrinth of stairways and corridors, and crossed the threshold into their private quarters. Fashang gasped at the opulence of the bridal chamber, where beautiful curtains covered the walls, and expensive furniture stood on every side. Food and drink were laid out on tables in vessels of silver, and an enormous gilt bed stood centrally in the room.

Taking his wife in his arms, he whispered, "I have longed for this day."

All the banter and cheekiness had gone from her face, and with glowing eyes she replied, "And so have I."

And thus, that night, two ancient dynasties were joined, albeit unconsciously. The Ming from the plains of north China bonded with the Monomotapa from the highlands of Africa, in the conjugal bed on the hilltop.

****

And so began one of the happiest chapters in the life of Wu Fashang – although it might be more accurate to describe it as the only happy chapter of his existence since his departure from Split Mountain.

Fashang soon found that Gamuchirai was singularly different from most African young women of her position. She decried the lifestyle of her sisters and half-sisters as boring. While they were content to perfect their embroidery and dancing skills, she was plying her husband with questions about the great world outside. Nor did she want to be confined to the palace grounds, but delighted Fashang by constantly begging him to take her exploring in the surrounding districts. Her slim body was extremely strong, and she could walk long distances with the best of the men.

It became a common sight for the two young people, the handsome Chinese man and the lovely African lady, to be seen striding through the populated valley to the quiet of the hills beyond. Not only did Gamuchirai show a strong intellect, but she also proved to be a sensitive and compassionate companion. She hung on every word of the saga of Fashang's long route from Shandong to Zimbabwe. When he was describing the demise of his friend Ah-Wang, she spontaneously burst into tears.

"You have suffered so much, my love. How awful to lose such

a good friend in such a manner!"

"Yes, I owe a great deal to him."

Shortly afterwards, Ibrahim Bin Sharif arrived on another trading expedition. His astonishment at Fashang's social elevation knew no bounds, and he repeatedly congratulated him. In view of the new situation, he released the Chinese from his employ, although allowing him to retain his workshop in the valley enclosure. He replaced Fashang with Simba, who by this time was sufficiently experienced to handle the work of an agent efficiently.

With the approval of his new father-in-law, Fashang spent a large amount of time in his workshop, fulfilling the vow he had made before his wedding. After a prolonged search, he found suitable layers of fine granite in a large boulder. Using explosives, he separated them from the parent rock, and then trimmed them to rectangular shapes. Recruiting a large contingent of workers, he moved these slabs to his workshop, and began to smooth the surfaces by grinding and polishing. Then, with fine chisels, he started to incise his life story onto the tablets in classical Chinese characters.

The Mambo had grandiose ideas for further building projects in his imperial capital, and requested Fashang to open new quarries for the necessary stone. Arrangements were made for Bin Sharif to send additional quantities of gunpowder up from Sofala, and the sound of blasting echoed around the hills day after day.

Gamuchirai showed great interest in all these ventures, and often accompanied her husband to the work sites. She found the whole concept of pyrotechnics quite fascinating, bearing in mind that her old tutor had talked of such knowledge in the distant past.

Fashang's cup of happiness overflowed. In his deep relationship with Gamuchirai, and his work in the community of the capital, he was deeply satisfied. He found the peace that had eluded him for so long. Their joy took a further leap, when it was revealed that she was with child, and the possibility of a family thrilled them.

Almost on their first anniversary, a son was born to them. Fashang held the tiny infant, and marvelled at his appearance which seemed to speak of both his parents. His skin colour was a light brown and his hair was black and curly, while his face combined the Chinese and African physiognomies in a most appealing way.

"It is your right to choose a name, beloved." Gamuchirai said gently.

"That is difficult. After all, who is he? He will be a man of two worlds. How shall we name him?"

"May I make a suggestion?"

"Of course. You know your culture better than I do."

"Let's call him Wang!"

"Why? That's not a Shona name!"

"But I have a deep affection for your good friend, Ah-Wang. Without him you'd not be here."

"But then the child will sound completely foreign."

She thought for a moment. "In our language we have a prefix which means 'little'. It is 'ka'. Why not name him Kawang? That sounds both Shona and Chinese. Also it means Little Wang."

"You are so thoughtful, my love," he replied, "and that is a wonderful idea."

With all the food, exercise and affection that he received, the child grew into a healthy toddler. Throughout the court, Kawang was a favourite. Even the stern Mambo was taken with this particular grandchild, despite having 147 others from which to choose.

Fashang and his treasured wife often reminisced about the

events that brought them together.

"If that bird's beak had not been smashed, I would never have found you. Actually mending it did not really save the city."

"I know."

"How do you know?"

With a laugh she explained, "I was watching you all the time, from above."

"What! Even with the Mhondoro there?"

"I'm not afraid of him. In fact I was sitting on the thatched roof of the sanctuary. There was a hole in the straw big enough for me to see what you were doing."

"You're quite a girl!"

"I saw the storm coming up quickly. It would have rained, even if you had not finished the bird repair."

"Now, you've deflated my ego," he chortled.

"But the rain came so fast, that it washed me down the roof. I had to hang onto a spike of rock to avoid ending up in the valley below."

"Really, you should have been a boy."

"But I'm glad I'm not!" she whispered, embracing him warmly.

****

About a year later, Bin Sharif passed through again, and Fashang renewed the old acquaintanceship. Among the many items of news from the world beyond the hills, he mentioned that the Chinese Treasure Fleet had arrived at Sofala once more.

"No need to worry, my friend," he said consolingly. "They will have forgotten about two deserters long ago. The admiral has other things to think about."

"I'm sure you're right. My life among the Chinese is now history. But I wonder why they've come back to Sofala."

"Trade and conquest. That's the motivation for those expeditions. Anyway, you are safe and settled here."

Despite the many demands on his time, Fashang managed to travel to the vast pasturelands that he owned by the Sabi River. His large staff of cattlemen kept his herd in fine form, and he was experimenting with breeding techniques to strengthen the strain of animals. This type of husbandry was completely new to him, and he thoroughly enjoyed the challenge and experience. To his surprise, Gamuchirai began to take a real interest in the zoology of the area, both wild and tame. Together they observed the varied fauna of the hills, plains and forests, and thus became quite expert in the study of the local ecology.

One evening, while the family was relaxing together in their hilltop eyrie, a message arrived from the valley. It was to the effect that Bin Sharif had sent a representative, who wished to talk with Fashang urgently. Sensing that this might be important, he descended the stairways and passages, crossed the valley, and arrived at Bin Sharif's compound. Simba was there, entertaining an elderly Arab with tea and refreshments. The man rose at Fashang's entrance, and salaamed.

"Greetings to you, sir. I come from Ibrahim Bin Sharif, my master."

"You are welcome – but what is your mission?"

"I bring news that I fear will greatly distress you."

Chapter 21

Imperial Invasion

Fashang waited uncertainly for the Arab to continue.

"It is reported that the Chinese army is proposing to attack Zimbabwe."

"But why?" replied Fashang hastily. "We are a long way from the sea, and this is a small state."

"Apparently news of the immense gold reserves of your king has reached the Chinese. They are mobilising a considerable force to march overland to this place."

"But, how big will this force be?"

"I do not know. My master obtained this intelligence from a spy on one of their ships, and at once sent me to warn you and your king."

Thanking the Arab, Fashang immediately requested an audience with the Mambo, which was granted at once. Despite the lateness of the hour, the king assembled his full court of officials and advisors. He had divined that there was urgency in the issue that Fashang wished to raise. As a member of the royal family, the king's son-in-law was permitted a seat in the great audience chamber. After the initial formalities, he was asked to present his matter.

"Great Mambo, I have received information that the Chinese army is proceeding this way, to attack our city. It is inferred that they have heard of our gold, and wish to seize it."

Showing a measure of alarm, the king queried, "And how reliable is your source?"

"It is someone known to me and to you, in whom we can put our trust. It appears that the threat is real."

"Induna, stand forth!" commanded the monarch.

An elderly African, dressed in rich skins and pelts, stepped from the crowd of officials. He knelt before the king, and Fashang recognised him as the commander of the armed forces.

"What are our capabilities to resist such an incursion?"

"Mighty Lord, I have heard of these warriors from China, and indeed they are much to be feared. However, your army has been kept in training, according to your command."

"How many men do we have now?"

After a brief calculation, the Induna replied, "I have four impis, each with four hundred men. Each impi has been coached by its officers very intensively. But may I suggest, Majesty, that the honourable Baba Fashang should inform us more accurately about these Chinese soldiers."

With a wave of the hand, the Mambo indicated Fashang.

"The revered Induna speaks truth, O king. The armies of the Dragon Emperor, as he is known, are formidable. But we have some advantages in our position. Firstly, the Chinese soldiers are accustomed to fighting great battles against disciplined enemies on the plains of China. Mostly, they are unfamiliar with mountains, particularly country which has great rocky outcrops and deep ravines. Secondly, their style of fighting is often at close quarters along extended fronts with the enemy. In contrast, your impis make use of swift dashes against their foes, and are skilled in the art of ambush. With strategy, we may repel the invaders."

Raising his hand, the Induna responded, "These things may be true – but until we know the strength and disposition of the Chinese army, we cannot be sure. With your agreement, sire, I will send a team of my trained spies to observe the enemy as they approach. My men move quickly and without trace."

The suggestion pleased the Mambo, who commissioned the Induna to expedite his plan with all speed. Fashang returned to his quarters, and detailed the events of the evening to Gamuchirai. She expressed her great fear.

"Do you think they know you are here? I am worried for you."

"No, light of my life, there is little chance that my location is known. We need not fear that."

Two days later, the Induna requested an interview with Fashang, and was invited to the reception room in the family's apartments. Gamuchirai served refreshment to the officer, who then expected her to leave. Fashang made an unprecedented request.

"If you will permit it, honourable Induna, I would like the Princess to remain while we talk. She and I have developed a relationship in which we function as a unit."

Somewhat surprised by this departure from convention, the Induna agreed.

"Baba Fashang, Princess, I have received the report of my spies. The Chinese army is marching overland from Sofala, instead of using the river. There are about five thousand infantry, of which six hundred appear to be archers."

"So possibly with our local knowledge we might be able to outwit them." Fashang countered.

"But they are carrying a large amount of baggage using local porters. My men did not recognise much of it. There is also a long tube…"

"A what?" remarked Fashang.

"A brass tube some four metres long and of thirty centimetres diameter. Its use is unknown to us."

Fashang rose, and walked about in agitation.

"But why is that so important?" Gamuchirai asked.

"Because… it means they have unshipped one of the cannons from a warship, and hope to use it here."

"Why is it so dangerous?"

"It uses gunpowder to fire a great ball with mighty force. Even the walls of the Great Circle could not withstand that!"

Now it was the Induna's turn to look alarmed.

"But I am thinking that perhaps we can devise a plan to thwart them. After all, they are only expecting a fairly primitive defence of this city. We will surprise them with their own technology!"

Throughout the hours of darkness, the three planners discussed their options. By morning they had a tentative stratagem. It was put to the Mambo, who wholeheartedly approved. He empowered Fashang to carry out whatever he wished for the defence of the Great Circle. Meanwhile, the Induna was to train his army in the special tactics that would be needed.

****

The life of the city was greatly disturbed when Fashang began to exert his plenipotentiary powers. Every able man was drafted into work-parties that were sent to the quarries over the hills. There they blasted great quantities of rock from the hillsides, and then produced a steady supply of stones conforming to the specifications set by Fashang. These were transported to the Great Circle, where a second wall was being built inside the outer fortification. Fashang copied the dry stone techniques of the original city builders, thereby constructing a stout rampart of equal height and thickness as the outer wall. Between the two walls was a gap of about a metre width, making a narrow longitudinal corridor.

"Why does your new wall only extend round part of the city?" one of the foremen asked.

Fashang explained, "We are protecting the direction down the valley. I expect the enemy will come that way."

The citizens were further mystified when work commenced on a tall tower just inside the inner wall. Fashang used hundreds of rocks to construct an interlocked structure of great strength, just slightly higher than the main walls of the metropolis.

Using the most skilled of his workmen, Fashang began to fashion pieces of granite into spheres about the size of water melons. He then drilled and chiselled holes into these balls, removing much of the central material. The void was then packed with gunpowder, to which a small fuse was attached. Fashang remembered the fearsome effects of the Chinese grenades on the warships. Time did not allow him to smelt iron for his bombs, and so instead he prepared a version in stone.

Once the mighty tower was completed, he set carpenters to work assembling a complicated frame on it. A long tree-trunk was centrally mounted on a hinge at the summit of the tower, and a huge boulder tied to one end. At the other extremity a small basket was fixed to carry a projectile. The lighter end was then pulled down and secured to anchors in the ground with strong ropes. Thus he produced a ballista, capable of hurling an object over the walls for a great distance. Adding a sighting system to the contraption, Fashang made many tests to calibrate the range and direction of his catapult.

During this time, the Induna was subjecting his warriors to gruelling manoeuvres on the rocky hillsides, and inculcating the strategies necessary to face the Chinese invaders. His spies reported that the invading column had reached the Ngezi River, and would be likely to attain the city in a couple of days.

All the inhabitants of the wide valley were evacuated to safety in the Great Circle, together with supplies of food and water. The city waited in readiness, with all eyes watching the far end of the valley apprehensively.

By means of a series of signals from the hills, the spies tracked the movement of the aggressors. Just after sunrise one morning, a glint of reflection from burnished armour could be seen moving in the distance. Then the bulk of the army came into sight, marching line-abreast towards the city. Fashang watched from the peak of his tower, and recognised the Chinese regimental symbols on the fluttering pennants of the advancing horde. Momentarily, his confidence departed, as he looked at the power and discipline of the army of the Dragon Emperor.

Events then took a turn which threatened to totally dishearten him. He feared that all his plans had been thwarted. Instead of heading straight for the Great Circle, as expected, the Chinese general turned his force away towards the hill palace. Obviously he had obtained intelligence that royalty lived there. Fashang watched in desperation as the army halted, and in the distance he watched a great cannon being mounted and loaded.

With a roar, the mighty weapon launched a cannonball towards the sacred hill. It crashed into some of the dwellings among the boulders halfway up the mountain. After a delay, a second missile followed it, causing further damage, and starting small fires. Fashang anxiously wondered how his family were faring, and how long the bombardment would continue.

As it happened, this phase was only a token show of force. Then the Chinese army moved to attack the Great Circle. Taking up the position that Fashang had anticipated, they adopted a standard formation. Rows of heavily-armed soldiers faced the city. Hidden among them, the cannon was positioned, aimed and primed. This scheme was employed so that the defenders would not be able to detect the position of the gun, and thereby make a sortie against it.

On the blast of a trumpet the ranks of Chinese soldiers opened to make a long corridor, down which the brass muzzle of the cannon was pointing. Within a few seconds, flame shot out of the barrel, and a smoke-shrouded metal ball flew towards the city. The artillery team was highly competent, and the ball crashed into the city wall a metre above the ground. Stones were flung in all directions, and then the weakened structure began to collapse. The massive wall came pouring down in a torrent of rocks, leaving a gap several metres wide.

With a resonating cheer, the enemy surged forward, climbed over the pile of rubble, and entered the city. But to their consternation, they immediately encountered a second wall of great resilience and height. The leading fighters shouted the news, but in the confusion more soldiers poured into the breach behind them. Seeing the corridors leading to right and left, the vanguard hurried along them. Just at that moment a rain of large rocks fell on their heads. The few who made it to the limits of the inner wall were despatched by archers.

A bugle sounded a recall, and the invaders re-formed before the city. Fashang knew that a second volley from the cannon would destroy the inner wall. Trembling a little, he carefully aligned his machine.

"Light the fuse!" he shouted.

A match was applied to the stone object in the basket, and the dried creeper began to splutter.

"Cut the ropes!"

After several swings of an axe, the restraints parted. The great boulder had its freedom to fall, and the massive tree-trunk reared upwards, carrying its projectile. Fashang watched with disappointment as the grenade was flung too far to the left of the target. But the trajectory suddenly changed, as a strong wind blew down the valley, and the flying object altered course. It then dropped heavily onto the ground a few metres from the cannon. The gunners were about to apply the taper to the touch hole of the great weapon, when the grenade exploded. Pieces of brass, wood, stone and flesh erupted into the air.

At this point, Fashang gave the order, "Black signal, now!" Instantly, a column of black smoke rose into the air. This triggered a sound, which both perplexed and frightened the invaders, who were now re-forming. The noise was that of a systematic tapping of great intensity. Little did the Chinese realise it was the synchronised impact of spears on shields. The next moment a swarm of gyrating warriors was skipping down the valley side, weaving among the rocks, waving their assegais. Orders were given for the Chinese troops to form up facing their attackers. Just as the two forces were about to engage, Fashang shouted, "White signal!"

A stream of rising white smoke galvanised the opposite hillside into action, as hundreds of other African fighters poured into the valley with loud cries. The Chinese force was caught in a pincer movement, and completely disoriented. The soldiers failed to hear the attempts of their officers to keep command.

Fashang had learned in his discussions with the Induna, that it was always wise to leave an escape route for a trapped enemy. This would minimise casualties on both sides of the conflict. Therefore the attacking impis concentrated on flanking movements, while leaving the route back down the valley wide open. Soon the Chinese troops, in their turmoil, saw that option as the only way out of the ambush, and began to run pell-mell away from the city. The Induna had stationed another impi at the point where the valley came out onto the plain, and this cohort harried the rear of the retreating militia for many miles. Eventually, the spies reported that the Chinese were making for the coast as fast they could.

****

By now, Fashang's prestige had reached an all-time high. He was a respected advisor to the king, and a much-loved member of the city's community. Together with Gamuchirai, he instituted several projects to benefit the health and well-being of people in the great valley. On occasions he became the Mambo's ambassador to the surrounding kingdoms, most of whom were in fealty to the sovereign of Zimbabwe.

Although not part of the military, he sometimes heard himself being called Induna Fashang, following his part in the repulsing of the Chinese army.

"It's funny how many names I've had in my life, Gamu," he mentioned, as the family sat in their family room, watching

Kawang playing with a pet warthog.

"You've had a very varied life – for someone of only thirty," she replied with a smile.

"Yes. Kong Jinwei... Wu Fashang... Baba Fashang... N'anga Fashang... and even Induna Fashang. I wonder who I really am – and where I belong."

"As far as I'm concerned, you belong here, and you belong to me."

"Recently I've had a strange dream, repeated several times. It was as though I'd become a bird, and was flying over the hills to the east. Then I saw Sofala below me, and headed across the great ocean. A small whitewashed town on the coast appeared, and I guessed it was Aden. After many more aerial miles, I flew across a great continent, which might have been India. I fancy that Calicut slipped by underneath me. Much later, I saw a port below, and from its shape it must have been Malacca. This strange dream mapped my life's journey, and eventually I came to land below the Split Mountain where I was born."

"Don't let it worry you, my beloved. You are secure here."

"I know – but I do wonder what the dream meant."

"By the way," she interrupted, with eyes of affection on their young son. "Kawang may have a sister or brother before long."

"How wonderful! Our family is growing!" exclaimed Fashang.

"Then we will have to think of yet another name that is both Shona and Chinese," she giggled.

Fashang suddenly became aware of a movement along the far wall of the ornate room. Focussing clearly, he saw a section of smooth round grey body sliding along the ground.

"Don't move!" he urged. "There's a snake in the room."

"It's a black mamba!" cried a terrified Gamuchirai. "Kawang come here at once!"

But the little boy was chasing his tiny warthog among the furniture, oblivious to his mother's command. Fashang realised that the child lay in the path of the snake's only exit from the room, making the reptile much more dangerous. Slowly the distraught father stood up, and moved gently towards his son. But this provoked an immediate response, causing the mamba to rear up, bringing its head a metre above the floor. Its gaze was fixed on Kawang, and slowly its mouth opened wide, revealing an inky-black interior and a set of sharp teeth at the top of the throat. It swayed back and forth a few times, obviously gathering momentum.

Knowing that nothing could prevent the attack, Fashang threw himself onto Kawang, shielding the child from the reptile. At the same moment the grey head lunged down, and fastened onto Fashang's neck. He could feel the fangs penetrating his skin, and the rush of liquid into his body. In vain he tried to prise the snake off, but the creature held on tightly.

In desperation, Gamuchirai grabbed a decorated ceremonial sword from the wall. Unmindful of her own danger, she slashed at the tail of the reptile, and continued beating until it relaxed its grip. It then wriggled its death throes in its own blood, and lay still.

Running to Fashang, she turned him over, and found a frightened, but unharmed, youngster underneath. Embracing her son tightly, she called for the servants to bring the court healer. But she watched with fading hope as Fashang struggled to breathe, and his eyes lost focus. Cradling him and her son in her arms, with the corpse of the grey attacker beside her, she felt the life ebb out of her lover. He gasped and rolled on the floor, but gradually became more tranquil as he lost consciousness. The shock was so great that she did not even shed a tear, but she knew that would come later.

The N'anga rushed into the room, following his peremptory summons. Falling on one knee beside the inert form, he felt the arms and chest for a while, before making his diagnosis.

"The honoured Baba Fashang has joined the ancestors."

****

Ululations rang out across the city from dawn to dusk – but this time they were cries of grief, not joy. The loss of this unique member of their society, and empathy for his stricken wife, moved the populace to a frenzy of mourning.

The Mambo decreed that no cooking fires would be lit for a period of ten days in honour of the departed hero. Gamuchirai walked somnambulantly around the palace with ash on her head. The only factor which prevented her grief from destroying her was the presence and needs of Kawang. For hours she sat nursing the boy, while tears streamed down her face. After a while she recognised that her sorrow was disorienting the child, and she began to play and talk with him as before.

The Mhondoro was ordered to divine a suitable site for the grave of such an important person, and preparations were made for a sumptuous state funeral. The body of Fashang was taken to the sanctuary, where under the watchful eyes of the sacred birds, it was anointed with oil and shrouded in yellow cloth.

The location of the tomb was fixed just outside the picket of stakes that marked the city boundary. It was argued that Fashang's ancestral spirits would be different from those of the local people, and therefore a grave further down the valley would be appropriate.

Gamuchirai approached her father with a request.

"Royal father, may I ask that my beloved's grave be covered in a special way?"

"What is this, my daughter?"

"For several years, my husband has been inscribing his life story on sheets of stone. Of course, we cannot read it, since it is in his Chinese writing. But I wish that these pieces of rock should be buried with him. Deep in my heart, I feel that someday a person will come who will be able to understand it. Then his story will not be lost for ever."

"Certainly, Gamuchirai, I will grant your request."

On the day of the funeral, the cortege set out from the palace with the covered body of Fashang on a stretcher of poles and bark. Drums and gongs accompanied the procession, to drive away evil spirits. Gradually the throng grew, as mourners from all parts of the city and beyond joined the movement of people. Such was the respect due to the deceased, that the Mambo himself made the unprecedented gesture of attending personally. Leading the grievers was Gamuchirai in drab clothes, covered in ash. It was considered inappropriate for children to be present, and so Kawang was left with his nurse.

On reaching the open grave, the corpse was gently placed in the earth, lying on its right side, with the head pointing north. At this point, Gamuchirai stepped forward, and addressed the Mhondoro.

"Blessed Mhondoro, I would like this object placed beside his head."

She held out a small stone cylinder.

"What is it, Princess?" he asked.

"It is what he called his 'chop'. The end has his personal sign on it, which he used to mark items as his own."

The shaman acted on this last request, and then ordered a team of labourers to lower the large granite tablets, covered in strange symbols, into the grave. The body of Fashang disappeared from sight below the grey sheets.

The Mambo strode to the edge of the pit, and turning to the watchers, addressed them in a thunderous voice.

"People of Zimbabwe, we say farewell to someone sent by the

spirits to bless and protect our land. This man we honour, and his children, and his children's children we will honour."

Taking a handful of earth from a servant, he threw it symbolically into the opening. At this cue, other officials started to toss soil onto the granite slabs until they were covered.

Assisted by her family members, Gamuchirai made her solitary way back to the palace. But she knew now that she had a future, and that it lay in her children. The memory of Fashang would be kept alive in them.

Chapter 22

Skeletal Evidence

Mududzo's revelation, that a skeleton had been found in the digging pit, electrified the three young people relaxing at the Jabulani Hotel.

"Wow, this is really getting exciting!" Alison enthused. "Let's get down there as fast as possible."

Alex, Alison and Meili leapt into the Land Rover, and turned onto the narrow road leading down to the Great Zimbabwe ruins. But their progress was impeded by two large vehicles rumbling along ahead of them. On the backs of both of them were the University of Zimbabwe badge, and the words "Department of Archaeology".

"Looks as if Prof. Mududzo is bringing in the heavy stuff. He's as excited as we are."

"This might be the find of the decade – at least for Zimbabwe."

"And to think I might look on the face of my brother!" waxed Meili lyrically.

After parking, they continued on foot down the valley towards the dig-site. Even in the few hours they had been away, the whole scene had changed. The crowd barrier had been moved further back, and the actual pit enshrouded with a huge white tent. Many more police and soldiers were in evidence, and the group was stopped by an officious sergeant.

"Sorry, but admission has been restricted. You cannot go

further!"

"But we are part of the archaeological team. Please let us through!"

"My orders are that no one enters the area."

Taking out his phone, Alex called Professor Mududzo, and explained the impasse. Shortly afterwards, the man himself appeared, and placated the officer.

"Sorry about that problem, Mr Hampstead – but we have stepped up security a lot. You and Dr. Hampstead are of course welcome to come to the site."

"And what about our Chinese friend here?" asked Alex.

"I regret that she is not part of the team – and she must wait outside."

"That's ridiculous!" Alison expostulated. "She is the key person, who alerted us to the value of the writing. She's now as much part of the operation as we are!"

Under Alison's vehemence, Mududzo relented, and all three were allowed to enter the marquee. Inside they found a quantity of specialist equipment, measuring and photographing each stage of the action. Of the granite slabs there was no sign, and it was inferred that they were already on their way to Harare.

"Professor, what were those vehicles we saw on the road?" asked Alex.

"It looks like this might be a lengthy job," Mududzo replied. "So we have brought down a mobile admin van with offices and a meeting room. The other is a dormitory, since we intend to stay on site till the end."

Moving to the edge of the hole, they saw that partially

hidden by the sand were a number of yellowish white bones. Two of the university staff were painstakingly removing the granules from what was obviously a skull, using small brushes and a hand vacuum cleaner. Mududzo explained the find.

"It appears to be a typical Shona burial. The skeleton is lying on its right side with its face towards the west. Within a few minutes we should be able to lift the cranium, and get it into the laboratory."

They watched breathlessly as the skull was gently released from its silicon surroundings. It was transferred to the mobile laboratory that had been on site since the morning. Alison commented that she could not see Dr. Mwonzi, and was informed that he had been sent back to Harare to take lecture classes.

"Despite all the excitement here, we still have students at UZ who expect to be taught!" joked Mududzo.

Alison felt slightly more comfortable with the absence of Daniel Mwonzi. Despite the valuable assistance that he had given, she still had a prickly sensation that he had not been transparent with them.

As darkness fell, Mududzo invited them to join a meeting of the staff to evaluate the day's finds. Entering one of the large vehicles, the trio were surprised to find a well-lit conference room with small office cubicles at each end. The departmental staff, numbering about a dozen, sat round a polished table. Professor Mududzo welcomed and introduced the members, and then signalled towards the door.

With an excess of showiness, one of the technicians brought in a covered platter, looking for all the world like a waiter in a smart restaurant. He placed the offering in the middle of the table, and Mududzo completed the pageantry by whipping off the cloth. Everyone gasped. Before them lay a skull, now carefully cleaned up. The surface of the bones was a mottled mixture of white and light brown, but they appeared to be undamaged. The eye sockets stared sightlessly at the company.

After the group had silently scrutinised the object for a while, an elderly white-haired African opined, "In my view this is not a Negroid skull. Neither is it Caucasian. Probably the shape indicates an Asian origin."

"Dr. Mutauranwa is our resident anthropologist," the professor explained. "and I feel that his opinion is to be taken seriously."

"So we have settled that this is the Chinese man mentioned in the writing on the slabs," offered one of the younger lecturers emphatically.

"Not so fast, young man! As professionals, we must move cautiously. That's why we need this high security. If we jump to the wrong conclusion, and the press gets hold of it, then it will be egg on our faces. You remember the infamous Piltdown Man case in the U.K., where a palaeological find was believed genuine for forty years, before being declared a hoax."

"If I may offer a suggestion," a quietly-spoken academic contributed, "I feel that we should keep this quiet, while at the same time seeking to get a carbon dating test on the skull."

"That makes good sense," observed Mududzo. "But it will mean sending it to Britain or America for that. Will be hard to keep the secret if we do that."

"With your permission, Prof, I feel there is another

possibility," Alex inserted. "My wife and I have a former colleague from Shorefield University, who is now working at the University of Cape Town. In fact, she is in charge of a nuclear testing unit there, and I believe they could do the carbon dating - without this skull leaving Africa."

"Sounds an excellent idea! Why don't you follow this up for us? If they can do this work, then I suggest we send the skull straight there to get an estimate of the age."

"But we must keep security in mind," observed one of the team. "Not only is there the publicity angle, but there are rumours of an international gang stealing and smuggling valuable finds like this."

"Quite right," replied Mududzo. "We will send it with a police guard. But who can take it? Most of us must stay on site, to work on the rest of the bones as they are disinterred. I wonder whether we could ask the Hampsteads to go to Cape Town. After all, they know the lady in charge of the unit there. Please make the necessary enquiries, and we will take it from there."

At that point the gathering was interrupted by one of the technicians, who apologetically came into the room.

"Sorry, Prof. But I thought you might like to see this. It was in the sand quite close to the head. What is it? Maybe a miniature of a god – a sort of idol?" he mused, turning over a small stone cylinder.

"Not at all," squeaked Meili with fervour. "It's a Chinese chop!"

Taking the item from the technician, she stared at the engraving on the end, and then burst into tears.

"What's the matter, Meili?" Alison asked anxiously.

"It's his chop. This is Kong Jinwei's special signature stone. Look carefully! This is 'Kong' down one side, with the other two characters of his personal name beside it."

"Looks like the confirmation is coming in fast," declared Mududzo. "All we need now is a historical date to fix the whole story."

The meeting broke up, and the Land Rover took the three of them back to the Jabulani Hotel. Alex spent the evening in a long Skype conversation with their erstwhile colleague at the southern tip of Africa.

"Well, what did she say?" asked Alison anxiously.

"You know Moira O'Clery, that wild Irish lady! She was over the moon about the idea – almost wanted to take the whole project over by herself. Certainly, she says, they can undertake carbon testing if the date is within the last two millennia. Already she's bubbling with schemes – so we won't be short of enthusiasm there."

"I say," interjected Meili, "d'you think I could come. My time at the school has finished, and I'm on my way home. But I could travel with you to Cape Town, and fly onward from there. I'd love to see what the tests prove."

"Why not," exclaimed Alex with gusto. "You're an honorary archaeologist now."

This conversation was reported to Prof. Mududzo the next morning. He immediately leapt into life, organising the necessary packing of the delicate skull in a special-purpose plastic container. The Zimbabwe Republican Police seconded a Detective-Inspector Gunda to accompany the group. It was agreed that Meili be permitted to accompany Alex and Alison to Cape Town, all at university expense.

Two days later, the mission set off in the Land Rover, with Gunda's considerable bulk filling one of the back seats. They soon found him to be a charming and witty companion, and surprisingly he got on well with Meili as they chatted animatedly. Their plan was to drive to Bulawayo Airport, whence they would fly via Johannesburg to their destination.

As the late afternoon sun illuminated Table Mountain, their plane circled over the vineyards, swooped past the light "tablecloth" of mist on the peak, and dropped towards Cape Town International Airport.

Meili squealed with delight. "That's the most beautiful sight I've ever seen! I'll never forget it."

Soon the aircraft was on the ground.

Chapter 23

Informative Isotopes

They passed easily through immigration and customs, although there was some delay with regard to Gunda's position. The South African authorities would not permit an armed policeman from a foreign state to enter, and so it was agreed that he would surrender his weapons. The S.A police would then provide the group with an escort to the university, to ensure that their precious cargo arrived intact.

All went according to plan, and they travelled in a police van to the prestigious institution nestling on the lower slopes of Table Mountain. Approaching the relevant campus building, they were met by a wildly-gesticulating red-headed woman in her mid-thirties. This was Moira O'Clery. Tumbling out of the vehicle, they were all grabbed, hugged and kissed – including Meili.

She had not changed in the least. Alex and Alison remembered their first encounters with her, in which they realised that the concept of staying motionless was quite foreign to this woman.

"Absolutely wonderful... really great to see you... made my day... you must be Meili... careful with that box... come inside all of you," rattled off a verbal torrent, while the speaker danced from foot to foot, and the red hair followed suit.

Soon they were settled in the office of the Director of the Light Isotope Unit of the University of Cape Town.

"This sounds like a unique find. I'm really jealous for you, turning up a skull like this. Well, I've done some thinking – and set some wheels in motion. By the way, would you like a cup of tea?" Moira jabbered.

They declined.

"We have set up the carbon-14 experiment, and should give you a result in a day or so. You said the cranium was probably seven hundred years old – in which case we can give you an accuracy of plus or minus twenty years."

"That sounds very good, and can be correlated with the known dates for Zheng He's Treasure Fleet," commented Alison.

"Actually, I'm burning to have a look at this find!" Moira said, indicating the box which had been deposited in her office.

"No problem!" Alex answered, and lifted it onto a table. As he raised the lid, and removed the polystyrene packing, Moira gasped.

"It's beautiful... almost pristine... no sign of damage... one of the finest specimens I've seen."

"How about security?" Alison enquired practically.

"Over there!"

They looked in puzzlement at a large bookcase, until Moira stepped up to it, and swung it forward. Behind stood a large metal safe, a metre tall. Dialling a combination, and then inserting a key, she opened the heavy door.

"Your Chinese friend will be very happy in there."

Changing briefly to a serious mien, she added, "There's

quite a bit of crime associated with items like this. We've had several reports of archaeological items disappearing into the hands of unscrupulous collectors."

Once the box and its contents were safely secured, the vivacious academic continued to gush.

"I've also had another idea."

"Oh, no," groaned Alex.

"Just you wait and see! I've sent out letters to all of them... expect responses tomorrow... the university clinic is primed... might get some fantastic results... we can publish lots of papers on this..."

"What on earth are you talking about?" Alison asked loudly.

"DNA, of course!"

"What's DNA got to do with all this?"

"So sorry! I get carried away, and then I gabble," Moira apologised. Then, continuing more slowly, "Since you say that Chinese folk with the surname Kong are possibly all related to Confucius, I thought we might try a DNA matching exercise."

"Matching whom with whom?"

"I've found about six hundred students here with surnames that sound Chinese. So I've invited them to participate in a voluntary survey in which we take a blood sample. We will then compare their DNA with a sample from your skull."

"What incredible imagination you've got!" exclaimed Alex. "But can you really find similarities over such a long time gap?"

"Well, it seemed to work in the case of King Richard III in the U.K. – and they found some of his modern relations by this means. The time between then and now is almost the same as with your Chinese person."

"But do you have facilities for this type of work in Cape Town?"

"I'll say we do! It's a brand new facility... only open a few months... and they'll love a project like this... it's called the Ancient DNA Department... the head is a pal of mine... so no problems..."

"But how long will all these tests take?" Alison enquired.

"We're trying to rush things along..."

"As always!" murmured Alex.

Ignoring his comment, she continued. "Maybe about a week, until we get both the radiocarbon and the DNA results."

"It all sounds terrific," said Alison with admiration. "So meanwhile we need somewhere to stay. Can you recommend a cheapish hotel?"

"Goodness me, you don't want a hotel! I've got a house for you."

"A what?"

"One of my staff has gone on sabbatical to Australia – and I have the use of his house. It's in the town of Muizenberg, about ten miles straight down the M3. In truth, it's not in the town, but on the mountainside above. It's yours for the week."

"You don't miss a trick, Moira! Just like the old days," breathed Alex.

"Excuse me," came a voice.

Guiltily, they realised that in their vibrant conversation, they had forgotten about Detective Inspector Gunda, who had been a silent spectator of the proceedings.

"It seems to me," he said, "that I don't really have a role at the present time. I have no real jurisdiction here, and wondered whether I could be released to visit some cousins of mine in Stellenbosch."

"I can't see why not," Alison acceded. "We do have your phone number."

"As soon as you're ready to return to Zim, give me a call, and I'll be right back. Thank you."

The resourceful Moira had even managed to borrow a car for their use, and following her detailed directions, the trio set off in the darkness. Gunda made his way independently to the main station to travel to his family.

After following a wide motorway, they turned onto a two-way road that began to climb up the side of a mountain. Just as it levelled off, Alison noted a sign.

"Must be just beyond here. Yes, that white gateway is it!"

Alex turned into the parking space in front of an isolated bungalow. After unloading, they entered the premises through the front door into a large lounge. Immediately, they stopped, astounded by the view. The large picture windows looked out on a galaxy of lights extending in a great curve.

"This must be False Bay, and we are high above it," Alison surmised.

Meili was entranced by the vista. "I thought Table Mountain was the finest scenery, but this rivals it."

The house was spacious and comfortable with three large bedrooms. The cupboards and fridge were stocked with food – all evidence of the indefatigable Moira.

After a good night, they rose to the sight of a splendid sunrise over the Hottentots Holland Mountains in the far distance. Below them lay a great bay, bordered by a sandy beach extending for many miles. Several towns were situated along this great strand.

For the next few days, the three friends hiked the mountains, explored the coastline, and swam in the warm sea. Constant contact was maintained with Moira O'Clery, who reported that 267 Chinese students had volunteered for the DNA blood test, although no details of the actual project had been released publicly.

One afternoon, while sitting on the stoep of the bungalow, looking across the bay, Meili asked about the testing procedures.

"How does this radiocarbon thing work?"

"Ask Alex! He should know!"

"No, ask Alison! She has the doctorate in this stuff!"

"Okay," explained Alison, "this is how it works. The sun's radiation affects the gas molecules in the upper atmosphere, so that some change to a version of carbon different from the usual. This carbon-14, as it is called, gets into the carbon dioxide that enters animals and plants. So, every living thing has a mixture of ordinary carbon and carbon-14 in a standard ratio. When a living organism dies, the carbon-14 begins to decrease at a steady rate – because it is actually radioactive."

"Is it dangerous?"

"Not at all. The amount is very small. If we take an ancient object, then by measuring the ratio of the two carbons, we can determine the time since the death of the organism."

"Sounds amazing!"

"It is. And it works, for a time range up to about fifty thousand years. But shorter times give better accuracy."

"I wish I'd studied science better at school – but music took all my energy," Meili reflected. "But when this is finished, where will my brother's head end up?"

"I'm really afraid that there will be a lot of controversy and unpleasantness, if we find that the skull is really from the Ming period," Alex observed gloomily. "Zimbabwe will want to keep the relic, since it was found on their ground. Because I discovered it while on a U.K. research grant, I guess there will be pressure to take it there. Even China might make noises about returning one of the ancestors! There's a lot of politics in academia."

"Does that mean he will end up in a glass case in a museum?"

"Quite possibly – just labelled 'Exhibit 999' or suchlike."

"That makes me quite sad. After all, he was a person – of the same race as me. He deserves better than to be on show for people to gawk at. I think he should be buried with dignity."

"It is sad. But, unfortunately, that's the way things go," agreed Alison.

****

After enjoying eight days of this splendid vacation, they were invited to meet Moira in her office. Hurrying back to the slopes of Table Mountain, they found an ecstatic Irish lady.

"Congrats to all of you... fantastic find... should shake the world..."

"D'you mind if we sit down?" asked Alison meekly.

"Of course, of course. I get so carried away. Well are you ready for the news?"

"That's why we're here," Alex remarked dryly.

For a brief period, Moira managed to still her effervescent movement. Sitting at her desk, she picked up a sheaf of papers.

"To make the carbon-14 measurements, we extracted a small piece of bone from the far interior of the cranium. This meant less chance of ash or dirt contaminating it, than if we had used exterior material."

"Sounds very sensible," agreed Alison.

"Carbon-14, as you know, is a radioactive isotope of carbon-12, with a nucleus containing six protons and eight neutrons. Our measurements of the ratio of the two types of carbon in your sample gave us a date, with an accuracy of plus or minus twelve years."

"Please tell us! I can't wait!" pleaded Meili.

"Well the median date that we have reached is the year 1425 AD."

Loud cheers rang out from the English and Chinese contingents, while the Irish applauded vigorously.

"How does that fit with the precise dates?" Moira asked.

Alex explained. "From Chinese records of the Fleet, we assume that our man arrived in Great Zimbabwe about 1419. Using your date of death, we can estimate that he probably lived there for about six years. But why he died is anyone's guess. He must have been about thirty."

"You have done a magnificent thing for my country, Moira. I am greatly indebted to you," Meili said solemnly.

"All in a day's work! Though I would like more days like this one! Now I want you to meet someone else…"

She led them out of her building onto the long campus that stretched across the lower slopes of Table Mountain. After a short walk along a roadway, they turned up some steep steps onto an open area.

"Good morning, sir!" Moira shouted cheekily.

Alex could not see anybody to be greeted.

"Who was that you were talking to?" he asked.

Pointing upward to a large stone statue of a seated man, she replied, "That grand old man, Cecil Rhodes. Father of South Africa, some would say! But actually one of your greedy English colonials seeking fame and gold."

They passed into another stone building with a Greek façade, and through dark corridors to a sign indicating "Department of Ancient DNA". Confidently leading the party to a large laboratory, she introduced everyone to the head of the unit, an Afrikaans gentleman.

"Welcome, my friends. Please sit down," he said politely, with a distinctly South African accent. "May I thank you for the opportunity to be part of this utterly intriguing study."

"You have already told me of your results, Mr. Potgieter,

but I would like these people to hear it first hand," Moira indicated.

"Certainly. In all, there were 259 students of Chinese extraction who turned out for the blood test. We used mitochondrial genome sequencing of the samples to look for common patterns in the DNA coding of these students and the skull which you have provided. Results indicated that thirty-nine student samples agreed with a DNA sequence in your relic."

"Wow, that sounds impressive!"

"And there's more. When we looked at the surnames, we found that thirty-three were called Kong, two Kung, and one Koong."

"And all those would be different English spellings of the same Chinese character," Meili added.

"Precisely. The few others that matched the DNA had a variety of surnames, possibly indicating cases of false-paternity. Overall, the evidence is strong that your ancient man was part of the Kong family. Of course, that does not link him linearly to Confucius, but he was certainly related... Even though there were two thousand years between them."

"A marvellous piece of work! Thank you, Mr Potgieter," Alison added warmly.

"In case you might be interested, the DNA showed that your man had brown eyes and black hair."

"How about his toenails?" Moira asked mischievously.

"Really, Miss O'Clery!" was the stern reply.

****

Back at the bungalow on the mountain, preparations were made for departure. Alex spent the evening sending e-mails to the various interested parties. Prof. Mududzo replied with hearty congratulations at the success of their mission, and requested them to return to Great Zimbabwe as soon as possible. Excavations there had turned up the remainder of the skeleton, but nothing else of note had been found. Prof. Oatman sent a quick reply from his iPad expressing his delight at Alex's research achievement.

Meili managed to book a flight out of Cape Town the following morning, which after many long hours, and several changes, would land her back home in Shandong. Alex contacted Detective Inspector Gunda, who agreed to meet them at Moira's office early in the day, and promised to arrange South African police protection while the skull was in transit to the airport.

With hugs and tears the three collaborators parted at the airport at five o'clock the next morning. As Meili passed into immigration, she promised to keep in touch with Alison and Alex. Quietly, the couple drove back into the city, nostalgic for the momentous things they had experienced with the young woman from the antipodes.

On arrival at Moira O'Clery's department, they found the precious box on her desk. She opened the top, and invited them to inspect the contents.

"There's your relic, safely packed for its journey back to the high veldt of Zimbabwe. Our tests have done no damage."

Resplendent in his uniform, Gunda was in attendance, together with two of the local constabulary.

Just before their departure, Moira asked Alex for a quiet word, and took him to an adjoining office. When he returned, Alison noticed that he looked distinctly worried.

"Is everything all right, love?" she asked.

"Yes, yes, of course. Just a few details I discussed with Moira," he stuttered unconvincingly.

Taking leave of the academic world of Cape Town, they were escorted to the airport. Having recovered his service revolver, Gunda took over their protection, as they flew across the country and into Zimbabwe. It was early evening, when they finally disembarked at Bulawayo Airport.

Chapter 24

Skullduggery

Alex messaged Mududzo to say that they were back in the country, and was urged to hurry back to the dig-site. After loading their precious cargo into the Land Rover, they began the five-hour drive through the hills of southern Zimbabwe. Darkness fell, but the strong headlights and spots on the vehicle illuminated the roadway clearly. Nevertheless, they kept an eye open for cows or goats who might be using the tarmac as their bedroom. Gunda described the hilarious time he had spent with his extended family, and Alison outlined the events of the past few days at the university. After a brief stop for sustenance at Zvishavane, they started on the last leg of the twisting road.

As they came round a bend, they saw ahead the reflective yellow jacket of a constable of the Zimbabwe Republic Police. Standing in the road, he signalled them to stop. Wearily, Gunda complained.

"Why is there a road-block at this time of night? Don't worry. When he sees my uniform, he'll soon jump aside!"

Somewhat stiffly, Gunda climbed out of the Land Rover, and drew near to the man. Suddenly a flash and a shot echoed through the night. Gunda fell, clutching his leg. At once, the bogus policeman reached down and grabbed the revolver from the stricken officer. Simultaneously, a second black figure emerged from the undergrowth, rushed towards the vehicle, and waved a weapon through the window.

"You! Get in back!" he shouted at Alex. Without complaint, Alex slid out of the driving position, and climbed into the rear seat. Alison quickly followed suit. Tearing off the yellow jacket, the first man dived behind the wheel. His companion stationed himself in the passenger seat, with his pistol pointing at the couple huddled behind him.

With a squeal of tyres, the vehicle took off along the dark highway. After about ten minutes, the driver slowed, and then turned onto a dust track. For nearly an hour, the vehicle and its occupants bounced along a rough road, while outside all was darkness. Alison estimated that they were passing through the farming area of Masvingo Province. Eventually, shaken and frightened, Alex and Alison saw a building ahead. The headlights lit up a solid brick house, typical of those in the rural areas.

Their captors parked by the front entrance, and then drove their prisoners at gun-point into the premises. They entered a bare room with windows on two sides, and Alex noticed at once that stout bars had been fixed across the openings. Without further conversation, the two men carried their entire luggage into the room, and then hastily backed out, shutting the door. The sound of a closing padlock could be heard, followed by the noise of a door being opened and closed at the back of the building.

Physically, mentally and emotionally drained, the couple clung together. Then they collapsed onto the floor in the impenetrable darkness. Alison was the first to recover her speech.

"What on earth has happened to us? Who are these men? What do they want? Oh, Alex, I'm so frightened!"

"I have no idea, my love. Perhaps they just want to steal

our vehicle – but then they would have dumped us in the bush. Anyway it sounds as though they're still somewhere in this building."

"My guess is that it's connected with the skull. But why did they put it here with our luggage, if they wanted to steal it."

****

The night was warm, and the mosquitoes active. After residing on the floor for a lengthy period, Alex staggered to his feet, and began an exploration of their prison. He soon determined that the wall comprised solid brickwork, the window bars were rigid, and the door was immovable.

"I suppose something will happen sooner or later. They won't just leave us here to rot. Maybe we are hostages or something. But for what reason?" Alison surmised.

Just as she uttered these words, they noticed a light through the trees. Peeping out of the window, they saw strong headlamps approaching. A car drew up to the house, and two men got out. As they approached in the light from the car, Alison gave a great cry.

"It can't be! My eyes have gone wrong! Maybe we are saved!"

Alex adjusted his eyes to the glare of the headlights. "By Jove, I think you could be right. It's incredible! And it means we can get out of here."

Peering more closely, they finally convinced themselves that one of the approaching figures was none other than Professor Horace Oatman. Their wonderment knew no bounds, and they were reinvigorated by the thought of imminent release.

After a seemingly interminable wait, the padlock was removed, and the door swung inward.

Alison leapt forward, crying, "Prof. Oatman, we are so glad to see you. We were beginning…"

Her words whimpered to nothing, as the light caught the face of Oatman. Instead of displaying his customary jovial expression, he glowered at them. Alison's eyes moved down to the small pistol that the portly academic held in his hand.

"Get back against that wall!" growled a voice, which was hardly recognisable as that of Horace Oatman.

"Now, you fools," he continued, "I tried to warn you – but you didn't listen. You're in way over your heads now."

He stepped further into the room, and was followed by a dark figure holding a torch. With a shock, they realised that this was Prof. Mududzo.

At last Alex persuaded his vocal muscles to operate. "What do you mean? Is there some mistake? Sir…"

"The mistake is yours. I'll tell you about it. We've got a few moments."

With both the gun and torch pointed in their direction, Alex and Alison listened to an extraordinary tale.

"I came to the conclusion very early on, that your software system, Alex, was extremely powerful. I used it, without your permission," he laughed. "And I noticed that particular spot in Great Zimbabwe which looked so promising. Sadly, you came to the same conclusion – so I tried to divert you to some other country. When you persisted in travelling here, I tried to get you expelled for carrying stolen artefacts across the border."

"Gosh, you mean you organised that problem at Beitbridge, when we ended up in prison?"

"Not me personally. Thank my good friend and accomplice, Bill Mududzo here. But you had an unexpected link to the highest authority, and our plan failed."

Truculently, Alex asked, "But what is your aim in all this?"

"It doesn't matter now whether you know or not. We are part of a powerful organisation which trades ancient artefacts and relics across borders. We have a number of millionaire customers who pay well for such items. But enough talking! Where is this famous cranium – for which several people are clamouring to give us a million dollars?"

Mududzo searched around the room, until he came across the special box.

"Here it is, Horace!"

"Well, open it then, Bill!"

As they removed the packing, their eyes glistened. Oatman gently lifted out the skull, and held it up to the sparse light in the room.

"Upon my word, this is a beautiful specimen, Bill. We can retire into obscurity when this goes for auction. Put it back carefully, and load it into the car."

Mududzo carried the prized box out of the room, while Oatman eyed them in a curious way.

"Really sorry, folks, but it can't be helped. You know too much about this business. One word from you could get us all into a penitentiary for a long time. But, it's your fault! If you'd gone to South America, or anywhere else, then you'd still have a future…"

"You're not saying that you will kill us?" burst out Alison.

"I don't appreciate your terminology, Alison. But, yes, you are expendable. In the grand scheme of things, two fewer archaeologists can be tolerated."

"You cannot do this!" she screamed.

"Don't worry. It will be quite painless," he pronounced with a sinister measure of sang froid.

Walking to the door, he shouted to Mududzo.

"Where are those men? We need them now!"

"I think they're in the back room – probably asleep. I'll give them a kick."

Within a short time two figures came through the door. Despite the only light being that reflected from the car's headlights, Alex recognised their two kidnappers. Mududzo had a long Shona conversation with them, and Oatman wanted to know what had been discussed.

"So, what's your plan, Bill? Do these fellows know what to do?"

"Yes, it's quite clear. They've done it before, and will take the Land Rover out to a very isolated spot, shoot the young folk, and then set the vehicle on fire."

On hearing this, Alison gave a shriek, and fainted onto the floor.

"They'll have to carry that one out. Get them tied up!"

said Oatman casually.

The two thugs clutched Alex's arms, but he leapt away from them. The bigger of the assailants then landed a blow on his jaw, knocking him to the floor. Hastily the men produced ropes, and tied their captives tightly. The two professors left the room, and drove away in their car, bearing the precious relic.

****

Consciousness returned slowly to both Alison and Alex, with the realisation that they were lying bound on the back seat of their Land Rover. Bucking and rattling, they sped along a rural road for several miles.

"Pull in here! This is as good as anywhere," commanded the man in the front passenger seat. "Sure you've got your matches?"

"Yes - and my gun! Don't fuss so much! It's not our first time."

"And how do we get out of here afterwards?"

"As I told you, I know this area. We walk across the fields to a remote village. At five o'clock, the morning bus passes through, and will take us well away."

Alex could hear the sounds of sobbing from Alison, and incendiary preparations from the men. Suddenly one of them sounded a warning.

"There's a light over there. It's coming down this road. What should we do?"

"Quick! Lift the bonnet – put your head inside! I'll tell them you're fiddling with the carburettor. Once they've passed we can finish the job."

The approaching vehicle turned out to be a small car, carrying two men. Slowing to a halt beside the stationary Land Rover, the driver called out in Shona.

"Do you need any help? What's the problem?"

"Thanks, shamwari, but we are fine. Just a little adjustment, and we'll be moving on."

"Maybe I can give a hand – I'm a mechanic," shouted the passenger in the car.

The man with his head in the engine compartment heard a door opening and footsteps approaching. His next sensation was that of a sharp object pressing against his ribs, and a quiet voice in his ear.

"Don't move at all if you value your life. Now… raise your hands in the air, and back away from the vehicle!"

At the same moment, his companion found himself seized by the throat, and thrown onto the ground. The newcomers hurriedly relieved the kidnappers of their weapons, and kept them pointing at the surprised thugs. One of the arrivals shone a torch around the interior of the Land Rover. A sharp exclamation followed.

"Good heavens, they are in here! Tied up!"

Wrenching open the door, he climbed in, and began untying the ropes that held the captives.

"Are you all right? What did they do to you?"

"Yes, nothing broken, I think," Alex replied groggily. "Ali, how are you?"

"Well, I've survived – but only just!"

The man helped them out onto the roadway. With some difficulty, they managed to stand, and massaged their limbs back to life.

"You arrived just in time," Alison said. "Otherwise we would have been burned alive."

"Sounds horrible…" the man commented.

"Wait a minute! That voice is familiar!" shouted Alex. "Who are you, anyway?"

The man swung his torch towards himself, and they recognised the features of Daniel Mwonzi.

"Daniel! Daniel! What are you doing here?"

"It's a tortuous story. I'll tell you later. But for now, we must get you to safety and comfort."

"What do we do with these two, sir?" asked the second of the rescuers.

"There's no way we can hold them," answered Daniel.

"Then I'll get them to start running down that road. A few shots will keep them going."

"Good idea."

Once the ruffians were well into the distance, Daniel suggested a plan.

"If you feel up to driving, Alex, we'd better get moving."

"Actually, I have a fearsome headache, and cannot focus properly at the moment. I'm not sure I can drive."

"No problem!" Alison contributed brightly. "I feel quite better now – so I'll do the driving."

"Where shall I take you? D'you need treatment?"

"I want to go home," whispered Alison plaintively.

"To Acacia Farm?"

"Yes."

"Well, if you are able to drive that far, we can go there. By travelling via Shurugwi, we won't need much more than an hour."

Daniel and his companion led the way in the small car, while Alison and Alex followed in the Land Rover. There was not much conversation, since they were both still dazed and shocked by the events of the night.

****

As the rays of the sun peeped over the mountains onto the stately homestead at Acacia Farm, Corrie was already actively supervising the early morning routines of the farm. Peter and Rutiziro had left the previous day for an excursion to Mana Pools in the north of the country, and Corrie was feeling a trifle lonely.

Having been slightly concerned about her daughter's trip to Cape Town, she was hoping for a message to reassure her of the couple's safe arrival back at Great Zimbabwe. Instead, she heard the throaty sound of a large diesel engine coming up the drive to the farm. She identified it at once as the noise of her own Land Rover, but was surprised to see it preceded by a small red saloon car.

She was looking forward to hearing news of the trip down south.

Chapter 25

Ethical Dilemma

The peace of the sunlit morning, among the mountains of her home, soon seeped into Alison's soul. The trauma of the previous night began to seem like a bad dream. Her mother had fussed around her, but was relieved to see that both Alex and Alison were rapidly recovering from their experience. Corrie remembered Daniel Mwonzi from his previous visit, and had invited him to stay on at the farm. His companion departed with the red car, soon after their arrival.

After breakfast, the four of them reclined on the sofas in the family lounge, as Alex narrated the events of the last few days. Corrie was in turn intrigued, amazed and aghast at the story. Finally, Alex looked across at Daniel.

"Please tell us, Daniel, how you happened to be on that road at that time?"

The tall African appeared somewhat embarrassed, and began in a slightly self-deprecating tone. "First, I must make a little apology to all of you. I have not been one hundred percent honest with you. You see, I have an alter ego."

"We had guessed there was more to you. So... are you a spy or something?" Alison queried.

"No, but I am attached to Interpol."

"Interpol! You mean you are some sort of global policeman?"

"Not at all! Interpol is not a police force. I have no power to arrest people, or do exciting exploits, as most people think. All that Interpol does is to provide a database on international crime, for use by national security agencies."

"And therefore, why are you involved?"

"When I was doing postgrad work in archaeology, I was approached. They asked if I would like to be an under-cover monitor, because there was a lot of crime connected with ancient artefacts in Africa."

"Don't we know," sighed Alex ruefully.

"So I went on a supposed Mediterranean holiday to the south of France. On the first night an unmarked car picked me up, and took me to Lyon."

"That's where the Interpol HQ is located."

Daniel smiled. "Quite correct. And I spent a month training there. It was mainly to do with surveillance techniques, both on the ground and on-line. There was particular concern about a ring of academics who were illegally selling historical artefacts."

"Now we're getting the picture," mused Alex.

"There was a general feeling that Oatman and Mududzo were collaborating in this affair – but no hard evidence had emerged. So as a member of the UZ department, I both did my job as a lecturer, and also kept an eye out for any clues."

Alison laughed wryly. "And to think that we thought you were the baddie. We received an anonymous note at Heathrow airport, warning us about you!"

It was Daniel's turn to look astonished. "Well, that is

interesting! I thought that perhaps my cover had been blown. So I guess it was Oatman who sent you that message. In fact, it's quite ironic. When you two arrived from the U.K., I wondered if you were part of Oatman's operation. That's why I went to Vic Falls to meet you, but I soon decided that you were clean."

"But why did you give us that package of artefacts that landed us in prison?"

"I had no idea what I was carrying. Just as I was leaving UZ, Mududzo asked me to give it to you to take into South Africa."

Corrie intervened. "This is quite laughable. Both of you were suspecting the other, then!"

"That's the way it seems," Daniel continued. "But when the dig got underway at Great Zim, I was still on the lookout for any suspicious features. Then Mududzo sent me back to Harare – ostensibly to teach the students, but actually to get me away from the site. Next thing I knew was that you had gone to Cape Town."

"I still don't see how you rescued us from those men last night," said a puzzled Alison.

"A few days ago, I received a message from Lyon – we have our own secure network – to the effect that Oatman had left Shorefield on a flight to Zim. My assistant, the man who was with me in the car, tailed Oatman as he left the airport to pick up a hire car. Without being seen, my man managed to attach a tracking device to the car."

"What's that," asked Corrie.

"It's a small magnetic unit that receives a GPS signal, and then transmits its location details by wireless. With a small receiver we can pick up this signal, and show the position of the unit on our satnav. After that, he followed Oatman to a hotel in Masvingo, where Mududzo was waiting. At that point I decided to drive down there immediately, since it seemed something was brewing."

"Go on!" a breathless Alison urged.

"Using the tracking system, we followed the hire car for a while, and then I realised that you would be returning that night along the same road. My unease for you deepened. Our system showed that the car had turned off the tar road into the bush, and we followed at a distance. At last we came to that remote house. Oatman's car was parked outside with the headlights shining on the place."

"Whew! You were so close, and we never knew."

"We hid our vehicle in a copse, and approached on foot. Then we saw your Land Rover parked there, with no sign of life. That made us really worried. After quite a long wait, we saw Oatman and Mududzo return to their vehicle and drive away. It was dark after that, and we could just see that some activity was taking place."

"You bet it was! We were being carried bound from the house," Alex added.

"Sorry we did not realise that. But when your vehicle tore away along a little side track, we rushed back to our car, and gave pursuit. The rest you know…"

After a silence, Alison looked Daniel in the eye, saying quietly, "Thank you, Daniel. We owe you our lives."

"The happy part is that you are both still alive. The sad part is that we have now lost the Chinese skull."

"Is there no chance it can be recovered?"

"Virtually none. It would have been out of Zim in a few

hours – and is probably winging its way to the U.S. right now."

"What a miserable ending," Alison concluded.

"By the way," Alex asked, "what happened to Detective Inspector Gunda? Did he survive?"

"Yes, he was picked up by a motorist later that night. He's now in Masvingo Hospital with a leg wound. But he'll make a good recovery."

"I'm so glad," Alison commented. "He is such a nice man."

After a further silence, Corrie pronounced brightly, "And now it's time for lunch. On the stoep in ten minutes..."

****

The afternoon was warm and bright, so Corrie suggested that the younger element should walk to a local hilltop, and enjoy a sundowner in that scenic spot. Taking a rucksack filled with drinks and snacks, they followed the river for a while, and then climbed up to a ridge. From there they scrambled up onto a prominent rock, with a commanding view of the neighbourhood. Both Alison and Daniel noticed that Alex seemed to be out of sorts.

"Are you feeling okay, darling," she asked protectively. "You don't appear to be yourself today."

"I am all right, really."

"Well, what is it? You have looked like this ever since we left Cape Town."

Alex heaved a great sigh, and settled on a piece of rock.

"You're right – ever since I left Moira."

"Whatever do you mean?" she asked incredulously.

He laughed. "Don't worry! I'm not missing Moira! It's something she said to me – and something I did."

"You do sound mysterious. Tell us more!"

"I was planning to tell you, Ali, as soon as we were alone."

Daniel interrupted. "Would it help if I gave you some time to yourselves?"

"Not at all, Daniel. My dilemma is whether I should share it with you. You might be shocked, and feel I did wrong."

"It's up to you, Alex. If you want to tell both of us, I'm happy to listen – and won't be judgemental," Daniel offered gently.

Taking a deep breath, Alex said slowly, "Oatman does not have the skull."

The other two jumped in astonishment.

"But we saw it! In Cape Town… and when Oatman stole it!" Alison screamed. "What's the matter with you, Alex?"

"Perhaps we should let Alex tell us the story," Daniel said in a pacifying tone.

"Very well," Alex started cautiously. "Moira O'Clery is a very astute woman, who keeps her ear firmly to the ground. She had received reports from her police contacts, that there might be an attempt to steal the skull en route from Cape Town to Great Zimbabwe. Even there, she felt it would not be safe. Her view was that a secure location somewhere should be found before it left her safekeeping."

"What a conceited attitude!" Alison gasped.

"But she may have had a point," Daniel put in. "I had heard similar intelligence."

"For that reason, she took some precautions. It appears they have a technician in their faculty, who is an expert in the area of 3-D printing."

Daniel nodded, but Alison looked baffled.

"A 3-D printer is a type of small robot which emits a stream of hot plastic. This cools very quickly, and as the arm moves it produces a three-dimensional surface. When controlled by a computer, the machine can generate complex shapes in solid form. Apparently this technician has perfected a technique for copying relics, such as bones, by scanning them with a laser. He uses it to make copies for students to handle."

"I read a paper about this," Daniel contributed. "It seems he can tint the plastic surface, so that it is almost indistinguishable from the original bone."

"I get it!" said Alison vehemently. "And so you decided to make a copy of that skull, didn't you, Alex?"

Holding his hands in a defensive position before his face, he replied, "Not guilty! I knew nothing of this till we went to pick up the box. It was all Moira's idea. She had it done without us having a clue. Fair play to her, she did offer me the choice of bringing back the original or the copy."

"She's an interfering, mad Irish woman!"

"So, then, did I do wrong in bringing the counterfeit one?"

"Sometimes the end justifies the means," said Daniel thoughtfully. "And the result is that Oatman has not got the skull."

"Where is it now?" asked Alison abruptly.

"In Moira's safe in Cape Town."

Alison put her head down for a while. Then, raising it, she smiled at her husband. "I do apologise, Alex. My reaction was wrong. Now I've thought about it, I think you made a courageous decision." Daniel looked away as they kissed passionately.

It took a while for this new information to sink in. Eventually Daniel said worriedly, "This moves the goal posts enormously."

"Why's that?"

"Up till now, we thought Oatman would keep away from us with his loot. But once he finds he's been tricked, he'll come after you to get the original. I wonder how long it will be before he realises that he has a fake. If he decided to gloat over his treasure by studying it, then he may already know. On the other hand, he may have sent it straight out of the country in its box. In that case it may be several days before someone overseas begins to raise a stink…"

"Is it really that serious for us?"

"Absolutely! These are powerful international criminals with strong connections. But there is one ray of light. I heard confidentially that the FBI in the U.S. are about to issue a warrant for the arrest of Oatman and Mududzo on other serious charges. This will result in extradition procedures, and most countries will hand them over for this type of crime. But it will take a few days, and in that time we could have trouble with them pursuing us. In fact, they may deduce that the skull is still in Cape Town, and try to steal it from there."

"So, it seems we are in danger, and the skull is also. What can be done quickly enough? If we can stall them for a few days, they may be safely behind bars," Alex pondered.

Alison turned a wet face towards them. "I'm sorry… but my emotions have overcome me. I was thinking of Meili's words about Kong Jinwei. She was sad that his head might end up in a museum - she said he was a person, and deserved dignity. I've just had this crazy idea. As far as the world's concerned this skull has vanished. It's now an unrecovered stolen object, and that's the end of it. Why shouldn't Jinwei, who's become very real to us, return to his birthplace?"

"What are you saying, Ali? Take the skull to China?"

"Well, why not? We have dug him up, and we ought to rebury him properly."

"Wow! It's a startling concept! Actually I do like it. But… wait a minute… where do we stand legally, Daniel? You are the policeman."

"Well, I haven't thought this through. We are all professional archaeologists. Speaking professionally, this is not acceptable – but speaking ethically, it may be the right thing to do. There is a precedent in the case of Richard III, who was dug up from a car park in Leicester. They didn't put his skeleton in a museum, but instead reburied him with full church honours. I can't see that Jinwei, who is significant in Chinese history, deserves less."

"But what about your job with Interpol?"

"I don't see a conflict. My assignment is to catch criminals, and going after Oatman and his ilk is my objective. I won't stand in your way if you want to repatriate this skull to China – but of course I can't openly support you."

"Before we go further, I suggest we try the idea out on Mother. I have always respected her sensible wisdom," suggested Alison.

"Good thought! If an advisor to the President of Zimbabwe agrees with us, then it's on!" exclaimed Alex with a laugh.

Returning to the farmhouse in the golden evening light, they sought out Corrie, and told her the strange tale of the counterfeit skull. They explained their dilemma and their plan. To their considerable surprise, she agreed with their logic that taking Jinwei's skull back to China was the decent thing to do.

"You two are not exactly rolling in cash, these days," she commented with a smile, "and so I'll be happy to pay your fares. But are you sure it's safe to do this, Daniel?"

"Mrs Robertson, I feel that if they move fast, there is little chance of Oatman locating them. And the further away the better. Within a week, Oatman and his gang will be running for their lives."

"Then, Daniel, how do you suggest we proceed?"

"To leave through Bulawayo Airport would be too risky. But, Mrs. Robertson, if you will lend me your Land Rover, then I will drive them over the border to Botswana early tomorrow. From Francistown, they can fly to Cape Town. After that, they are in the apparently capable hands of this Irish woman they talk about. Then I must return to Harare, since I have work to do – teaching students and catching criminals!"

It was settled, and they all retired for the night, wondering what the next few days would bring.

Chapter 26

Continental Drift

The faithful Land Rover roared along the smooth tarmac to the border post near Plumtree. Daniel had judged it carefully, so that they arrived at six o'clock, just as the frontier was opening. They were among the first to cross into Botswana, and did so with a minimum of difficulty. From there, an hour's drive took them to Francistown Airport. As they parted, Daniel promised to keep them informed about any developments that came to his notice.

In the departure lounge, Alex texted Moira with a simple phrase: *"Coming CT urgently, A&A."* Knowing the Irish firebrand as he did, there was no doubt that she would take action of some sort.

Three hours later, his expectations were fulfilled as they passed into the arrivals hall at Cape Town. A frenzied waving of arm and red hair directed them straight to Moira.

"Good to see you. Now follow me!" was her welcome, as she led them at a fast trot to the car park. Once safely inside her personal car, she turned onto the motorway leading towards the city.

"My guess is that you got into trouble because we sent the plastic version of the skull," she suggested.

"That's not half of it, Moira! We've been kidnapped, tied up and almost shot."

"Heavens! Who did all that?"

"An international cartel that wanted to steal the skull. And they succeeded – but they failed!"

"So my information was right! I'm glad we took that precaution."

"By the way, Moira," asked Alison, "are we on the right road? We'd like to get our hands on the skull as quickly as possible."

"Don't worry! You will. But I feared that others might be after it, so your Chinese man has gone for a walk. He's enjoying the view of False Bay."

"You mean you've moved the relic to the house at Muizenberg?"

"Correct! You can stay there while we decide on a plan. That's also why I am using my own car, instead of my university vehicle which is too obvious."

Soon they were comfortably settled overlooking the brilliant blue of the expansive bay. Moira wanted every detail of the eventful story in Zimbabwe. Their rehearsal of it was punctuated by Celtic expressions of surprise, horror and anger. When Alison introduced their idea of taking the real skull back to Asia, Moira at first looked appalled. But then, in the same way as Daniel, she began to see the logic of the stratagem, and gradually warmed to the concept.

"It seems to me that if you are going to make this journey, it would be best to contact that Chinese girl. What was her name?"

"Pang Meili."

"Right. I believe she lives in the same area from which this Kong Jinwei hailed. Maybe she can be of help."

"Good idea," agreed Alex, and reached for his phone. "D'you think the phone service will work all the way into north China?"

"Only one way to find out! But, yes, communication is excellent there."

After some thought, Alex typed in a message. *"Bringing your brother home. Can you meet us? Which airport best? A&A"*

"Will Meili understand that, d'you think?" Alison asked.

"The Chinese are the best code-breakers in the world," Moira reassured her.

After twenty minutes of further conversation, Moira was proved right. Alex's phone beeped loudly, and he grabbed it.

"Look forward to seeing all three of you. Fly to Jinan. Will meet you. Give flight number. Love, M."

"This all needs some thinking through, my dears," Moira said at length. "Why don't we sleep on it, and finalise things in the morning?"

They agreed, and Moira left, ostensibly to go home. In fact, she returned to her office on Table Mountain, and spent hours in front of her computer screen.

****

As Alex and Alison were breakfasting on the veranda of the bungalow, Moira arrived.

"Here we are... It's all done... Looks good... and not too visible..."

"Moira, please! What are you talking about?" Alison enquired.

"Your flights, of course. They're all booked."

"What? Already?"

"I went on line, and found you a route using small airlines – just in case your nasty professors are watching the obvious ones"

"You are a wonder!"

"No matter! I chose national airlines or private operations with few planes. It'll make the trip much longer – but, we hope, much safer."

"So, when do we start?"

"Tonight, from here to Joberg. Then a late night one onward."

She produced a pile of computer printouts, which the couple scanned avidly.

"Almost like a world tour – this half of the world anyway!" enthused Alex.

Lifting a bag onto the table, Moira said, "Your big challenge is to get the skull through all those airport security systems. Fortunately, on the route I've chosen, I guess the technology is fairly old."

"What's in this bag?"

"It's some cloth which has an X-ray density similar to bone. We obviously cannot stop the scanners from seeing the skull, but we can adjust its shape to look like a harmless bundle. If we wrap the item loosely in this material it will not have a clearly-defined outline."

"Will it work?"

"Not a hundred percent. But unless the scrutinisers are super awake, it should."

"Do we put it in the hold baggage, or carry it as hand luggage?"

"Keep it in sight at all times. Definitely hand luggage."

****

That evening a Kulula jetliner took off from Cape Town, carrying a complement of passengers who preferred cut-price travel to the luxury alternative. Among them were the Hampsteads - and a skull. After a brief stop-over at Oliver Tambo Airport in Johannesburg, they boarded a small Bombardier jet. Throughout the hours of darkness, it flew north along the eastern seaboard of Africa.

"Good morning, dear passengers! We hope you have had a good night. Shortly we will be arriving at Aden Airport. Please make preparations for landing."

Alex and Alison roused themselves drowsily, but came round quickly when they noticed the scene through the windows of the plane. A dazzling white city lay along the fringe of an ultramarine bay. Behind the metropolis, desert sands extended to the hazy horizon.

An hour later, they were sipping drinks in the transit lounge.

"Can this be for real?" exclaimed Alison.

"What's that?"

"I've been checking the tickets, and the itinerary from here on. Our next flight is with Airy Faerie Airways!"

"Gosh, is there such an airline?"

"Apparently – and it will take us to Kozhikode."

Picking up his phone Alex began to search for information.

"Ah! Yes. Airy Faerie does exist – it is owned by an Englishman resident in Aden, and it has two planes. Does a regular run from here to India."

"Where is this Kozhikode place?"

"It says near the southern tip of India – its ancient name was Calicut."

"Let's hope the aircraft isn't a Tiger Moth!"

Six hours later, after a bumpy ride in a twenty-seater jet, they landed in India. Almost immediately, they boarded a sleek airliner belonging to TajAir, which carried them across the Bay of Bengal to the tiny airport at Malacca. Weary and jet-lagged, they tumbled off the plane, and found they had a twenty-four hour wait before the next leg of the journey.

"Let's find a cheap hotel, and get a good break."

"Spot on!"

Following a restful night, they made a brief exploration of the town that had such a long, rich history. The amalgam of Muslim, Buddhist, Hindu, Chinese and Portuguese cultural features made them aware of the strategic importance of the little outpost. Late in the evening, they boarded a Hainan Airlines flight for the final stage of their tortuous passage across the globe.

****

Leaving behind the dark green forests of Malaysia, their aircraft climbed over the Himalayas, and swept across the yellow paddy fields of central China. As dawn broke over a mountainous landscape, the flight attendant announced that they were dropping down into Jinan.

Emerging from the modern, stylish facilities of Jinan Airport, they were confronted with a sea of faces waiting to welcome passengers. At first it seemed that there were scores of young women looking identical to Meili. The black hair, round faces and bright smiles all seemed very familiar. After a short period of indecision, they spotted the real Meili skipping through the crowd. Dancing up to them, and enveloping them in a warm embrace, she was obviously overjoyed at the reunion.

"This is really wonderful. This way... that's my car over there."

She led them to a smart little vehicle, and loaded them aboard.

"Is this really your car, Meili?"

"Absolutely. I bought it as soon as I came back."

"But how could you afford such a lovely means of transport?"

"In Zimbabwe I saved my salary carefully. In China these days, cars are quite cheap. The global recession has cut our exports."

"And so, where are you taking us now, Meili?"

"Come to my family home. My parents are dying to meet you. It'll take us about an hour to get to our town."

During the hour, Alex and Alison filled Meili in with details of the happenings since she left Africa the previous week. She was dumbfounded by the drama that had unfolded, and by the identity of the criminals who had finally shown their hands.

"I always felt deep down inside me that Daniel Mwonzi was a good man. I'm glad he turned out to be on the right side."

Winding through the centre of a small town of high-rise

apartments, she parked in front of a doorway. A lift took them up to the ninth floor, where she ushered them into her home. A Chinese couple came forward smiling, and Meili made the introductions.

"My father and my mother. He speaks some English, but my mother does not – so I will be your interpreter."

Although Meili's father looked to be in his mid-forties, the visitors initially mistook the other woman for Meili's sister. The two looked so similar that the generation gap appeared to be invisible. Meili's parents were charming and welcoming. Her father was a production manager in a local chemical processing plant, while her mother taught in a kindergarten. Their flat was quite spacious and airy, with a wide view across the hills and plains of Shandong. To her embarrassment, Alison discovered that the elder Pangs had vacated their master bedroom in favour of their guests.

The midday meal was a time of great nourishment, and considerable hilarity. The manipulation of the chopsticks looked so simple in the hands of the indigenous diners, but proved frustratingly awkward for the newcomers. In the end persistence paid off, and the delicate flavours of the food were greatly enjoyed.

Following the lunch, the family relaxed on the balcony, far above the hooting traffic in the streets below. Meili was keen to talk.

"I have discovered some very interesting background concerning our friend – I mean my brother – Kong Jinwei. My mother told me this, but she wants to tell you herself. I will translate for her."

"This sounds fascinating," said Alison.

"I want to thank you first for all your kindness to my daughter in Africa. We are greatly indebted to you and your family."

"But she was the one who helped us out," interposed Alex.

"I want to tell you about my childhood," the translation continued. "I was born in 1960, and grew up during that terrible time called the Cultural Revolution. We lived in great fear. As a young teenager, I was forced to attend many meetings of the Young Pioneers. We had to learn special songs and wear red scarves. At that time a number of new operas were written. They used the old Beijing style, but had novel themes. I well remember one that was called 'The Mason and Landlord'. It was especially popular round here, because it was set in Shandong."

"Do you mean that it might connect with our Jinwei?" Alex asked breathlessly.

"Quiet! Just listen!" Alison admonished him.

"When my daughter told us the story of your discovery in Africa, I realised that the narratives were similar. In the musical, a man tried to save his sister from rape on her wedding night. The aggressor was the local landlord of the district. The message of the opera was the heroism of the peasantry in overcoming the bourgeoisie. In some ways the star of the story was seen as an early Communist."

"Wow, that is comparable with what we found on the stone tablets!" exclaimed Alex.

"But there is more," Meili said, picking up the story. "After an Internet search, we found a historian in Qinghua University who had studied the myths of old China. He confirmed that the revolutionary opera was based on a folk tale from south Shandong. Here comes the interesting bit... the legend says that the village was called Split Mountain."

"Fantastic!" chorused Alex and Alison. "Just the same as in our story. Does it exist now?"

"Using our version of Google Maps, we searched for a long while, and discovered the village about five miles from a major town."

"So what next," asked Alison.

At that moment, Alex's phone started to beep. Quickly he grabbed it, and began silently to read a message on the screen. As he did so, his countenance darkened and he looked worried. Finally he turned to the others.

"Sorry folks, but we seem to have some genuinely bad news!"

Chapter 27

Returned Hero

"What's up?" Alison cried. "Who's it from?"

"It's from Daniel. I'll read it to you.

"Warrants issued in US. Mududzo arrested. Oatman believed to be on flight to Shanghai. Possible links with triads. Seems to have discovered your intentions and destination. Be careful."

"Heavens!" Meili uttered emphatically. "They're chasing you – to get the skull back, no doubt. What should we do?"

"But, what does 'triad' mean?" Alison asked.

"They are the secret societies that have dominated the Chinese underworld for centuries."

"I thought they were abolished in the revolution."

"In theory, yes. But the reality is that they still have great influence in the country."

"How can Oatman be linked to these societies?"

"There's a global network, where the Mafia, the triads and some other gangs collaborate. So Oatman has probably had an introduction."

Thoughtfully, Alex said, "He also has the translation of the script from the slabs. That means he knows the location of the village, and he has heard that we might go there. So we can assume that he hopes to catch us, and grab the skull. He can read the map, just like us."

After a period of confused conversation, a plan began to form. Meili outlined her ideas.

"I propose that the three of us travel to Split Mountain

tomorrow. The roads are good, and it will take about three hours. We can lay my brother in peace again. Hopefully, we can be there and away before Oatman shows up."

During the afternoon, Meili organised a sight-seeing tour of the environment. The many hills and ridges surrounded small valleys, where rural communities were active in farming and light industry. The soil was good, and the area appeared relatively prosperous. They visited some relatives of the extended Pang family, and saw a variety of life-styles, accommodation and dress. Everyone was very welcoming, and Alex and Alison found the whole afternoon very enriching.

During the evening back in the flat, Meili's parents asked hesitantly whether it would be possible for them to view the relic. Alison brought it into the living room, and carefully unwrapped the special material that had slipped it through so many X-ray scanners. As she held up the skull, the Chinese members were overcome with wonderment. Instead of shouting their joy, they just stared at it, each with their own thoughts.

"This is more meaningful to us than you can imagine," Meili sighed. "It takes us far back into the roots of our heritage. My parents fully agree that he should be buried with dignity in his home."

The following morning, preparations were made for the trip to the south of the province. Mr Pang made it clear that he expected Alison and Alex to return in the evening, and spend several more days with the family. The Hampsteads were overwhelmed by the hospitality shown to them, and looked forward to a chance to unwind when it was all over.

Just before departure, Alex received another text from Daniel, which he read out.

"Oatman apparently joined up with 14K. Seen boarding flight for Qingdao. Chinese authorities agreed to extradition if he can be found."

Meili decoded the message for them. "The 14K is one of the more notorious secret societies. Very active in Shanghai, but also up here."

"Where is this place Qingdao?"

"On the south coast of Shandong. It's about two hundred miles from where we are going."

"So, it seems we are in a race. But the stakes are rather high," observed Alex laconically.

"But I think we should still go," stressed Meili. "If we don't win the contest, the 14K will be staked out there – and we'll never get another chance."

"Right-ho!" yelled Alison. "To the road!"

****

The motorway was new and empty, so they made good time on the journey south. Realising that their adventure may be reaching its termination, Meili asked about the future.

"What does this all mean for your career, Alex? It seems your research has been disrupted. Anyway, the main exhibit has disappeared."

"I'm not too worried. Back at UZ they will still have all the other parts of the skeleton. Everyone will know that the skull was misappropriated by unscrupulous men. We have the photos, as well as the carbon-14 and DNA results from Cape Town. I have enough material for my thesis, certainly."

"I'm glad that we are not ruining your prospects by doing this."

"Not at all. I'm convinced, like you, that this is the fair thing to do in the situation."

After passing over a range of hills, their route took them through a small town.

"This is Jining," Meili announced. "Does it mean anything to you?"

"Sorry, doesn't ring a bell."

"This name actually appears on the granite slabs. I'm going to stop for a moment, despite our urgency."

Twisting through the middle of the busy town centre, she followed a Chinese signpost to the outskirts. She stopped before a high embankment.

"Now, a short walk!"

Leaving the car, she led them up a small path to a wide expanse of water.

"Tread carefully. Perhaps we should have taken our shoes off! This is probably where Jinwei came on that fateful morning."

"This is the Grand Canal!" Alison breathed.

"Correct. In his day, there would have been lots of traffic – not just the small boats you see now. Much of the waterway has silted up along its length."

"To think that Jinwei may have stood here – and boarded a barge moored on this bank!"

Silently, they returned to the car, and drove on. As they sped along the arterial road, Meili pointed along the valley which they were following.

"We can assume that this is the way Jinwei came on his horse…"

"… the night he escaped from the town prison," finished Alison.

In the distance they could see indications of a large town. Well before they reached it, Meili began to drive very attentively, looking at the road signs.

"There it is! Pikai Shan, Split Mountain. Here comes the

turning for the village.

Feeling that they were driving over hallowed ground, they peered expectantly as they entered the village. It was a compact little settlement, dominated on one side by two hills. Their facing slopes were almost vertical, explaining why the village had been so named. Standing in the narrow main street, they looked at the geography around them. Meili commented on the scene.

"You may not remember this, but the carving on the stones gave a good description of Jinwei's home. It said that his house stood on a hill directly opposite the split in the mountains."

Looking in the other direction, Alex concluded, "So that hillside behind us must have been the place."

The access to the designated hillside was obstructed by several new houses and a small factory. Thus, they decided to drive back onto the main road, and then walk up the back of the knoll. Parking beside the highway, they carefully removed the precious relic from the car, as well as two spades from the boot. A short stretch of strenuous climbing brought them out onto the top of the prominence.

"This must be the place," Alex enthused. "Didn't it say that the bridegroom's party came straight towards them through the defile between the hills?"

"Where should we bury him?"

"How about that copse of trees? That's roughly where his house must have stood. Also, we should be unobserved."

Taking it in turns, they dug down into the thick brown earth. Deciding that half a metre would be an adequate depth, the two girls carefully unwrapped the skull. Meili produced a length of white cloth, and began to wrap the relic in it.

"This is silk. In China, white is the colour of death and burial."

Meanwhile, Alex was studying the village through his

binoculars. Abruptly, he gave a warning shout.

"Keep under cover! We may have companions."

"What can you see?"

"A smart black car has stopped in the village. Three Chinese men... and a European. My gosh, it's Oatman!"

"Oatman, himself?"

"There! Look for yourself!" he ordered, handing the binoculars to Alison.

"You're right!"

"Well, let's finish the job – and get away!" suggested Meili urgently.

Quickly placing the precious relic into the hole, they refilled it, and tamped down the earth.

"Fetch branches and leaves to cover it up!"

Happily, the undergrowth was very thick, and it was possible to drag enough vegetation to completely conceal the grave. Just as they finished, Meili happened to glance away from the village to the main road behind them.

"Look at that!" she cried.

Following the direction of her finger, they saw three sleek white cars slowing down near the turn-off for the village. Each vehicle had a large curved stripe painted on its side, as well as two distinctive Chinese characters.

"The police have arrived!"

Remaining inconspicuous among the trees, they looked down on the drama unfolding in the village. One of the police vehicles came along the main street towards the group around the black car. Immediately, the men, including Oatman, bounded into the vehicle, and sped off along the road. Round the corner, they suddenly encountered a second white car blocking the street. As they braked to a halt, two men jumped from the moving car and ran up a side street. Shots rang out, and they crumpled to the ground.

The final image that the hilltop watchers retained was that of three men with raised hands standing in the street. They were surrounded by armed Chinese police. One of the arrested parties was the portly academic from Shorefield.

"Best to get out – before people ask questions," urged Meili, while hurrying them back down the slope to their car on the road below.

Scrambling into the vehicle, they set off along the fast thoroughfare. But after a few seconds, Meili slowed the car, and then pulled off to the side of the road. Alison looked at her with anxiety, and then saw tears streaming down her face. But at the same time, she was smiling broadly, and staring up at the hilltop they had just vacated.

"Welcome home, my brother," she whispered in Chinese. "Welcome home, after seven hundred years."

THE END

Printed in Great Britain
by Amazon.co.uk, Ltd.,
Marston Gate.